DROWNING
A WHY CHOOSE
FORBIDDEN DARK ROMANCE

Book Cover by A.eM.—Instagram: iam_a_em

Character Art & NSFW ART by: PGA Illustrations

2nd edition, 2024

Blurb

DROWNING

Resisting temptation is harder than she thought.

Darkness. Death. Temptation. Forbidden.

Four words that perfectly describe Emerson Cole.

After enduring an abusive boyfriend, the death of her parents, and a relentless, unhinged stalker, Emerson feels like she's drowning, and there's no one there to save her.

Or is there?

When she's voluntarily trapped with four forbidden men who she was always warned to stay away from, she finds herself slowly emerging from the darkness that was drowning her. Each

MAN BRINGS HIS OWN DEPTH AND DESIRE INTO HER LIFE, AND SHE'S UNABLE TO RESIST THE TEMPTATION.

IN THIS TANGLED WEB OF LOSS, LOVE, AND EXTREME LUST, CAN KANE, SEVEN, STONE, AND ACE RESCUE EMERSON FROM DESPAIR BEFORE SHE'S COMPLETELY CONSUMED? OR WILL SHE DROWN IN THE DARKNESS OF HER PAST?

Content Warnings

Dear Reader,

This book explores a lot of dark and triggering elements. And although Drowning isn't as dark as Trick or Treat or Breaking Boston, it's still pretty dark. Make sure to scan the QR code, click on my website, and read the *entire* list carefully. If you're not comfortable with *any* of them, *please* choose a different book to read. Your mental health always matters. My book isn't for everyone, and that's okay, but *please* don't read it if you have even one of the triggers listed below. If you do, great, but *please* don't come at me saying you hated the book or dnf'd it.

Because. You. Were. Warned.

If you have *no* triggers, *love* the why choose trope, and live for the dark side of things, then by all means, be a good girl or boy, and check out the shopping list of content warnings and tropes listed below to see what you're signing up for, Fucker.

For the full list, visit my website:

Drowning Playlist

...that made me wanna fuck and cry at the same damn time.

Or Nah—Ty Dolla Sign
Hard For—Kevin Gates
Confessions Part II—Usher
Luv Bug—Kevin Gates
Bitch—Tech N9ne
Drowning—A boogie Wit Da Hoodie
Work—Rihanna
Take You Down—Chris Brown
Ride—Ciara
Ace Hood—Body to Body
Hey Daddy—Usher
Chase Atlantic—Into It
Nice and Slow—Usher
Cute Girl—D[illegible]y Graves
Pony—Ginuwine
Bust it Baby—Plies
The Hills—The Weekend
Truth be Told—Kevin Gates

Dirt Nap—Diggy Graves

Sure Thing—Miguel

Unsteady—X Ambassadors

Bad for Me—Kevin Gates

Papercut—Linkin Park

I Can Tell—504 Boyz

Burn—Usher

One Thing—Kevin Gates

The Way—Mac Miller + Ariana Grande

Me Too—Kevin Gates

Lovin on me—Jack Harlow

Car Underwater—Armor For Sleep

OTW—DJ Luke Nasty

I Invented Sex—Trey Songz

Take Your Halo—Tech N9ne

U Got it Bad—Usher

Boyfriend #2—Pleasure P

Razor's Edge—Masked Wolf + X Ambassadors

Listen here:

Hold your breath and dive right in, Little One. I hope you're not afraid to get wet...

Stay dark, stay twisted, stay smutty!

Prologue

Emerson

December

Gentle hands rove over my body, attempting to slide beneath my snug black dress. I try to evade the touch, but I'm gently pulled and turned around, my back pressed against the door of my bedroom.

"Not now, Damon," I say to my long-time boyfriend, trying to compose myself before going back downstairs.

"It'll help get your mind off things," he tells me with a smile, evoking memories of the boy I fell in love with years ago, the same melting glint in his hazel eyes.

But he's not that same boy anymore.

And I'm not that same girl anymore.

A lot's changed between us, and around us, cracking the comfortable foundation we built together.

When I don't respond, his expression transforms into anger as he pushes off the door behind me.

"It's always 'not right now,' Emerson. Damn it, I have fucking needs too," he states before grabbing his black hoodie and storming out, leaving me reeling against the wall from the force of the door slamming behind him.

The sound echoes in my ears long after he's gone, and with my back pressed against the wall, I sink to the floor, shaking, with tears streaming down my face, smudging the hours of makeup I carefully applied. My long chestnut curls are tangled from Damon's grip.

But at this moment, my appearance is inconsequential.

Nothing matters anymore.

My parents are gone, never coming back. They won't care about how I look because they're not here to see me.

The pain of their loss pierces my heart once more, as I obsess over the fatal car accident that ended their lives, leaving my brother and me all alone.

Now I'm trapped here with a boyfriend who can't comprehend my grief or support me when I need him the most.

I wipe away my tears and stand up, realizing that I need to be strong for Eli and myself, even though I can't see how that's fucking possible.

The music from downstairs fills the house—my parents' song—serving as a reminder of their absence.

I need to escape.

Flinging open my bedroom door with tear-blurred vision, I collide with a solid chest, my nose taking the brunt of the impact.

"Fuck!" I exclaim, tears clouding my vision and making it difficult to discern who it is... Yet I know without a doubt just by the way he smells.

"Apologies, Emerson," Seven, my brother's best friend, says as he steadies me with his hands on my shoulders.

"I'm fine. I just didn't see you there," I say, wiping the tears from my eyes as the world comes back into focus. "What are you doing up here?"

"Checking on you. We saw Damon leave, so I wanted to make sure you're okay," he explains, his smile causing my broken heart to flutter.

Seven— eleven years my senior—has always been off-limits. With piercing blue eyes reminiscent of the ocean, light hair just long enough to pull, and a perfectly tanned, tattooed physique, he's undeniably attractive. Yet anything beyond a platonic relationship between us would irrevocably upset Eli.

"Are you okay?" Seven asks, bringing me back to the present, standing at the top of the stairs.

"Not really, but I will be," I admit, feeling submerged in sorrow yet hoping I can overcome it.

"Did he hurt you?" His voice becomes hushed, ensuring no one in my family downstairs can overhear.

I shake my head, wishing to put it behind me. "No, he's just upset," I say, brushing it off and attempting to walk past him.

"Wait, Em," he says, holding me tighter, pulling me near to his chest.

As much as I want to lay my head against him and embrace him with all my might, I hesitate. If Damon were to witness, he'd erupt. If Eli were to see us, it would lead to chaos. A fucking hug isn't worth the fallout.

"I should go back," I begin, but I'm unable to finish my sentence before his lips softly meet mine, his hand resting protectively on my hip.

The kiss may be brief, but it's enough to make me question everything. His tongue glides with ease around in my mouth, sending tingles all the way down to my toes.

"What... what was *that* for?" I ask as he pulls away, touching my tingling lips with my fingers.

"You know *exactly* what it was, Princess. After all these years, can't you figure out why I did that?" he chuckles, intertwining his fingers with mine and guiding me downstairs.

En route, I'm engulfed by various family members offering their condolences, recounting tales of my parents, and giving me money to help, even though I don't need it. .

I lost my parents; nothing will ever completely heal that wound.

A flute of champagne is placed into my hand, and I accept it without a second thought, needing to numb myself before facing people I'd rather not see. In the background, the hushed whispers of my brother, Seven, and our friend Stone are unmistakable.

I decide to step outside for some air and pass by the room where photos of my parents are scattered across the tables. I resist the urge to look, quickly grabbing a bottle of wine from the bar.

I push open the back patio door, stumble outside, and hope to keep my tears at bay until I can be alone.

The snow crunches beneath my heels as I descend the porch steps, making my way toward the fire flickering in the backyard firepit. Sitting down, I allow the warmth of the flames to envelop me. Besides the pain of losing my parents, I can't get the simple kiss from Seven out of my mind.

"Would you like some company?" A deep, resonant voice filled with sensuality and danger startles me, and moments later, my father's best friend Kane appears, holding a bottle of his own.

"Sure, sit." I motion to the empty spot beside me, taking a generous swig from the wine bottle.

Kane joins me, sitting so close that our shoulders touch. Instinctively, I rest my head on his shoulder and exhale heavily, the weight of everything still feeling like a fucking elephant on my chest.

Kane remains silent for a while, simply being there for me before speaking. "If you ever need me, Little One, you call me. I won't hesitate to come." He kisses my temple, wraps his arm around me, and does his best to bring a smile to my face.

And he does.

With his other hand, he runs it down my thigh, giving my knee a playful squeeze. The intriguing look he gives me makes me swallow slowly and hard, unable to pull my eyes off of him, wondering what he's thinking about. His gaze then drops to my lips and nervously I lick them, trying to keep my eyes off of his.

He was my father's best friend and my closest confidant when me and my parents didn't see eye-to-eye.

Kane, his son, Stone, and my father were in the same MC club together; riding bikes was their life. My mother wasn't a fan of it, especially since my brother and I got bikes of our own. She was terrified something would happen to us—the irony.

My parents meant everything to me, especially my father. Even at twenty-two, I still lived at home because I couldn't bear the thought of leaving them. And now, because of a drunk driver who fled the scene, they're no longer with us. Eli and I are alone now, but at least we have each other.

"You're going to be okay, kiddo," Kane reassures me, breaking the silence, his hand resting on my knee and his fingers dragging lazily up and down my arm. An innocent gesture is turning into so much more in my mind, and I know I need to put a stop to it before it gets out of control.

He leans in, kissing my cheek, the stubble on his face scratching against my skin, a shiver wracking my body.

"I'll *always* be here."

One by one, my brother, Seven, and Stone join me and Kane around the fire, offering silent support. I keep drinking, trying to escape the pain—to forget the loss even just for one night.

I already feel myself falling into a dark hole and I fear what might happen if I can't find a way out.

How am I going to carry on without my parents? I guess I'll figure it out one way or another.

The warmth of the fire and the company of those around me start to ease the pain, if only just a little. I look at everyone, feeling grateful for their presence. And especially for Kane, who seems to be looking out for me in his own way.

The weight of the wine in the bottle is a reminder of the dark hole I'm trying to avoid, but for now, it offers some sort of fleeting relief.

I take a deep breath, trying to focus on the warmth of the fire as I come to terms with the fact that I'll need to figure out how the fuck I'm going to live without my parents.

ONE

BLACK EYES

Emerson (22)

SIX MONTHS LATER— JUNE

I gently pat the foundation onto my skin, concealing the bruise around my eye as much as possible. A touch of black eyeshadow and a thick line of eyeliner make the bruise less noticeable. But I can't hide the bruises covering my body—my clothes will have to do that.

However, wearing a hoodie and leggings in the summer makes it difficult to avoid questions. Especially from Eli, Seven, and Kane. They understand Damon's situation, but they also recognize that there is more to the story.

As I stand up from my vanity, the bedroom door opens, and Damon enters in wet swim trunks. He locks the door and rushes over, a chilling look in his eyes.

"Hey, baby. I've missed you," he says, pulling me close to him, my body smacking against his wet chest.

"I've missed you too, babe," I reply with a forced smile, hoping he doesn't see through my facade.

He kisses me passionately and rubs his hands over my aching body, pushing me toward the bed. He hovers above me, tearing down my leggings with one hand and a wild expression in his eyes.

"Show me how much you missed me," he demanded, biting the side of my neck hard.

"I'm not feeling it, Damon, but I still missed you," I respond hesitantly, forcing another painful smile.

"Nice try. If you really missed me, you would let me fuck you. What the fuck are you hiding?" He glares at me and grabs my throat, cutting off my airflow. His paranoia is disturbing, but I refuse to show fear in my eyes. *Not anymore.*

"Damon, I really miss my parents."

"They are fucking gone, Em. There's nothing you can do, so you might as well get on your fucking knees. I'll make you feel better," he says sternly, pulling his pistol out as if to scare me.

The look in his eyes tells me he's dead serious. I reluctantly turn onto my stomach and rise to my knees, bracing myself for what lies ahead. He approaches me from behind and enters me forcefully, causing searing pain to spread throughout my body. I bite my lip to keep from crying, his grip still tight on my throat.

"If you deny me again, you are going to fucking regret it," he growls. "You're *my* fucking girlfriend, so I can fuck you whenever I want." *Thrust.* "Do you fucking understand?" *Another thrust.*

"Yes, Damon," I say, catching my breath and closing my eyes, wishing it would end.

"And if you even consider leaving me, you will end up like your parents," he says in a chillingly calm tone, sending a shiver down my spine. "And I'm *dead* fucking serious."

I struggle to hold back my tears as he continues to use me, his threats echoing in my mind. I feel shattered, but I know I have to stay strong.

Once he is gone and the room is quiet, I wipe away my tears and take a deep breath. The suffocating fear that has consumed my life is more damaging than the bruises on my body. But I am too terrified to leave.

I descend the stairs, dressed in a cozy hoodie and black leggings, fingers crossed that the house is empty. However, just as I get to the bottom of the stairs, Seven is waiting for me in the foyer.

As I turn to walk away from him, I try to avoid him by keeping my head down, but his deep voice stops me cold.

"It's hot as *hell* outside, Princess. Why are you dressed for winter?" His voice contains a hint of anger, but he does not raise it.

I return to face him, hoping my makeup has not been smudged by my tears. "All I wanted was to be comfortable. The AC makes it *freezing* in here," I reply, hoping he believes me.

"Right... Well, are we ever going to talk about what happened between us the night of your parents' funeral?" As he speaks, he moves closer.

Knowing that this conversation was bound to happen, I freeze. I was hoping it would happen later rather than sooner.

He holds my waist, gently pressing me against the wall and studying my face intently, his surfer boy physique so close to mine. "I meant what I said, Emerson." He kisses my cheek and walks away as my brother turns the corner, saying, "You deserve better than that asshole."

"Emerson, I didn't know you were here," Eli exclaims, giving me a look of intrigue as he watches Seven disappear.

"Yeah, but I'm leaving for a bit. I'm going to take my bike out." Riding has always made me feel relaxed. The sensation of the wind blowing through my hair and the vibrations of the bike throughout my body make me feel alive.

Seven and Eli look at me, knowing I'm hiding something. But I can not bear to tell my brother that my boyfriend is beating the shit out of me. He'd be so disappointed that I haven't left him; he wouldn't understand.

"Well, if you want to stop by, Kane, Stone, Seven, and I will be at the bar." He kisses my forehead and turns away, saying, "Do not bring that fucking asshole, though."

Seven looks at me with admiration in his eyes, which breaks my heart. I have been in love with my brother's best friend since I was thirteen, but I have never told anyone. Is he really implying that he feels the same way? Is all of this innocent flirting and playful banter real, rather than a harmless game, as I had assumed?

"You know I'm always here, Princess. At the drop of a hat, I'll be by your side. Simply say the word." He takes another step closer to me, cups my cheek, and looks deeply into my eyes.

"Seven, I'm fine. I promise." I smile back, never taking my gaze away from his. "But whatever you're thinking, stop. It will never work. Eli would kill us both. You're eleven years older, and it just... it wouldn't go over well with him." I choked out, feeling my heart break even more.

"Who cares about the age difference? And I'm sure Eli would come around *eventually*. I want you, Emerson, and I will not stop trying." He gently kisses my lips before walking away, just like he did six months ago.

Finally, in the garage, I get on my bike and start it, feeling the rumble between my bruised thighs. After putting on my helmet, I press the door opener and slowly walk my bike out, feeling the heat of the sun's rays on me.

Fuck it.

I take off, paying no attention to my speed. Right now, the throttle is my best friend, and I squeeze it as I zip down the back roads of Boston.

What would happen if I wrapped myself around a tree right now? I would be with my parents and would not have to deal with Damon. But then I would have to leave my brother to pick up the pieces, which I simply cannot do.

So I just ride.

I ride for my parents.

I ride for *me*.

I let the serenity envelope me like an aura, feeling at peace with myself.

I ride to escape the negative aspects of my life.

I ride for the sensation of wind in my hair and adrenaline coursing through my veins.

I just fucking ride.

Two

Killer Thoughts

Kane (42)

I watch the whiskey swirl elegantly in my glass, absent-mindedly twirling it in circles with my fingers. The pulsating music fills the room, causing my foot to tap lightly on the bar floor. With each step, my black Jordans adhere to the tile, clinging to some spilled liquor. As I inhale deeply, the familiar aroma of cigarette smoke, marijuana, and alcohol floods my senses.

Leaning back against the booth, I watch the young crowd dance, laugh, and enjoy their escape from the past. I particularly notice Eli, who is working tirelessly to support his devastated sister, Emerson, while also dealing with his own grief as a result of their parents' deaths. It fucking hurts me to see them like this.

But Emerson. *Fuck.*

I shouldn't be feeling these things I feel for her. She has a model's body, perfect perky tits, a juicy little ass you could set a glass on, and eyes that make my cock hard every time she looks at me.

She's only twenty-two, though. Would she even consider a man twice her age? I had not noticed her until a few years ago, when she joined the SSB—the biker crew her father and I founded twenty years ago.

I finally paid attention when I saw her riding a bike in tight leather pants and a crop top.

And she hasn't left my thoughts since.

But her fucking boyfriend has her under his control, and she is too afraid to leave. She hasn't said anything, but she doesn't have to. I noticed the bruises. I can see the tears—we all do. But, in light of her parents' deaths, we do not want to say anything that could send her into another downward spiral.

Something else is lurking in the shadows of their relationship, but we haven't discovered it yet.

"What's up?" Stone, my son, who is about Emerson's age, inquires as he slides into the booth across from me. He stands over six feet tall, tattooed and pierced, with slicked-back black hair and hazel eyes, reminding me of myself when I was his age.

My hair is now long and dark, with silver streaks visible on random strands. My eyes are no longer as bright green as they once were; instead, they are dark and dull, with hidden secrets lurking beneath my irises. My entire body, covered in tattoos, remains largely unchanged: muscular and broad, with the same sharp, defined jawline and sculpted chest that I've worked hard to maintain.

"Business," I respond, still watching the kids dance. "I need you and Ace to make a run for me tonight." I finally look at him, finishing the remainder of my drink without making a face.

"Where to?" He takes out his phone and texts Ace, his friend, and another member of the club.

"Down to New Bedford. Take your bikes; they'll get you there faster."

"Alright, Ace is on his way." He puts his phone down and refills my glass before taking a swig from the bottle. "Are we still on track for Nantasket?"

"As long as Eli says it is good, yeah. I'll talk to him sometime tonight."

He nods, his jaw slightly ajar, his gaze fixed on something behind me. Shifting in my seat, I notice Emerson entering the bar... alone. She has obviously been crying, though, and I already knew why.

Stone and I watched as she went to the bar, got a drink, looked around the group until she saw her brother and Seven, and then turned to come toward us. Eli stays put even though he sees her, his eyes widening with shock and rage.

"Surprised to see you here, Blue Eyes." Stone stands up and embraces her, kissing the top of her head as he towers over her by a foot.

"I felt like having a drink. Besides, I wanted to speak with Eli, but then I changed my mind," she laughs, looking at me.

The look she gives me makes me want to bend her over the table and fuck her sadness away.

Of course, I resisted.

"Kane, do you have any jobs?" Her lips curl into a smirk as she holds the glass to her mouth and sips like a pro. Even hotter.

"Sit down, Little One. We'll talk."

Ace walks in, the bell on the door chiming.

"Looks like I should head out. I'll be in touch."

Emerson watches Stone walk away, both he and Ace turning to look at her.

She's like a really bad car wreck or a murder scene; you know you shouldn't look, but you do, and then you can't look the fuck away. All the bikers in the club want her, but she's off limits because she's Eli's baby sister.

But rules were made to be broken, and with Emerson, I intend to break every fucking one.

"So, about those jobs," she says sweetly, batting her innocent lashes and licking her lips, unintentionally making my cock rock hard.

"Do you feel well enough to go for a run? You know how important it is for my riders to have the right mindset. No distractions, Little One." I extend my hand and place it on top of hers, feeling her pulse against my thumb.

"Well, I've never been one to be easily distracted," Emerson says with a sly grin. "Especially not when I'm out on the road, feeling the wind in my hair and the thrill of that freedom that comes with it. I'm ready, Kane. I'm always ready."

I can't help but notice the fire in her eyes as she speaks. The same fire that has drawn me in since the first time I truly saw her for who she was. As much as I want to protect her and keep her away from the darkness and dangers of this life, a part of me wants to let her in.

"Alright, Little One," I say, firmly squeezing her hand before letting go. "I have a Southie run."

"But that's not even far away." Her nose scrunches and her brow furrows, and it is the most adorable fucking thing ever.

"It's a twenty-grand pick-up, Emerson; it's a big job."

"I'll take it." She smiles as she slides out of the booth, pulling a cigarette from her pack. "I'm going out back for a smoke."

"Let me join you," I offer, sliding out of my side of the booth and following her towards the back exit, my gaze fixed on her ass.

Eli notices us and gives me a curious look, but I raise my finger and walk out the back door with his little sister.

She lights her cigarette and hands me her lighter for mine. She leans against the graffiti-covered building and looks up at the sky, as if nothing is wrong.

"Nice try." I lean next to her, blowing smoke rings into the air.

"What are you saying?" She turns to me, perplexed, her cute nose scrunching.

"Your makeup is starting to wear off. I can see the bruises, Little One," I say softly, trying not to upset her.

"Kane, please," she begs, casting her gaze downward.

I step in front of her and slide my hand under her chin, causing her head to tilt slightly back. My blood boils as I examine the collection of bruises, and it feels as if acid is coursing through my veins.

"Did *he* fucking do that to you?"

She nods, but doesn't say anything.

"I'll fucking kill him," I growl, pressing my forehead against hers, wanting so fucking bad to kiss her.

"He'll k–"

"What the fuck, Emerson?" Damon yells, "I have been looking everywhere for you," as he storms over to us and rips her away from me.

"Don't ever fucking grab her like that again," I threaten, noticing Emerson's fearful expression.

"She's *my* fucking girl, and I've told her to stay the fuck away from this place unless *I'm* with her."

"Kane, it's okay. Just please, stop," Emerson begs, her gaze drawn to Damon's waistband and the Glock tucked inside.

I want to fucking kill him.

But I stop provoking him and let it go, as much as it fucking kills me. Cus she's right. He's unhinged tonight, and no one knows what he's capable of. These killer thoughts inside my head keep screaming at me to kill him, but Emerson has seen enough death lately.

Nonetheless, he must be dealt with.

I take a step back, my fists clenched at my sides, watching Damon pull her back into the bar. Eli appears behind me, a worried expression on his face as he searches for his sister.

"Kane, I didn't know you were outside," he starts, but I cut him off.

"I just wanted some air," I say, avoiding his gaze as I walk toward the back door. The walk is difficult, with tension filling every void in my mind. Emerson's face, her bruises. Damon's possessive nature. I need to make it right.

Back in the bar's garage, the guys are preparing for thc evening when Emerson enters, her head held high but the same sadness lingering in her glass blue eyes. She is apprehensive at first, watching the men prepare their bikes and generally just kind of existing from the sidelines for the most part. I can tell it's her way of gauging the situation. But I know she is willing and ready when I watch her fiddling with the bullets scattered all over the table.

As we gear up, I pull her aside. "You don't have to go with us, Little One. You don't have to do this. What did you even tell Damon?" I ask her.

She looks me dead in the eye with a smirk and says, "I don't want to talk about it." After that, she mounts her bike beside mine, and I give her a shoulder pat before we fire up our engines.

We've got a ride to make. And it's not just for the run. We've got some rules to fucking break.

The teasing summer breeze pushes my bike as I ride, gripping the handlebar with one hand, my other resting on my hip. Looking beside me, I watch Emerson ride, lost in her own little world as she becomes one with the open road. Even through her helmet, I can tell she's distracted, even though she swore to me she was fine. I can tell something other than Damon is bothering her, but her stubborn ass won't tell me.

...unless I force it out of her.

Filthy thoughts begin to bombard my mind, and I start to become distracted as I ride, thinking of all the ways I'd be able to convince her.

When we come up to a light only miles away from the pickup site, Emerson stops on one side of me and Seven on the other, the rumble of the bikes drowning out the rest of the city noise around us. With Emerson's visor open, I pierce my eyes deeply into hers, but she looks away, immediately breaking eye contact. I can see the internal struggle fucking with her and her feelings for the forbidden, making her question her morals.

She speeds off as the light turns green, leaving a cloud of dirt in her wake from her bike's back tire. Seven and I eventually catch up to her just as she's pulling down the long, dark driveway, which leads to a secluded three story house set in the cut. Dogs bark upon our arrival, being yanked back by the chains looped around their necks as we stand in front of the gated yard.

"Is everything okay?" I ask, pulling off my helmet and setting it on the seat of my bike.

She shrugs, keeping her helmet on. "Fine," she says, again, walking ahead of Seven and I with determination in her gait.

"What's with her all of a sudden?" Seven questions, pulling off his helmet to reveal his face.

"Not sure, but let's get this shit done so we can get out of here. I don't have a good feeling about it." I look around, retrieving my gun as we walk up to the door.

There's a risk we take with any job, but we always manage to get them done. This isn't the first time I've done business here. Whether it's doing a large cocaine drop-off or a huge cash pick-up, we've never encountered any trouble, but there's something about tonight that just feels... off.

The second I walk up to the front door and raise my hand to knock, the porch light flips off, and the sound of gunfire roars from behind the door, inside the house. In a panic, the three of us duck and rush to find cover, hoping not to be hit by the flying array of bullets aimed right at us.

"What the fuck is happening?" Seven seethes, opening fire to try and defend us.

"I don't fucking know!" I scream, firing back while frantically looking around to see if Emerson is safe.

Ducking behind the PODS storage container, she fires back in the direction of the flashes we see through the door's glass panes, her helmet still covering her face.

After minutes that feel like an eternity, the gunfire comes to an abrupt stop. I peek out from behind cover and see Emerson taking off her helmet, her face pale and her eyes filled with fear. But when I try to embrace her, hoping to comfort her, she pulls away from me.

"Emerson, are you hurt?" I can feel my arm burning as I ask, already knowing I had been grazed by a bullet.

"I... I'm fine. But, Kane," she gasps, her jaw dropping. "You're bleeding."

"It's just a graze," I assure her, watching her eyes darting back and forth between my face and my arm.

"Stay here while we see what the fuck happened." Seven just stares at her, afraid to leave her alone.

But we cautiously approach the door and slowly push it open. What we find is a scene of chaos and destruction, and I feel a pit form in my stomach. This job was supposed to be routine, so how did it go so fucking wrong?

We quickly search the house, but the 20 grand we were supposed to pick up is gone, along with any answers. And the dealer lies dead on the living room floor.

"Let's get the fuck out of here," I hiss, trying to figure out what the fuck happened.

As we ride back to the bar, my mind races with thoughts and possibilities. Who could have known about this job, and how did they find out? And the most pressing question of all, who is going to pay for this fucking disaster?

Seven leaves as soon as we get back, leaving me and Emerson alone at the closed bar. I sit down and grab a bottle of Jack, not even bothering with a glass. I begin to panic when I don't see Emerson, but before I can get up and look for her, she emerges from the hall with the first aid kit in her hand, a grim expression still painted on her pretty face. Without saying anything, she rolls my sleeve up to assess the wound, pulling out the necessary items to bandage me up.

"I'm fine, Little One." I flash a smile at her, but she shakes her head, ignoring me.

Pouring rubbing alcohol over the laceration across my bicep, I hiss, getting a grin out of her. "Stop being a baby, Kane."

"How about you get shot, and I'll pour alcohol on it?"

"You got grazed, remember?" She finally smiles, cleaning the area thoroughly.

And then an awkward silence falls around us, and another look of concern flickers in her eyes. I can tell she's holding back, but from what? When I try to tug her onto my lap, she resists, refusing to give in to temptation.

"We can't, Kane," is all she says, finally wrapping a bandage around my arm to stop the bleeding.

"I just want to make sure you're okay. Tonight was a lot to take in; it shouldn't have fucking happened." I shake my head, still utterly confused about the situation.

"It shouldn't have, but it did," she says, looking at me through shame-filled eyes. "And I think it was all my fault."

"How the fuck is it your fault? You were there on a job that had nothing to do with you."

Shaking her head, she whispers, "it had everything to do with me, Kane. I'm pretty sure it was Damon inside that house, and I think he was trying to kill me."

•••••••••••

THREE

CAVING

Emerson

Damon and I ended things.

I know he's fixated on me and refuses to let go. He has threatened to kill me if I leave, and I believe him. His obsession has only gotten worse over time, and now it's just fucking scary.

I'm not sure what made him reconsider letting me go, and I'm too afraid to fucking ask now, especially after what happened on the job last night. I know it was Damon inside that house, shooting at us.

After last night, when he snatched me away from Kane, Damon took me to the side lot, where he proceeded to remind me how much he loved me and that he'd kill anyone who tried to take me away from him. When I tried to walk away, he grabbed my throat and threw me to the ground, giving me a few kicks in the ribs to remind me who was in charge.

As he beat me, I blurted out, "I want to leave." He paused and looked at me as if I had slapped him across the face,

then helped me up and gave me a deadly, chilling look that I still cannot get out of my head.

I was determined to break free from the chains of fear and control that had wrapped themselves around me. When I told him I wanted out again, he laughed and nodded before walking away. He never spoke to me again after that, and the fact that he let me go so easily made me even more afraid of what he had planned. I knew there was something, but I had no idea what or when.

So, now I'm sticking around at the bar until my brother goes home; it's the safest option for me.

My legs are numb from the journey, and my head is spinning as I lie on the couch in the back room. Despite the bitter burn of each sip, I keep drinking from the bottle of whiskey, wanting to be numb so I don't have to feel the physical and emotional pain I'm suffering through.

Suddenly, I feel uneasy, and the hairs on the back of my neck stand up. Despite the fact that the room is spinning, I sit up and push through the discomfort to get to my feet.

Swinging open the door, I stumble down the hall in search of Eli, but instead run into Seven, as we have so many times before. He holds me tightly, keeping me steady.

"Where is my brother?" I can hear the slurred words coming from my mouth, but I smile regardless.

"He ran upstairs with Ace and Nova." Seven smiles, wiggling his brows.

"Ah, gotcha." I nod along with the beat of 'Body to Body' playing through the speakers.

"Where are you heading, Princess?" He shouts above the music, his warm breath sending shivers down my spine.

"Dance with me," I blurted out, eager to forget what had happened last night.

He appears surprised at first, but a smile spreads across his face as he leads me to the dance floor and twirls me around, my ass fitting perfectly against his groin. I can feel his already hard cock against me, and as his hands grip my hips, all of my worries melt away. I feel the thrill of his touch deep within my being.

Fuck, I'm in trouble.

As we dance, thoughts of Damon and my brother fade away, and I concentrate solely on the sense of liberation and excitement of being close to Seven. The music pulses through me, and I close my eyes to immerse myself in the moment. I can tell he feels it as well, and I enjoy knowing that I am eliciting a similar reaction from him.

My body moves seductively, and I roll my hips, eliciting a growl from his lips that sends a jolt right into my ear.

"I left him," I suddenly whisper.

Seven's eyes brighten, slightly widening as we continue to dance.

"Now kiss me like you've been wanting to, Seven," I taunt, hoping he will take the initiative.

"You're drunk, Princess. I can't do that." He offers a smile, but it's not good enough.

I want him, and resisting temptation will be impossible.

I move away from him and lace my fingers with his, guiding him to the back room. When we are inside and the door is closed, I push Seven against it and kiss him, asserting control over what I want.

But he pulls his mouth away from mine and holds my face in his tattooed hands. "Emerson, baby, we can't do this. You're... too drunk, and I don't want to take advantage."

"I'm drunk, yeah, but I know that I want this, Seven. I've wanted this for so fucking long now, but we never had the chance. I'm free now, and I know what I want."

He smiles, his lips curling deviously, making his deep blue eyes glisten under the LED lighting. "Then be a good girl and kiss me. Take what you want, Princess."

The moment he gives me permission, I lose it. I push him toward the couch, pulling on his clothes to get them off. He manages to pull down my leggings, but when he reaches for my sweatshirt, I stop him, my gaze sweeping over the tattoos that cover almost every inch of his naked, sculpted body. He gently pushes me onto the couch and stands there, staring at me sternly.

"Take it off, Princess. I want to see you—all of you." He stares at my naked lower half, his gaze drawn to the ring pierced through my clit, his mouth watering.

"Just fuck me, Seven." I reach up and grab his arm, attempting to pull him down.

"What, I can't admire you before I ruin you?" He laughs, leaning down a little more, his cock sliding against my thigh.

I shiver, my pussy dripping and clit pulsing, ready for him to fuck me. "Are you not capable of multitasking?" I try to make a joke to keep him from seeing the bruises under my sweatshirt.

Still, he hovers over me and spreads my legs wide, rubbing the tip of his pierced dick up and down my slit, coating it in my arousal. My lips parted, and as I was about to moan, he seized them and destroyed my mouth with his tongue. He kisses me until he sucks every last ounce of air from my lungs, leaving me breathless as he pulls away.

"Fuck, baby. I've been waiting for this day for a long time," he whispers softly into my ear as he tugs my lobe between his teeth.

"Then Fuck me, Seven. Show me how much you want this. Show me how much you want me." My eyes flutter as his cock head presses against my opening, gradually easing inside.

"This greedy little pussy feels so fucking good," he grunts, bottoming out inside of me.

He remains motionless, allowing me to wiggle my hips and adjust to his size and the sensation of his piercings gliding against my inner walls. My back arches, and I start to buck my hips, wanting nothing more than to chase the feeling of his cock stretching my pussy out.

"Do you want this dick, Princess?" Seven licks my collar-bone and works his way down to my breasts.

I nod, attempting to find my voice. "Yes," I moan, digging my nails into his back as he starts to move slowly inside of me.

I put my legs around him and drew him in without waiting for him to finish. He picks up the pace, his hips thrusting into mine with a purpose that leaves me gasping for breath and on the edge of something so powerful that I can't look away. My body tingles, with waves of pleasure building and crashing over me as we move in perfect harmony.

Every touch—every thrust—draws us closer to something so intense and consuming that we lose ourselves in each other, the weight of the world falling away as we succumb to the fire between us. With Seven's hands gripping my hips and his gaze never leaving mine, I lose myself in pure bliss, surrendering to the raw, unfiltered pleasure that only he can provide. In that moment, nothing else in the world seems to matter.

All of my feelings for him, which I had never known how to deal with, suddenly made sense.

He fucks me sweetly at first, admiring my body as if he were my fucking king. But as he quickens his pace and fucks me with deep, powerful strokes, I notice the darkness flicker in his eyes as he loses control. His lips find a place on mine as my pussy clenches around him, strangling his cock as he fucks me harder, battling through my tight muscles.

"Come for me, Princess. I want to feel that sweet cum soaking my cock so I can leave it there overnight."

I shuddered at his words, his hand slowly pushing my sweatshirt up. In this moment, I didn't care about bruises painting my skin. My orgasm overtakes me, causing me to cling to him for dear life as our eyes lock with intensity.

"Emerson," a whisper escapes his lips as more skin shows, my climax on the verge of exploding. "I'm going to fucking kill him." He slams into me one more time, and the damn inside me bursts, my cum soaking him and dripping onto the couch beneath my ass. It's the most amazing thing I've ever felt, and I don't want it to end.

He grunts and groans against my lips while twisting my nipple and pounding into me, fucking me through my climax.

I bask in the afterglow, knowing that I have finally let go of everything that has been haunting me for so long. For the first time in my life, I feel truly liberated. The bruises on my skin are simply reminders of a past that I am leaving behind.

I close my eyes and let the sound of his breathing lull me into a peaceful state. My heart beats, attempting to return to normal, but he pulls out, leaving me feeling empty. He strokes himself, aiming for my pussy, with a gleam in his eyes that makes me melt all over again. He comes, hot, thick fluid pooling all over my pussy, sliding down my lips. He takes his hand and smears his cum all over my pussy lips, rubbing it in like lotion.

"Don't wash this off until I tell you," he demands, gasping as he shudders from his orgasm, his body collapsing on top of mine.

"You want me to walk around with dried cum on my pussy?"

"My cum, Princess. I want you wearing *my* cum," he says proudly as he kisses me one more time, his tongue gently dancing with mine in unison.

Once we are dressed and sitting down with a drink in our hands, I light a cigarette to satisfy the craving that has been torturing my soul. We sit close together, silence enveloping us, but nothing needs to be said.

Again, I feel a sense of unease creeping in, and the hair on my body rises. Shaking slightly, I turn to look out the window, hoping no one is there. I'm hoping I don't see Damon out there.

"What is it?" He taps my shoulder; his voice hoarse.

"N... nothing." I look away from the window and lock eyes with him again, trying to conceal my fear.

"He's not going to fucking touch you, Emerson."

As he wraps his arm around my back and gently tugs me against him, I close my eyes, wanting to believe him.

But I know that with Damon, anything is possible, and I don't like the feeling.

Four

Keeping Secrets

Seven (33)

After making sure Emerson is safely tucked away in the meeting room, I make my way back to the bar. As I walk out of the hallway, I spot Eli, Stone, Ace, and Kane. Taking a seat, a drink is promptly placed in front of me. Kylie walks away to the other end of the bar, gives a cheeky wink, and licks her lips, making me cringe in disgust. The women in this bar have nearly fucked every member or customer that walks in. I've fucked my share of the club girls, but my dick's been dry for the last year—until Emerson soaked it just moments ago.

"Where were you, fucker?" Eli asks, his bloodshot eyes piercing into mine as if he knows the answer but doesn't want to hear it.

"I was talking with your sister until she fell asleep. She's safe in the meeting room, passed out," I admit, knowing he'll buy it.

The six of us had known each other for years, and Eli had always told us that Em was off limits, so if he found out I had fucked his precious baby sister, he would kill me.

So I have no plans to tell him just yet.

"Did she tell you she dumped Damon?" I nodded to him, noting the shocked expressions on his, Kane's, and Stone's faces.

"Nah, she hasn't yet," he deeply growls, slightly angry.

"She had to, Eli. His ass was beating her. He was going to kill her if she didn't get out now," Kane speaks up, enraging Eli even more.

He was aware of the kind of predicament she was in—we all were, but none of us wanted to make her feel worse by bringing it up.

"I'm going to fucking kill his ass." After slamming his empty glass against the bar, Eli draws Kylie's attention and causes her to rush back towards us.

"Get in fucking line. I want to kill him too," I say through clenched teeth, remembering her beautiful body and all the bruises that covered it.

"If anyone is killing him, it's me," Kane commands, a murderous glare in his eyes.

"Can I get you boys another drink? Maybe a dance too?" Smiling, Kylie licks her lips once more before putting her curly red hair up in a high ponytail.

"Yes, a drink. Not a dance. Fuck outta here with that." Averting the ill-looking glance she is giving me, I slide my glass towards her.

"Another round for all of us," Eli orders, his anger boiling just beneath the surface.

Kylie gives a nod and gets to work preparing our drinks. Eli gives me a cold look as she comes back with the glasses refilled.

"Once Em wakes up, we're going to have a little talk about this," he says, his tone leaving no room for argument.

I give a nod, understanding that things with Damon are far from over. But for now, Kane is staring at me as if he knows that I just painted Emerson's cunt with my cum, but does he really? We sit in the darkened bar, nursing our drinks and secretly planning our next move.

After we've all had more drinks than we can count, Nova, Eli's girlfriend, comes over and wraps her arms around him from behind. He smiles, a drunken look washing over his face.

"Ready for me to take you home?" she asks, giving him a shiver as she kisses the side of his neck.

"Yeah, I'm ready." He stands up, wobbly on his feet, but Ace steps in just in time to keep him from falling.

"Thanks, bro," Eli mumbled, hugging Ace haphazardly.

"Anytime. Let me help walk you out to the car." Ace gets into position to help him walk out, but they look at us before leaving.

"Anyone else need a ride? Nova is the DD tonight."

I shake my head no, and so does Kane, but Stone and Ace decide to go with them.

"Oh, don't forget, the beach house on Nantasket is ready, so ya'll can head over whenever. I still have to get Em on board, so go without us." Eli salutes us as they walk away, leaving thick tension in the air between Kane and I.

Kane was Emerson's father's best friend, and since his death, he has been like a father figure to Emerson and Eli. I can tell there is more lurking beneath the surface, but Kane is not the one you want to start shit with; he is vicious, ruthless, and downright savage.

"What the fuck is that look for?" he growls, tossing back his glass of whiskey.

"Nothing, just thinking," I admit, even if it is a lie.

"You fucked her?" he chuckles, darkly and deeply, patting me on the back.

"What? What makes you say that?" My jaw drops slightly, but I remain calm, trying not to give myself away.

"Come on, Seven. You're fucking glowing, and I haven't seen that stupid look in a year... not since you gave up pussy like a pussy." Shaking his head, Kane orders another drink, his eyes casting down the hall toward the meeting room.

I sigh heavily, feeling the liquor doing its job of making me warm, numb, and stupidly open about shit. "Yeah, we fucked, but she wanted to do it. I told her no, that we should wait, but she knew what she wanted, and so I gave it to her," I whisper simply, feeling a weight lift off my shoulders.

"Eli is going to fucking kill you," he begins, "but I can't lie, I've been wanting to fuck her too." He looks at me with a straight face, and I know he's being honest.

It's not surprising that Kane wants to fuck Em. Every biker in the SSB has wanted Emerson for as long as I can fucking remember. She's fucking gorgeous—too gorgeous to ignore.

She's got that innocent beauty—the kind where she has no idea how fucking beautiful she is.

"You never know what will happen this summer at the beach house," I slurred, winking as I finished off my last drink of the night.

"It ain't gonna be that simple with her brother there. But we can still try." Kane shrugs, standing to slip his black hoodie over his head.

I follow suit, pulling on my hoodie too, and throwing a few bills on the bar for a tip.

"I'm going to stay in the office with her tonight. I'll make sure she's safe," he tells me, even though that was my plan.

"I'll stay too. She was worried, looking out the windows when we were in there, so we can never be too safe."

We stride down the hall, nervous, anxious steps the entire way. As we unlock the door and open it, panic sets in when I don't see her anywhere.

"I thought she was in here?" Kane seethes, searching high and low.

But when we spot an open window, we both panic, not knowing if she left on her own or if someone took her. We share a look, murder and rage clouding our eyes as we clench our jaws in unison.

"Let's go fucking look for her," Kane orders, and for once, I'm not arguing with him about it—I follow him, eager to find her... and find her safely.

Five

Backpacks & Kisses

Emerson

I don't even remember leaving the bar. I have no idea how I did either. I can't even walk straight, so me taking off was the dumbest thing I could've done, especially with an angry, unhinged Damon on the loose.

I just had to get out of there after what happened with Seven.

I have no regrets whatsoever. But I know deep down I shouldn't have done it. I never go against my brother. But this time, I did, and I was afraid of disappointing him, so I ran to avoid having to face him.

The warm summer night air kisses my body sweetly, engulfing me in its comforting embrace as I walk down the sidewalk, constantly checking over my shoulder.

The hairs on my neck and arms don't rise, but when I hear the rumble of bikes behind me, my heart starts to thunder inside my chest because I already know who it is; I can tell by the sound of their bikes.

Coming up to a bus bench, I sit down and wait for them to pull up to the curb, knowing them all too well. Sure enough,

Kane and Seven dismount their Kawasaki Ninja 650s and walk over, a mixture of relief and concern on their beautiful faces.

Both men, of different ages, are covered from head to toe in piercings on the best parts of their bodies. Kane, with his dark hair and sexy gray streaks, massive, broad physique, and emerald green eyes that turn me into mush, is the first to arrive and sit beside me on the bench.

Seven stands in front of us, his beautiful inked body obscured by black ripped jeans and a black hoodie, his hands buried in his pockets as he scans our surroundings. He catches my smile and returns it, flashing a subtle wink that causes goosebumps to appear all over my body, despite the fact that I'm not cold.

"Hey, Emerson," Kane says, reaching out to gently touch my arm. "Are you okay?"

I nod, feeling a pang of guilt at the thought of their worry. "I'm fine," I reply, hoping it sounds more convincing than it feels. "I just needed some air."

Seven chuckles softly and takes a seat on my other side, his muscular arms resting against mine. "You know you can't just disappear like that, especially with Damon on the warpath."

I sigh and lean back, the adrenaline and alcohol in my system beginning to wear off, leaving me exhausted and aching. "Yes, I understand. I fucked up."

Kane's piercing gaze meets mine, and his concern is evident. "How about we get you home? We'll deal with the fallout together. I'll let you be my backpack tonight," he says flirtatiously, licking his thick lips with his long, thick tongue that makes me clench my thighs to stop the ache between them.

But it only intensifies it.

I manage a faint smile, thankful for their presence. As we stand and start walking towards the bikes, I know that facing Damon is going to be hell, and I hope that I won't have to. But having Kane and Seven by my side gives me the courage to face the approaching storm.

But will they be enough?

Kane and Seven split up just down the street from the house I share with my brother—our parents' home. I close my eyes and wrap my arms around Kane, hugging him as tight as I can while my cheek rests against his back.

As I breathe in, an overwhelming scent of sandalwood and whiskey fills my nose, causing my insides to tingle. But I love it; it's comforting. The ride woke me up, bringing back all of my feelings of guilt, terror, and sorrow.

Kane cuts his bike off and dismounts as we pull into the driveway, helping me off the back like a gentleman, because he is.

"Oh, you don't have to walk me. I'm fine." I smile, tucking a dark curl behind my ear as he walks me to the door, anyway.

"You fucking know me better than that, Little One," he said, taking my hand and walking me into the quiet house.

I know my brother is here, even though his bike isn't in the driveway. So as we climb the stairs, trying to be quiet, I try to pull my hand out of Kane's, but he refuses to let go. I don't fight it. In the dark, I smile, knowing he can't see me. But as we enter my room, I flip the lights on and dim them down, wiping the smile off my face.

I sit down on my bed and pull my boots off as Kane sits down right beside me, our arms touching. A shiver hits me, and my heart begins to race for reasons I'm not quite sure of.

"So, you ended things with fuckface, huh?" His green eyes bore into mine, searching for the depth inside.

"Yeah, I needed to," I admit softly, not wanting to get into everything.

But Kane, being the grown, wise man he is, won't leave unless I talk to him. There's times I've loved our talks and times when I didn't. He was always the person I could go to when I wasn't seeing eye-to-eye with my father. His advice was always spot on, and he helped me see things more clearly than I had. Kane, my father's best friend, stepped up and took over the role after my father died. And I'm fucking thankful for it.

"Say the word, and I'll fucking kill him," he simply says, keeping a straight face.

"Kane, as much as I want him dead, I would never ask you to do that." I shake my head, the hair on the back of my neck stiffening.

"No man can put a frown on your face and bruises on your fucking body and get away with it, Emerson," he growls, his chest heaving heavily.

He moves closer, scorching heat emanating from his toned, bulky body. My gaze moves across it, noticing his nipple piercings through the white wife-beater he's wearing. A not-so-subtle cough escapes his mouth, accompanied by a smirk that tugs at the corners of his lips.

"My eyes are up here, Little One. Now, be a good girl and fucking look at me," he demands in a seductive, stern tone that has confusion filling my head.

I slowly look up, taking in every inch of him from his chest up, until our gazes finally meet. Kane slides his large, tattooed hand under my chin and raises it slightly before firmly grasping it.

Then he brings his mouth closer to mine... and closer... until our lips are only a few inches apart. I swallow hard, attempting to maintain my composure and keep my body from trembling with excitement.

Is he going to kiss me? Shit, would I let him kiss me?

"Emerson, sweetheart, I love you. It fucking kills me that he has ever touched you. But I'm not mad at you, okay? You should never be afraid to talk to me, your brother, Seven, or anyone else—because we all want to hear what you have to say." He reaches his thumb toward my lips and softly sweeps it across my lower one as he tugs his between his perfect white teeth.

"I know, Kane. It's just difficult for me to admit that I need help or that I made a mistake that needs to be corrected. I don't want to be that weak girl that Damon turned me into anymore. I want to be able to stand on my own two feet and deal with my problems like a fucking strong woman." I take a deep breath, feeling a little weight lifting off my shoulders, but I'm still being weighed down.

He smiles as he traces my lip with the calloused pad of his thumb. He then leans in and presses his lips against mine, breathing heavily as his tongue slides into and around my mouth. I pause briefly, unsure of how to proceed. It's my father's best friend, who's twenty years older than me. But as my shy tongue brushes against his, I throw caution to the wind and plunge into a black hole of pleasure. It's wrong on so many levels, but rules were meant to be broken, so why not fucking break them?

He cupped my face in his hands, holding it in place as he deepened the kiss and eased me onto my back, my hands running up and down his sides. It's hard not to feel his dick pressing against my stomach, but I focus on the kiss and the way he devours my mouth as if he's craving it. But just as I start to get lost in the smooth, quick movements of his tongue and electrifying touch, he pulls away, his lips glistening with my spit.

"Kane," I whispered, my heart pounding in my ears.

"Shh, Little One. Get some rest. We'll talk tomorrow, but just so you know, before the summer is over, I'm going to make you fucking mine." He gently squeezes my hand before releasing it. "I'll let you get some rest. But if you need anything, just call me, okay?"

Startled, I nod as he quietly shuts the door behind him. Alone in my room, I took a deep breath and sank into my bed. After such a long day, the things that happened are still replaying in my head.

I lie there, tired, my eyes slowly closing as fatigue takes hold of me. I know there are still many unanswered questions and challenges ahead, but for the time being, I allow myself to drift off into a dreamless sleep, comforted by the knowledge that the ones who matter the most are only a phone call away.

Six

South Side Bikers

Stone (22)

"Where the fuck is it, Kilo?" I seethed and pressed the muzzle of my Glock against his temple, enjoying watching him tremble like a fucking bitch. Ace and Eli rummage through his shithole apartment, which is typical for Southie.

Needles and crack pipes are fucking everywhere, and this motherfucker's eyes are large, black, and wild, most likely from hitting the crack pipe just before we broke through the door. Noticing how pissed the guys are getting, I press the gun harder against his head, switching the safety off so he knows I'm not here to fuck around.

"I'm going to ask you one more fucking time. Where. Is. The. Fucking. Money?" I get in his face, our noses touching, and fear flashes through his eyes.

"I... I don't have it, Stone," he manages to croak out in between sobs as he continues to shake like a fucking leaf.

"Well, you had it. You did the fucking run for my old man, and when he finds out you don't have his [illegible], he's not going to think twice about putting a fucking bullet into your

skull." I look over at Ace, who raises his hands and shakes his head, still unable to find what we came for.

"It ain't here, man. We've turned this place upside down, and there's not a fucking cent," Eli roars, angry, irritated, and his mind occupied. "Call your father and see what he wants us to do."

"Watch him," I said, moving away from Kilo, who was tied to one of his kitchen table chairs, his face covered in bruises that had cut and bloodied my knuckles.

Stepping into the bedroom, I close the door, light a cigarette, and call my father while looking out the window at Boston's bright city lights illuminating the dark sky.

"What is it?"

"Kilo doesn't have your money. How do you want us to move forward?"

"Where exactly did he say it was? That's ten grand, Stone; it didn't just fucking disappear," he growls, extremely pissed off.

"He didn't. The fucker is high out of his mind. He can't remember shit, or he just doesn't want to tell me."

"Ask him again. If he doesn't answer, fucking kill him." He hangs up, leaving me heaving a sigh as I try to prepare myself for another kill.

It's not like it's my first one, but shit, each kill takes a fucking toll on me; it never gets easier.

I knew what I was signing up for when I begged my father at eighteen to let me into the SSB, but after I was initiated in, I realized I had no idea what the fuck I was actually signing up for. My father and Colt—Emerson and Eli's father—were once among the most feared men in Boston, and after Colt was murdered, my father became even more ruthless.

I puff heavily on my cigarette as I return to the crack den of a living room, my Glock still in my hand and my finger on the trigger. I stand behind Kilo, remaining silent as I nod to Eli.

"Where is the fucking money, Kilo? That's all we want to know," Eli tells him as he and Ace step back and to the side, out of the path of the blood spatter that's about to paint his crummy carpet.

"I told you, I don't have—"

I press the gun against the back of his head and pull the trigger without blinking, blowing mentholated smoke into the open, bloody wound as his body slumps forward.

"I had an order," I explained, as the guys looked at me in shock.

They shrugged and wiped down everything they touched, even though they were wearing gloves, before we slipped back into the darkness, the warm air embracing us like a mother's hug.

We knew it would be a long night spent cleaning, disposing of evidence, and burying the body. But in the life of an SSB, it was just another day. There was always more work to do. This was our world, and we were the predators. And I was always prepared for the next hunt.

We walk a few blocks to where our bikes are parked, enjoying the summer breeze and the echo of multiple gunshots in the night.

"You all going to Nantasket tonight?" Swinging my leg over my bike, I ask.

"I still need to talk with Em about it, so we will probably ride up there tomorrow, but you can go tonight." Eli puts his helmet on and inserts his key into the ignition. "I'm going to Nova's tonight for a bit before I go home, so I'll see you bastards later." Ace and I watch him ride off into the night as the roar of his bike pierces my ears.

The thought of Emerson being alone entices me, but with Ace here, I can't risk someone finding out that I went behind Eli's back to see her.

But... fuck. I desperately want to.

She has at least four of us obsessed with her, and she has no idea. Oh, but she will, especially if we are all stuck at the beach house for the summer.

"You want to go to the bar?" Peering through his open visor, Ace asks.

"Fuck it. Why not?"

Pushing Blue Eyes out of my mind, Ace and I ride side by side down the street, the wind whipping harder the faster we go.

We pull into the bar's parking lot, live music and conversation filling the warm summer night. As we walk in, I can't help but wonder if Emerson will be coming. But I quickly dismiss the thought, instead focusing on the drinks and the good times ahead.

We find a table near the stage and settle in, the energy of the room drowning out the lingering thoughts of what could have been. For now, I'm content to enjoy the night, the music, and the company around me.

But the thought of Emerson lingers in the back of my mind, and I cannot shake the feeling that this summer will change everything.

Ace (27)

Stone and I enter the crowded bar and head straight for our usual booth in the back, noting that Seven is the only one sitting there. As soon as Kylie notices us sitting down, she walks over and places a bottle of Crown and four shot glasses on the table before sauntering away with a wink and flipping her hair over her shoulders.

Seven goes for the bottle first, stuck in a zone without blinking.

"What is your fucking problem?" I ask, pushing a shot glass toward him to fill.

"Not shit. I'm just in a mood," he huffs, taking a shot before filling mine. "It has just been a long night. Where the fuck have you both been?

"Doing a job for dad," Stone replies in a monotone, still shaken up by yet another kill.

I reach under the table and place my hand on his knee, gently grazing it up his thigh. He relaxes slightly against my touch, and I know exactly what he needs. Even though we're both attracted to women, we've been attracted to each other since fucking high-school, and it's no secret either.

"Where are your father and Eli?" Seven tosses another shot back, sliding the bottle over to us as the music pulsates throughout the bar and the bass vibrates through our bodies.

"Eli is with Nova, but I have no idea where my old man is."

"He was here, but he took a call and left without saying anything." Seven studies Stone as I palm his cock beneath the table, feeling it grow against my hand.

As I slip my hand down his pants and grab his cock, Seven turns toward the entrance, his jaw dropping open. Stone and I exchange looks, my hand stroking him firm and slow, just the way he likes it. He spreads his legs and leans against the back of the booth, causing his shoulders to slump.

Kane enters the room with a furious expression on his face and a step that shouts "fury." Stone tenses up as my hand continues to stroke him under the table, trying to keep him steady. Ignorant of the situation, Seven grabs the bottle and fills his glass once more.

"What the hell are you doing here, looking like that?" Stone's voice is low and dangerous as he tries to suppress a moan as I squeeze the tip of his dick, smearing little beads of moisture all around it.

"I'm here for a drink. What's it to you?" Kane retorts, his tone defensive as he glares at his son..

His eyes narrow as he glares at us, his jaw clenched. I can feel Stone's heart racing under my touch as the tension in the booth grows, my hand sliding up and down his dick. Seven just stares at the door, looking for Emerson, not even bothering to hide his obsession with her anymore.

"Where the fuck is Eli?" Kane looks around, trying to find him in the crowd.

"Not here. He went and met up with Nova after we finished the job," I answer, since Stone is gripping the edge of the table, fighting through the orgasm that's bubbling to the surface.

I feel hot cum spurt from his cock, and I use it as lube to finish him off, stroking fast and hard until Stone goes limp and begins to pant. I pull my hand out of his boxers and wipe his cum on my pants, a grin on my face as I take another shot.

"I need to talk with the two of you," Kane demands, glaring at us sternly.

Taking a minute to regain his composure, Stone nods, takes one more shot, and slides out of the booth with me right behind him.

"I needed more than just a fucking rub and tug, Ace," he whispers as we follow his father to the back room.

"I gotchu, baby boy. Just wait until later."

SEVEN

MISSING UNDERWEAR

Emerson

Scalding water cascades over me, setting fire to my bruised skin. I lower my head and stand beneath the stream of the pulsating water, strands of wet hair falling into my face.

Tears fall down my cheeks, but the water masks them, making it look like I haven't been crying in the shower for the last thirty minutes.

I miss my parents. I'm so fucking lost without them. There is an emptiness inside of me that will never go away, or at least it does not seem like it will, even with my big brother. I feel as though I am drowning and am unable to reach the surface to breathe. I thought I was strong enough to handle their deaths, but boy, was I fucking wrong.

I eventually turn off the shower and reach for my towel on the rack when my hands start to get wrinkly and my skin turns bright red from the boiling water. After wrapping it around myself and wringing out my hair, I step out of the shower, putting my feet down on the memory foam bath mat and avoiding my reflection in the slightly fogged-up mirror.

I tiptoe down the hall, my bare feet tapping the hardwood, and notice how strangely quiet the house is. I walk into my room and flip the light on, going right for my walk-in closet to get dressed for the night. But when I pull open my dresser drawer to find a matching bra and underwear, my jaw drops to the floor when I see my entire drawer empty—except for one pink thong shoved toward the back.

What the fuck?

I grab the underwear and feel a gooey substance soaking them, causing them to fall from my hand onto the floor. My hand shines under the light, and without a doubt, I know I just touched cum.

Someone stole all of my underwear and came in with the only pair they left—*Damon.*

Frozen in fear, afraid that he's still in the house, I hug my towel closer to my body and dial my brother's number with quivering hands. He doesn't answer. So I call Kane, hoping he's close enough to swing by and check the place out.

"I was wondering when I was going to hear from you. What's going on?" he asks, yelling over loud music, probably at the bar.

"Damon was here... or is here... I don't know."

"I'll be right there. Grab your gun and get in your closet."

"I already am, Kane. Just hurry, *please*," I beg, trying to hide the panic in my tone as every little sound begins to freak me out.

"Good girl. Don't worry, Emerson. I'm coming."

I slump to the floor with my back against my full-length mirror, hugging my knees to my chest. Reaching behind it, I grab my gun and click the safety off, laying it beside me just in case.

I close my eyes, trying to calm down and focus on my breathing. Minutes feel like hours as I wait for Kane to arrive, my heart pounding in my chest. Finally, I hear the sound of his footsteps approaching, and I take a deep breath, feeling relieved for the first time since I found out Damon had been in my house. Kane bursts into the room with a concerned look on his face, but as soon as he sees me, his expression softens.

"Shit, are you okay?" he asks, crouching down beside me.

I nod, feeling a sense of safety wash over me, and my heartbeat slowly returns to normal. Kane wraps his arm around my shoulders and helps me to my feet, leading me out of the room and through the house to make sure Damon is nowhere to be found.

Once we're sure the house is clear, Kane stays with me while I get dressed, minus a bra and underwear.

"I'm going to fucking kill him," is all he keeps saying, chain smoking and pacing near the closet door as I finish getting decent, his gun in his hand, ready to use.

"I don't know how he got in. We had the locks changed and all the windows are locked. The alarm didn't even go off." I run a brush through my wet hair, letting it fall perfectly down my back, trying to figure out the mystery of the missing underwear.

"Did he leave you anything or take anything?" Kane asks, watching with curiosity as I put my makeup on, smacking my lips as I finish off with a layer of red lipstick and gloss to make them shine.

I turn to face him, shaking my head in disgust and embarrassment. "Yeah, he took all of my bras and panties. Oh, but he left me one pair, which he fucking left his cum all over." I cringe, walking out of my closet with Kane right behind me, his eyes burning a hole into my back.

"What a fucking pervert! You're not staying here tonight, not unless your brother comes home."

"I'm sure Eli will be home late, but he'll be here." I slide my feet into my black-heeled boots that match the black leather pants and red, lacy crop top I have on, feeling good about myself for the first time in a while, despite the invasion of privacy.

The look Kane gives me as I stand up, ready to go, makes me shiver—in a good way, though. He takes a step toward me, a devious smirk tugging at the corners of his lips.

"Fucking hell, Little One. Why do you make it so damn hard for me?" He growls, raking his eyes the length of my body with a torturous look swirling in them.

"What?" I laugh, trying to hide the nerves that threaten to cripple me.

He stops in front of me and reaches out, dragging his fingers down the front of my body in a teasing manner. slightly getting me worked up.

"You know exactly what the fuck I'm talking about. Your father always told us—everyone—to stay away from you, but you make it *so* fucking hard for us." His words hit me hard, bringing back memories from the other night with Seven, and that fucking guilt started to consume me again.

He backs me up until my back hits the wall, his six-foot figure towering over me. I grip the hem of his soft black shirt, clutching it in my hands with a slight tug. And when I look at him, catching his lustful eyes with mine, I know that we're both in the same boat.

It's fucking impossible to stay away from them too. *Case in point: Seven.*

"One of these days you're going to let me have that pussy, Little One, and I'll show you exactly how a real man fucks," he whispers into my ear as he leans in, peppering soft kisses on the side of my neck with his palm pressing against my throat.

"I fucked Seven," I blurted out, holding my breath in anticipation of his reaction.

He grins, lets out a deep chuckle, and licks the shell of my ear. "I know all about it, but don't worry; your secret's safe with me."

I stood there, shocked by his response. Kane took a step back, still grinning and leaving me flustered as I tried to play it off.

"So now it's my turn, Little One." And with that, he grabs me by the waist, pulling me close with such force that my breath hitches in my dry throat. I press my lips against his, engulfed by the burning desire that's been beneath the surface for years. I can't hide from it any longer. At that very moment, we shattered the thin wall between the friendship we had and the forbidden lust we shared.

Pulling away breathlessly, Kane licks his lips, dropping his intense gaze to mine, sending a shiver down my spine.

"Kane..." I moan as he puts his finger to my lips to silence me.

"I'm not going to fuck you tonight, but mark my fucking words, that pussy is going to be mine, and when it happens, I ain't going to hold shit back." He backs away, slides his hand into mine, and gently pulls me behind him as we make our way through the house to the front door, my mind still clouded with desire.

Eight

Lucky Number Seven

Seven

The entire time Kane, Stone, and Ace were in the office at the end of the hall, I sat in the booth alone and drank. Even when Kane rushed the fuck out of here as if the bar was on fire, I didn't get up. But I noticed Stone and Ace weren't with him. Which means they're probably fucking in the back somewhere.

I can feel Kylie's eyes on me as she stands behind the bar, not doing her fucking job, but every time I turn around to look, she rips her gaze away quickly.

The bass reverberates throughout the bar as the current Tech N9ne song goes hard, blaring loudly and spilling out onto the street. Bikers from all over are gathered here to drink, bringing their latest groupies who I want nothing to do with.

I fucking want Emerson.

I take another shot, savoring the familiar burn as it smoothly slides down my throat, making my buzz more intense. Shaking my head at a wave of heat that rushes over

me, I look toward the door just in time to see Emerson and Kane walking in... *together*.

Emerson's eyes lock onto mine as they enter, a smug smile playing on her lips. Kane, on the other hand, looks irritated and agitated—like a man on a mission. I can sense the tension between them, but I don't care. All I want is for Emerson to come over to me and let me kiss her, to feel her body against mine.

I down the rest of my drink and push myself out of the booth, deliberately avoiding eye contact with Kylie as I make my way through the crowded bar towards the exit. I need some fresh air and a moment to clear my head.

Outside, I lean against the wall and take in deep breaths of the cool night air. As I close my eyes, all I can see is Emerson's face, her laughter, and the way she looks at me when she thinks no one is watching.

"How come you're out here?" Emerson's voice makes my eyes fling open, coming face-to-face with her bright smile and her red-painted lips.

Her tight red top clings to her curvy body, making her tits pop out of the top of it. Her hard nipples are poking through the lacy fabric, making it obvious she isn't wearing a bra. And those leather pants—fuck—are tight, showing off her ass and every bounce her cheeks do as she moves. Hanging just below her hips, I trace her tattoos with my eyes, her sparkling belly piercing my eye.

"Seven?" she asks, taking a step closer and tucking her curly brown hair behind her ear.

"Fuck, Princess. You look good enough to fuck against the wall right here." My words are slurred and I know she can hear them, but she doesn't care.

She steps closer, gripping the waist of my jeans with her fingers, grazing the skin inside them. I slide my hand behind her neck and squeeze until my fingers press against her pulsing veins. Pulling her mouth to meet mine, I seize her lips and thrust my tongue between them, tasting the mint from her gum as I explore every inch with hunger.

My other hand finds its way to her hip, pulling her closer to me as we kiss, lost in the heat of the moment. The sound of the bar fades away as we focus on each other, the tension from earlier melting away as our bodies press together in a seductive dance of desire that we're both drowning in.

Breathlessly, and with red lipstick smeared around her puffy lips, she smirks and inches her hand down my pants even further, her blue eyes piercing into my fucking soul.

"Fuck me, Seven. I bet you won't," she teases, her long, innocent lashes fluttering as she playfully bats her eyes.

Challenge accepted.

"You shouldn't have bet me, Princess." I spin her around and press her chest against the back of the building, roughly tugging her tight pants down, only to realize she isn't wearing underwear either. "Um, is there a reason your not wearing a bra or panties tonight?" I whisper right into her ear as I flick her lobe with the tip of my tongue, making her body shudder against mine.

"Long story... but Damon stole all of them," she moans as I kick her legs open slightly and pull out my cock, running the pierced tip along the crack of her ass before pushing against her wet opening.

I drive into her fiercely; the friction sends pleasure shuddering through my body. A guttural moan escapes her lips as I grip her hips and thrust into her harder and deeper. The air is thick with lust and longing as we move together in a rhythmic, primal dance, keeping in tune with the beat still blaring from inside.

I slide my cock out of her tight, wet cunt, hold tightly onto her hips as she wiggles them, and slam back in with a forceful thrust that surges her into the building. Her hands go on the wall above her head, and she leans back, pushing her ass out for more.

"Mhm, Seven," she softly moans, making my balls tighten from the heavenly sound of her voice.

"What is it, Princess? Tell me what you fucking want," I growl, sinking my teeth into the side of her neck as I repeatedly slam her back on my cock, her tight inner walls gripping me like a vice.

"Harder," she begs, on the verge of losing all the control she's been trying to hold onto. "Fuck me harder."

"Ah, my dirty little slut wants it harder, huh?" I pound into her until I bottom out in her warmth, ripping a low moan from her dry throat.

"Yes, please."

"Take this dick, Princess. Come all over it while I paint your cunt with mine." Holding her hip, I reach around to the front of her body and push my hand between her shaky thighs.

Finding her clit, I rub and roll circles over it with the pad of my thumb, still slamming into her with everything I've got.

Her moans echo in the alley, sending shivers throughout me and making my cock throb while buried deep in her cunt. Her walls grip me in a heartbeat-like rhythm as she begins to unravel before me.

"Good fucking girl," I grunt in between thrusts, feeling her warm release start to soak my dick. "You're such a good little slut, letting me fuck this pussy for anyone to see," I groan, feeling my muscles tighten all through my body as tingles begin torturing my toes.

With a final full-body thrust that makes her rise on her toes, trying to chase the feeling of my cock ripping her apart, I burst, spilling every drop of my cum as deep inside of her as I can get it, holding her in place.

Before long, our bodies reach a crescendo, and we both tumble over the edge, waves of ecstasy washing over us. We stand there, breathless and dazed, in the quiet alley behind the bar, our secret shared only between us.

Emerson turns to me, pulling up her pants, her eyes sparkling with satisfaction. "You win," she smirks, a playful glint in her hooded blue eyes.

As I tuck my cock back into my pants, I pull her close and kiss her, tasting the sweetness of her lips and the desperation on her tongue. "If this is what winning feels like, I never want to lose," I whisper against her skin, savoring the warmth of her body pressed against mine.

"I hate to burst your bubble, Seven, but everyone loses sometimes."

With a smirk, she walks into the bar, leaving me standing in the alley alone with a smoldering arousal that keeps burning inside of me. I can't believe her sassy provocations are getting under my skin. But I don't want them to stop. And I'll be fucking damned if I lose anytime soon. I'm a fucking winner, and I get what I want. And right now, the only thing I fucking want is Emerson.

After regaining my composure and waiting until my cock went slightly soft, I walked into the bar after Emerson, my eyes glued to her every swift move. I secure another drink and then make my way over to her, flashing her a smile that makes her eyes sparkle. She knows that I won't fucking back down, and I'm ready to show her just how willing I am to fight for her. She's a fucking challenge, and I love a good challenge.

Determined, I walk up to her and whisper in her ear, "I never fucking lose, Emerson. And I'll prove it to your ass." With that, I grab her hand and lead her over to the booth, confident that whatever comes our way, I'm not backing down. And as I look at her and feel her hand in mine, I know that the only thing I want is Emerson. And I'm going to make sure that she fucking knows it too.

Nine

Tasting the Forbidden

Kane

The cold leather couch shocks my body as my back hits it, cooling me off and calming down the raging storm of emotions brewing inside of me. Drink after drink, I try to get the bullshit with Damon out of my head, but I can't. He fucked with Emerson again, and he needs to be fucking stopped.

Pulling out my phone, I bring up Eli's message thread and type out a new one, trying to control the anger in my words.

We need to fucking talk about your sister's ex.

Why, what happened now?

He broke into your fucking house, Eli. He's stalking her ass, and she's fucking terrified.

Take her home tonight and stay with her. I won't be home until morning.

I thought you were taking her to the beach house tomorrow.

I am, but I had to drive down there tonight to let Ace and Stone in. Tell Seven to head over tonight.

Fine. But we need to talk about how we're going to handle that motherfucker.

We will, trust me. Just take her home and fucking protect her for me.

Will do.

I toss my phone on the cushion beside me, a cunning grin on my face I can't wipe away. He just gave me an in with Em, and he doesn't even know it.

Standing up, I tuck my gun in the back of my pants and cover it with my shirt, clutching the bottle of Crown as I head for the door. But it opens before I can get to it, and a tipsy Emerson walks in with Seven's hands protectively holding hers.

"Daddy Kane!" she squeals, dropping Seven's hand and rushing over to me, nearly knocking me over as she jumps into my arms.

Hearing her call me Daddy makes my cock jump against her stomach and my blood rushes like a tidal wave through my veins. Seven winks, licking his lips as his eyes lock onto her ass, leaning against the closed door.

"Someone's feeling better." I laugh, brushing her silky brown curls out of her face so I can see her better. And fuck, *she's gorgeous.*

"I am, thank you." She kisses my cheek and goes to take a step back, but I snatch her wrist and yank her against my chest, feeling her hard nipples poking against me.

"Easy there, Little One," I warn with a smirk, running my hand up her back and pulling her closer. "Let's save the fun for when we get back to your house, huh?"

"What do you mean?" Her perfectly sculpted brows pinch in confusion as her racing heart thumps against my chest.

I lean in close, my lips brushing against her ear. "I mean, I have orders to take you home tonight and stay with you until your brother arrives." As I whisper into her ear, I can see the fire in her eyes igniting. She nods, biting her plump lips as a sly smile plays on them.

"Now be a good girl for me and go give this to Ryker or Kylie, whoever is behind the bar." I hand her an envelope of cash for the night, and as she takes it and spins on her heel, I slap her ass and watch it bounce as she saunters away seductively.

"I'll be right back," she says, turning to look at me one more time over her shoulder.

"Hurry back because I want to get going." My order comes out more demanding than I wanted it to, but she listens well and scurries off, making sure to give Seven and me a show as she leaves.

Alone, Seven turns to me, a slightly confused look on his face, his eyes drunk and bloodshot. "What was that all about?" He pulls out a smoke and lights it, tucking a thick blunt behind his ear.

"Eli wants you to ride out to the beach house tonight to meet him, Stone, and Ace."

"I need to sober up some, but yeah, I'll be out there tonight. Take care of Emerson, Kane," he warns me, his tone turning serious. "She's struggling but won't admit it."

"I know; believe me."

As Seven stumbled out the door, I picked up the crown and capped it, my mind racing with the plans I had in store for Emerson tonight. She needed someone to protect her—to make her feel good—and I was more than fucking willing to play that role.

With a smirk, I waited for her bubbly ass to come back before we headed out the door, ready to take care of business—finally.

Back at Emerson's house, we head right for the stairs and run up them, her hand in mine as she pulls me behind her. I don't know what she thinks is going to happen tonight, but I already told her I wasn't going to fuck her.

Don't get me wrong, I want to, but I want her to be sober so she remembers it. I want her to want me while she's in the right frame of mind, and I don't want it to seem like I'm taking advantage.

I ignore all of the guilt from the promises I made her father, feeling like a piece of shit for wanting to ruin his little girl in the most sinful, depraved ways.

But even I can't resist temptation forever.

As she collapses on her bed and pulls her boots off, I scan her room to make sure there aren't any more surprises from Damon.

"I'll be right back, Little One. I'm going to do a walk-through to make sure that motherfucker hasn't been back." I lean down and press a soft kiss to her forehead, hearing a small sigh of relief slip from her red lips.

"I'll be right here when you get back." She grins and leans back on her elbows, my eyes darting to her pointy nipples still poking through her top.

I quickly tear my gaze away and head out of her room, making my way through the rest of the house to ensure that everything is secure. As I finish my walk through, a wave of unease washes over me. What if Damon had already been back? What if he had found some other way to torment Emerson? I push the thoughts aside and return to her room, relieved to find her exactly where I left her. Maybe it was time to finally give in to the overwhelming desire that had been building between us—one that we had been hiding for a while.

I strip down to my underwear, watching her hungrily take in the sight of my body, mesmerized by the tattoos covering almost every inch of my skin. Climbing into bed with her, I put my gun under the pillow and turn on my side, slowly pulling at her clothes until they come off, and she's left ass naked beside me, her cheeks red as she begins to become shy.

Before she can speak, I roll on top of her, hovering my body over hers with our lips inches apart. She holds onto my hips and locks her legs around me, trying to pull me as close to her as she can.

"Kiss me, Kane," she begs, her eyes pleading with desire.

And so I do, fusing our mouths as my tongue slips between her lips, finding hers in a wild dance of need and hunger. My cock grows and pokes into her, but I ignore my own needs and focus on her—focus on making her feel good.

Breaking the kiss, she whimpers, clawing at my back as I slide down her body, roughly pushing her legs open. The smell of her arousal fills my nose as I dip my head between her thighs and lick from the bottom of her cunt to the top, making her back rise off the bed.

"Ahh, Kane!" she gasps, letting herself fall flat on her back as I suck her swollen little clit between my teeth.

"I love hearing my name come from those lips, Little One. Scream it all you want because tonight, I'm going to eat this pretty pink cunt until you squirt all over my tongue."

She shivers, looking at me, not knowing what to say until she blurts out, "I fucked Seven tonight again."

"I know, and I don't give a fuck. We're all grown." I spread her pussy lips open and push my tongue inside her, getting a taste of her sweetness that begins to drive me fucking wild. "We can all share," I mumble against her cunt, the vibrations from my voice making her eyes roll back.

With each flick of my tongue, Emerson's moans grew louder and more desperate, her body writhing in pleasure beneath me. I could feel her getting closer, her hips buckling against my face as she teetered on the edge of release. My fingers fucked her while my tongue lapped up her slick juices, her scent burning into my nose. She pulled my hair and cried out as I pinched her clit and used my fingers and tongue to destroy her.

Her body shook. Her back rose and fell. Her legs tried to clamp around my head, but I roughly pushed them open and pinned them to the mattress. I didn't stop until she cried out my name, her body shaking with the force of her orgasm. I sucked her cum out of her and held it on my tongue until her pussy was dry and begging me for a break. Climbing back up her body, I captured her lips and forced my cum-covered tongue between them, wanting her to taste how fucking sweet she was.

As she lay there, breathless and sated, I looked into her eyes, a surge of desire washing over me once again. I knew that tonight was just the beginning for us, despite the complicated situation we found ourselves in.

A mix of emotions and thoughts flooded my mind as I gazed down at her, but in that moment, I knew that I wanted to protect her and be there for her in ways she couldn't even imagine.

And I was willing to do whatever the fuck it took to keep her safe, no matter the cost.

••••••••••••

Ten

Surprise, Surprise

Emerson

I wake up wearing a long, loose t-shirt that smells just like Kane. And when I open my eyes, rubbing the sleep out of them, blinded by the bright sun peeking in through the windows, I turn and see Kane still sleeping soundly beside me. I watch as his perfectly sculpted, tattooed chest rises and falls with each breath he takes, fixating my eyes on the shiny platinum piercings he has through his nipples.

He's fucking gorgeous, especially for a man in his forties. His short, dark hair with silver streaks on random strands is all tousled, making him look fucking stunning. I've always thought that Kane was attractive for someone his age, very well built, with a figure that towers over me.

To be honest, I never looked at him the way I have been lately. I mean, he was my father's best friend, and I knew nothing would ever happen between us.

But after the events that took place last night in my childhood bed proved otherwise. And even though I'm feeling plenty guilty over my actions with Kane *and* S[illegible]n, I want

them even more, despite my brother and father's rule that they were off limits to me and I to them.

I hate letting them down, but at the same time, I can't ignore the new, intense feelings I've been keeping in—and I don't fucking want to.

Yes, I've been struggling and slowly spiraling since the murder of my parents over six months ago, and I have no idea how to move on and find happiness again.

But Seven and Kane have helped immensely, and I'd be lying if I said I didn't want to explore more to see where things could go. I need to move on from Damon, and they've helped with that too. Getting over your first love is hard—harder than I thought—but they make it so much easier for me. I know I deserved better than Damon and his cruel and unusual beatings.

So, I guess I'll have to figure things out as I go along. And if that means exploring these new and unconventional feelings with Kane and Seven, then so be it. Because I refuse to let anyone hold me back from finding happiness again, especially not my own guilt.

As I look at Kane sleeping next to me, I can't help but feel a rush of emotions, a perfect storm drowning me from the inside. But I know if anyone can pull me out of the water, it's them two.

Maybe it's time to take a risk and see where this goes. I can't keep living in the past, and perhaps Kane and Seven are what I need to move forward. I know it won't be easy, and there will be consequences, but I have to try. I owe it to myself to find some sort of peace and happiness after everything I've been through, even if it is with the two men I was told to stay away from. The heart wants what it wants, and if Eli wants me to be happy, he'll come around to the idea of us... *eventually.*

Scanning Kane's half-naked body, my eyes fixate on the scarred bullet wounds from all the times he's been shot, and all I want to do is brush my lips against them.

His eyes flutter open, a warm smile spreading across his lips as he looks at me. I smile back and let out a deep breath, knowing that I'm ready to take a chance on what we have. Kane reaches out and takes my hand, giving it a gentle squeeze.

"Hey," he says softly, letting my hand go and grazing his under my shirt and up my stomach, making me shiver from the deep chill penetrating my bones.

"Hey," I reply, feeling a sense of peace wash over me, relaxing against his touch, not wanting to move from my spot.

This might be complicated, but I know it's worth it. And besides, the way Kane ate my pussy until I squirted and came all over his face, is worth any kind of disappointment that I'll be facing from my brother.

Before either of us can say anything else, my bedroom door opens, and Eli walks in, a mix of shock and anger twisted into his facial features. "What the fuck is this?" He glares at Kane, taking note of him only in his tight-fitting boxer briefs and me in nothing but a t-shirt that barely covers my ass.

"Relax, Eli. We fell asleep as soon as we got home," Kane says, sitting up, trying to diffuse the situation we both know is about to blow up.

"Emerson, is this true?" Eli looks deeply into my eyes as I sit up beside Kane, my back against the headboard.

"Yes, we fell asleep. I'm sorry for what it looks like."

Out of nowhere, Kane secretly slides his hand between my legs and eases his fingers into my pussy, boldly fingering me right in front of my unsuspecting brother.

"You'd better not be lying," he sneers, rolling his eyes.

"What are you doing at home anyway? I thought you were with Nova." I sit there for a moment, trying not to moan as Kane's fingers dig deeper inside of me, getting soaked in my arousal as he glides them between my walls. Feeling like I'm going to come, I manage to push him away and compose myself before Eli can put two and two together. I swing my legs over the edge of the bed and slide my feet into my black Victoria's Secret slippers that warm them immediately.

"Well, I have a surprise for you, Em. I need you to get dressed and pack a bag for a couple weeks." He grins mischievously which makes me nervous, but I try to remain calm.

"Where are we going?"

"You'll find out. Get ready because we leave in an hour, and I want to beat the rain since we're taking our bikes," he says cryptically. "And Kane, while Emerson is getting ready, I need to talk to you downstairs."

"Sure thing, Eli. Let me throw my clothes back on and I'll meet you on the balcony." Kane looks back at me and winks, making me smile even though I try hard not to.

I quickly change into light, ripped jeans and a cropped white T-shirt that shows off the tattoos on my stomach and the piercing in my navel, my heart pounding with the sense of unease that Eli's sudden appearance and news has brought on. But Kane gave me a reassuring smile as he left to talk to Eli, so I took a deep breath, deciding to focus more on what comes next.

With my bag packed, I take a few steadying breaths and head downstairs to find out what Eli's big surprise is.

Eli is standing next to Kane, arms folded across his chest, as I make my way down the staircase. Kane sends me an encouraging smile before turning to Eli, engaging in what seems to be a serious conversation.

"What's going on, Eli?" I ask as I approach them, my voice showcasing a blend of emotions—curiosity, anxiety, and a hint of hope.

"I can't tell you just yet, Em, but I promise it's for the best. Trust me," he replies, his eyes expressing sincerity, yet holding back some hidden worry.

I nod, trying my best to stifle the waves of uncertainty that are threatening to crash over me. I know Eli always has my best interests at heart, but the unknown is always unsettling. With a brief glance at Kane, who offers me a reassuring smile, I make a mental note to have a conversation with him as soon as I have a moment alone. I need to talk to him about what happened between us, about how I feel, and about the uncertainties that lie ahead. I'm not sure where this is all going, but I know one thing for certain—I have to take a chance and see what happens.

As Eli hurries us out the door to beat the impending rain, I feel a tinge of anxiety and a flicker of excitement. This might be the beginning of a new chapter, and I have to be brave enough to turn the page. And as the three of us depart on our bikes, I silently hope that this adventure will bring clarity, healing, and maybe even a glimpse of happiness.

Eleven

House of Memories

Emerson

Before we even get there, I know where we're going. The roads to our family beach house on Nantasket are burned into my brain by now.

But why would Eli bring me here, and with Kane of all people?

When we finally pull into the garage, I remove my helmet and gape, taking in the other bikes parked next to us.

Seven. Stone. Ace. Their bikes are all here, which must mean they are too. Is spending the summer at the beach house with Eli and the guys Eli's big surprise?

Fuck, if that's the case, then I'm in fucking trouble.

When the sound of the bikes stops rumbling, I get off of mine and turn to face my brother, who has a big, sly smile on his face. I can already feel my resolve eroding as temptation tightens its grip around my neck as Kane stands behind him, looking devilish in the most delicious way.

"I figured getting away for the summer might help." My brother walks over and wraps his arm around me, ushering me toward the door to go inside.

"With everyone here, though?" I mumble, avoiding Kane's intense gaze as best I can.

"Why not? They're all our family too, Emerson. We all want you to be happy and safe, and you won't be if you were to stay in Dorchester with Damon on the loose." Eli opens the door, and we enter a room filled with complete chaos where Seven, Nova, Stone, and Ace are playing pool in a room off the back balcony and drinking like fish. Though it is not overbearing, the music is loud enough for them to miss us when we enter, giving me time to get used to the sudden discomfort I'm feeling. These guys have been in my life for as long as I can remember, but after having intimate relationships with two of them, a feeling of unease rises in me and I begin to panic.

I cast a quick glance at Kane, who remains lingering nearby, his gaze piercing my own. The memories of our past seem to hang in the air between us. I take a deep breath and try to push them away as I follow Eli further into the chaos, trying to put on a smile even though my heart feels like it's about to burst out of my chest.

However, as I look around the room, a sense of dread creeps in. Being here, surrounded by these familiar faces, awakens memories and emotions that I thought I had buried deep within myself. I take a deep breath and try to push all of the negativity aside, wanting to enjoy my time here even if I don't know how to do it.

"Here's to a summer we'll never forget," Seven says, thrusting a red solo cup into my empty hand, giving me a smoldering look over the brim of his cup as he takes a drink.

I nod, taking a large sip to try to alleviate the anxiety coursing through my veins. Nova approaches Eli, loops her arm through his, and kisses his cheek.

"Glad you guys made it safe. Emmy, I'm glad you decided to come. This summer is going to be so much fun," she laughs, dragging my brother away and leaving me alone so anyone can approach me.

And they do.

"So, Blue Eyes, what do you think?" Stone asks, bumping his shoulder against mine as I scan the room, watching the small crowd sway to the music's beat.

"I think I was ambushed," I laughed, taking another swig of the rum in my cup. "But who knows, this could be fun."

"Nah," Ace speaks up, wrapping me in a hug. "It *will* be fun, Em."

"I'm going to put my things in my room. I'll be right back," I muttered, pushing through the guys.

I climbed the stairs, trying to hold back tears as I passed pictures of my family on the wall. Eli might have thought this was a good idea, but deep down, I was already regretting it. Every step I took toward my room felt like my heart was breaking and shattering all over again. At this rate, I will never be able to pick up all of the pieces and put my heart back together. I hated thinking negatively, but I couldn't bring myself to see the good in anything.

Walking into my room, I wiped my tears and looked around, realizing that everything was exactly as I had left it last summer. Putting my bag on the floor beside my bed, I walk to the floor-to-ceiling windows and gaze out at the beach, the massive waves crashing against the shoreline.

Putting on my Linkin Park playlist, I abruptly changed moods and began tearing apart my room, wanting no trace of the girl I used to be. I rip pictures and posters down, shatter little glass collectibles I'd been saving since I was little, and I don't stop until I'm out of breath, a sobbing mess on the floor, and until my room is unrecognizable.

At that moment, I didn't care what anyone else said. I was going to make it my goal to make my time here as difficult as possible. What I needed to do was devise a strategy for getting through the summer. I had to be strong to keep from falling deeper into the black hole that was swallowing me.

I stared out at the ocean, watching the waves crash into the shore, wishing I could be anywhere but here. Because being here only reminded me of my parents and the summers we spent here as a family. It was incredibly painful to reflect on the good times, so I refused to do so any longer. I didn't care if I'd ever heal. At least I knew that I wasn't going to wallow in self-pity. I wanted to make the most of my summer, especially since I would be trapped in a house with some of the most forbidden, dangerous men my father had warned me to avoid.

But I also couldn't wait to get out of this place. I needed to get out of the house and away from the suffocating memories it held. I glanced at the door, hoping to make a quick escape, but I knew that running into the guys was inevitable. I desperately needed a change of scenery. After a few moments, I stood up and made my way to the door to the balcony off my room. I couldn't stay here for another minute. I walked out of the house and down the stairs to the beach, hoping that the sound of the waves would help me relax.

Twelve

Blue Eyes & Cloudy Skies

Stone

As Ace and I emerge from one of the spare rooms, we notice my little blue-eyed beauty sitting on the beach, her feet in the water and her head pointing toward the cloudy sky. We come to a halt and stare out the window at her, knowing she is already struggling just being here. With my father and Seven on a booze run and Eli and Nova occupied, the brilliant idea of keeping her company comes to mind.

"I know you want to go down there," Ace says, noticing how intently my gaze is focused on her.

"Yeah, I just want to make sure she's okay. You want to join me?" I offered, walking down the hall to the back deck, which leads directly to the beach.

Saying nothing, Ace follows, both of us eager to spend some alone time with her before everyone returns and chaos reignites. We grab a pitcher of margaritas and a towel and head outside, the hot air enveloping us as we walk

through the white sand, being careful not to step on broken seashells.

When she turns around, I can tell she has been crying, but she smiles through the pain and wipes the makeup from beneath her eyes.

"What are you guys doing? I assumed you would be inside with everyone else." Her voice cracks, but she does an excellent job of maintaining her composure as we take seats on either side of her.

"They are on a run, and your brother is... busy. We wanted to make sure you were alright." I offer her the pitcher, which she accepts without hesitation, digging her black painted toes into the sand.

"Fuck, that's strong. Are you trying to get me drunk?" Genuine laughter escapes her throat, and I can tell she is gradually loosening up.

"Maybe, but we have the entire summer for that, Blue Eyes. Right now, we just want to make sure you're doing okay."

She sighs, looks at me with teary eyes, and hands me back the pitcher. "It's rough being back here, but I'm trying to put that shit behind me so I can enjoy myself." She leans her head on my shoulder and adjusts her position so that her feet are comfortably resting on Ace's lap.

"Thank you for being here, guys. It means a lot to me." Her voice is gentle and vulnerable, and her guard is completely down.

"Anytime, brat. We're here for you," Ace says, his hands gently running through her hair.

The three of us sit there in silence, the sound of waves crashing against the shore serving as a soothing background. And as the hidden sun begins to set, painting the sky in drab shades of orange and pink, I can feel Emerson's body relax against us, the stress slowly fading with each sip. I lower my head, our mouths inches apart, but I don't kiss her.

I want to, but I know she is vulnerable, and Emerson is the last person I want to take advantage of. But the look she gives me indicates that she wants something, so I leave the decision up to her.

"Tell me something, Stone," she says in a low whisper, shivering against me and Ace as a gust of warm wind blows heavily around us.

"Anything." I brush my knuckles against her cheek, tracing her jawline as she instinctively licks her lips, a distant, needy look in her ocean-blue eyes.

"How long have you wanted me?" she asks softly, confidence radiating from her half-naked body, and my gaze moves to the tattoos covering her tanned skin.

"For a long fucking time," I admit, breathing heavily as I stare out at the ocean, perplexed as to why she is now asking this.

"What about you, Ace?" Turning her head and shifting her focus away from me and toward him, she cracks a small smile that makes her dimples pop, eager to hear what he has to say.

"How did you know that I wanted you?" He teases, running his hand up her bare legs and staring at her with a darkness I have never seen before.

Yeah, Ace and I have fucked before, but we are both into women, too, and the prospect of the three of us being together begins to weigh heavily on my shoulders.

Maybe she will be up for it this summer, but Emerson fucking Cole is unpredictable.

"Ace, I can see how you look at me. Damon and Seven have given me that look before..." She pauses and returns my gaze, her cheeks flushing with nervousness. "And your father, too."

I shake my head and chuckle, aware of my father's fascination with her but unconcerned.

"Blue Eyes, we all fucking want you. Okay? How could we not? You're the total package: funny, caring, a total badass, and fucking sexy as sin."

Emerson sits up, giggles, and pauses to think. "I appreciate it," she says, leaning in and kissing my cheek.

Ace intertwined his fingers with hers before bringing her hand up to his lips with a gentle kiss. I raise an eyebrow, curious about where this is going.

"Have you ever thought about this before?" I ask, shifting slightly. "Do you want us as much as we want you?"

Emerson bites her lip and smiles before looking at me. "Maybe a little. "Time will tell," she says mysteriously, tugging her bottom lip between her teeth and casting an alluring look in her eyes.

The three of us sit there, caught up in the sexual tension that pervades the humid air. As the sun sinks further below the horizon, the last traces of red and yellow are quickly swallowed up by the darkness of night, and the anticipation of what is to come begins to swarm in my stomach.

I am ready to ruin her, to give her everything she wants, but one question haunts me: What the fuck are we going to do with her brother? Because as long as he is here, watching over her—over us—it will be difficult to have the fun that we all know we want.

The thought of Eli watching over us like a hawk makes me restrain myself from making any moves. It's clear Emerson is interested, but I don't want to complicate things more than they already are. With Eli around, things could quickly spiral out of control.

I give Ace a look before returning my attention to Emerson. "We will figure it out," I assure her, hoping she understands how complicated things could become.

The stuffy air around us is charged with desire, temptation, and anticipation, and as night falls and the town falls asleep, I can only hope that we can navigate this emotional minefield without causing irreversible damage.

But one thing's for sure: it's going to be an interesting fucking summer.

Once the pitcher is gone and we have all had a good buzz, we walk hand in hand back to the house, noting that no one has returned yet.

The trees sway in the wind, and the waves crash loudly behind us, like angry thunderclaps reverberating across the beach.

Nothing but darkness and the flames of the roaring fire in the fireplace greet us as we walk inside, stomping our sandy feet on the mat in front of the sliding glass doors. We walk through the house together, turning on random lights to help us find our way up the steps. Ace looks at me over Em's head, giving me an intriguing yet playful look as if he's wondering if the same thing on her mind is the same thing on our mind.

He gets his answer as we come to a halt in the middle of the hall in front of her room, her hands gradually slipping from our grasp. With her back against the closed door, she crosses her tattooed arms over her chest, pushing her tits out and giving us a menacing look that makes my cock hard again.

"What's that look for, Blue Eyes?" I step toward her slowly, rubbing my hands together without taking my eyes off her face.

"We still have a few minutes before they should be back..." She winks at me and then looks at Ace, giving him the same look that makes us both want to fall to our fucking knees and worship her.

"So, what does that mean?" I ask, playing along as I take a final step toward her, stopping mere inches away.

"Yeah, Brat. What's on that dirty, little mind of yours? Me and Stone are fucking *dying* to hear," Ace mutters, taking a few steps closer.

"It means," she says with such dominance that it almost makes me bust a load in my shorts. "If you want to kiss me, then fucking do it." She licks her lips and waits, while Ace and I try to figure out our next move.

Without hesitation, I lean in and press my lips against hers, sensing the warmth and urgency between us. Ace brushes his hand against her cheek before joining in, our three-way kiss full of passion and desire. The sound of the front door opening interrupts our moment, but we couldn't care less.

We are completely engrossed in each other, consumed by the intense pleasure and addictive flicks of our tongues against one another.

When we hear Eli calling out to us, we reluctantly break away from the kiss. He stands in the doorway, looking at us with a mix of shock, anger, and irritation. "Seriously, guys? What the fuck?" he seethes, shaking his head.

Ace smirks and takes a step towards him, separating himself from Emerson. "Well, maybe if you didn't leave us alone for so long," he teases, playfully patting him on the back as he walks away, leaving Eli glaring at me and Emerson.

"I get it, Eli, but come on. You have to know your sister is old enough to make her own decisions."

"That's not the fucking point, Stone, and you know it." Eli storms off, shaking his head and muttering under his breath loud enough for us to hear.

Turning back to Emerson, a lost look consumes her pretty blue eyes and the vulnerability radiating off of her tugs at the thin heartstrings I do have. "Blue Eyes," I whisper, tucking her hair behind her ear to showcase her stunning face. "Don't let Eli ruin this for you. This trip is for you, *not* for him."

"I guess you're right, but still," She clears her throat and wipes the wetness away from her eyes. "I hate disappointing my brother."

I pull her in for a hug and linger for a bit, taking the time to inhale the way she smells, savoring it for as long as I can. I know this isn't the way she wanted her brother to find out, but now that it's out in the open, none of us have to hide anything anymore...

Thirteen

The Rebel

Emerson

It took me a minute to compose myself after my brother walked in on me, Stone, and Ace making out.

Fuck.

I didn't want him to find out that way or this soon. He still doesn't know about Kane or Seven, and when he finds out, it'll be much fucking worse.

Anxiously, I run a brush through my long, dark hair, looking nervously at my reflection in the mirror. I can see the sadness in my eyes—the pain I am trying to mask; it is written all over my fucking face. I reapply my makeup, trying to look presentable, wiping the smeared lipstick from around my mouth, which is also stained on the guy's lips.

Fuck.

After popping a Xanax and an Ambien, I wash them down with the last sip of water in the bottle, crushing it and tossing it into the garbage when I'm done. The alcohol still vigorously courses through me, giving me a slight boost of liquid courage, but I know that as soon as I see [illegible], all that

shit will dissipate and I'll crumble like a weak bitch under his feet.

With my back to the door and my eyes on the beach out the window, flashbacks of my parents dance heavenly in my mind, making the pain of not having them here much worse. There are times when I don't think about them as much, but being here, at the beach house, is bringing up all the past trauma I have been trying to work through. I don't know why Eli thought this was a good idea, but I hope he knows what he's doing.

"Knock, knock."

I turn around, dropping the tube of mascara, a blush covering my tanned cheeks, when I see Seven standing in my doorway, leaning against the frame. The smile on his beautiful face gives me fucking butterflies, but it also brings up all the nerves I've been working on pushing to the side since I've been locked in my room, afraid to face the real world downstairs.

"Hey," I finally manage, my voice coming out in a cracked whisper.

"So, is it true, Princess?" he asks, stepping into my room and walking closer, never taking his eyes off of mine.

"Is what true?" I swallow hard, forcing my feet to move so I can meet him halfway.

"Is it true that Eli walked in on you, Stone, and fucking Ace making out?" he chuckles, reaching out to clasp his heavily tattooed hand around my hip.

"What do you think?" I raise my brow, trying to challenge him and show him that I'm not afraid. But I am. And he knows it too.

"You're a bad little girl, aren't you?" He brushes his nose along the crook of my neck, sending a shiver up and down my spine.

Leaning in to the comfort of his touch and the familiar smell that puts me at ease, I sigh, feeling a little weight lifting off my shoulders as I let my guard down. "You know I'm a bad girl, Seven," I whisper, running my hand over the bulge in his jeans, feeling it grow beneath my touch. "But what are you going to do about it?"

"Just fucking wait, Princess. Just. Fucking. Wait," he growls, slipping his hand into mine and giving it a slight tug, dragging me out of my room.

"Where are we going?"

"Down to join the party. I'll show you what I do to bad girls later, trust me." He smirks, making my pussy wet and my knees weak, almost forgetting about the shit with Eli.

...until we hit the bottom steps and walk right into him as we go to enter the living room.

I freeze at the sight of Eli, Stone, Kane, and Ace sitting on the couch, their eyes turning to us as we make our entrance. Seven doesn't even flinch, his confident smile never leaving his face as he tugs me closer to him. I bite my lip nervously, feeling the tension in the room skyrocket as Eli's gaze shifts from Seven to me.

"Where have you two been?" Eli asks, his voice tight and controlled as he angrily eyes us up and down, his eyes stuck on our intertwined hands

"We were just up in Emerson's room, having a little chat," Seven replies smoothly, his hand tightening around mine. "Is there a problem with that?"

Eli's jaw clenches, but before he can respond, Kane cuts in, his eyes flickering with a mix of concern, desire, and amusement.

"Let's not start a fight, Eli," he says, his voice calming. "We're all here to have a good time, remember? We're all here to support Emerson, not make shit worse."

I glance at Ace, who is sitting quietly, observing the situation with a neutral expression. Suddenly, I realize that this might be my chance to distract Eli from what happened earlier. I take a step forward, mustering up all the courage I have left.

"Hey, Eli," I say, forcing a smile. "Why don't we all just relax and enjoy the party? Maybe have a few drinks? We can talk later."

Eli's gaze softens as he looks at me, and for a moment, I see the pain and worry in his eyes. He nods slowly, as if coming to a decision, his shoulders visibly relaxing as he lets a sigh slip from his throat.

"You're my fucking baby sister. But you're right, Em," he says, his voice gentler now. "Let's just have a good time."

As the music bellows and the tension in the room eases, I feel a wave of relief wash over me, mostly because my meds are kicking in. Maybe I can navigate through this mess after all. I glance at Seven, who gives me a sly wink, and I can't help but smile back. Despite the chaos and the unresolved issues lingering in the air, I'm starting to feel like we can make it through the night unscathed.

After a few drinks and a few games of beer pong in the game room, the seven of us head for the beach. Tension and stress, nowhere to be found. While Eli and Nova hold hands and skip ahead of us into the darkness, Ace and Stone flirt their way behind them, grabbing each other's asses as if they think we can't see them as we follow behind them; it's cute, really.

Sandwiched between Kane and Seven, I walk with my bare feet sinking into the warm sand, the comforting ocean breeze blowing fiercely, guiding our way to the water. Kane reaches behind me, his large hand cupping my ass and squeezing firmly, ripping a squeal from me as my body jumps from the sudden touch. Seven grins, mischief flashing in his drunken eyes, while his pierced tongue darts out from his mouth to lick his full lips, as if he's fucking hungry or something—hungry for me.

As another gust of wind blows, my thin wrap that's around my waist blows, showing off my ass that's squeezed into the bathing suit bottoms I put on. When the four disappear into the darkness ahead, Kane stops me, putting his arm in front of my chest, then pushing me against Seven. His hands hold my hips, pulling my ass against his cock, fitting perfectly in his groin. Kane steps in front of me, his hand grabbing my throat like a necklace, while his other slips down the front of my bathing suit, finding my clit right away.

"Already fucking wet," he growls, rubbing until my body twitches against Seven's.

Kane leans in and captures my lips, slipping his thick tongue into my mouth and taking charge right away. Leaning back against Seven for support, I reach up and grasp Kane's biceps, holding on tightly as our tongues tangle in a heated battle of desire that we're both trying to win. Warm lips brush against the nape of my neck, skating across my skin with sensual kisses that have me moaning into Kane's mouth as he sinks his teeth into my tongue.

I reach back for Seven and pull him closer, feeling the heat of both men against my body. As the waves crash against the shore, I let the intoxicating sensation of desire wash over me, surrendering to the fiery passion that ignites between the three of us.

As we stand there on the edge of the ocean, our bodies entwined in a sensual dance, I realize that this is where I want to be—between the two men who set my soul on fucking fire.

Kane's fingers slide down my pussy lips, spreading them open. And as he eases his fingers inside me, pushing them as deep as they'll go, I find myself falling into the darkness with them, all worries and cares pushed aside because the pleasure ripping through me trumps everything. He pumps his thick fingers in and out of my pussy, arousal dripping down the inside of my tender thighs. I shiver uncontrollably, wanting more than his fingers inside me. And I think he knows it too.

"Here's what's going to happen, Little One," he murmurs against my swollen lips, slowly pulling his hand out of my bathing suit, leaving me feeling empty and craving his touch more than ever before. "We're going to go down to the beach and sneak off where we can be alone." He grins, sucking his soaked fingers into his mouth and licking off my arousal, making my body shudder from the gesture as Seven lets me go.

"I like the sound of that," I admit, as the three of us continue to walk, me being held up by the both of them in fear that my knees will buckle from underneath me and send me crashing to the sand.

"Ah, someone's being a little rebel tonight," Seven chuckles, lighting a thick blunt and taking a hit before passing it.

"I wouldn't say rebel, just that I'm tired of my life trying to be controlled—my every move trying to be decided for me. I know what the fuck I want, and I'll be damned if I let someone tell me I can't have it."

The beach stretches out before us, the moon casting a silvery glow on the water as the sounds of the waves crashing against the shore fill the air. I can feel the heat of desire burning within me, knowing that this night is going to be nothing short of unforgettable.

As we make our way further down the beach, the anticipation builds quickly within me, feeling the soft sand between my toes and the warm breeze on my skin. It's like time stands still as we find a secluded spot away from prying eyes, surrounded by the darkness and the intoxicating scent of saltwater as it sprays all over us with each wave that crashes against the shoreline.

Kane and Seven waste no time as they pull me into their embrace, hands and lips exploring every inch of my body. The sensation of their touch sends shivers down my spine as I lose myself in the raw, passionate energy that surrounds us.

This is where I belong—caught between the two men who have awakened a hunger within me that I never knew existed. And as we give in to the electricity that crackles between us, I surrender to the pleasure that threatens to consume me whole, sending me deeper into a different kind of darkness that I never want to find my way out of.

Fourteen

Corrupting Emerson

Kane

My darkened eyes locked onto Emerson's, taking note of the high that's glazed over her pretty blues. Sitting with her ass in the sand and her toes touching broken seashells, I get swept up in her allure, unable to focus on anything else.

But I don't want to anyway.

She hums 'I Can Tell', bringing me back to the good old days when music was actually music and not the shit it is today. Her eyes flutter, her long, dark lashes casting a shadow under her lids as her blue orbs roll back.

Forcefully ripping my gaze away from her, when Seven deliberately clears his throat to grab my attention, I notice the menacing look in his eyes as he goes to stand up.

"I'm gonna go see what the others are doing." He grins, flashing me a wink that Emerson can't see. "Y'all enjoy your alone time."

Smooth, I think to myself, a crooked grin spreading across my lips. Finally, Em turns to look at Seven, reaching her arms up to try and pull him down.

"Give me a hug before you go," she begs, tugging on the drawstring of his bathing suit as he lowers himself to her level.

Wrapping her in a giant hug that seems to ease the stress consuming her, he places a gentle kiss on the top of her head and pulls away.

"Have fun with Kane, Princess. Who knows when you'll get the chance to be alone again," he says smoothly, his voice ringing like a lullaby and almost making Emerson's eyes shut again.

"Keep Eli occupied then," she laughs, scooting closer to me as he stands back up, brushing the sand off his ass.

Seven and I share a knowing nod before he walks away, eventually disappearing into the thick cloud of dark fog sweeping along the beach. Once we're alone, Emerson turns and looks at me, resting her hand on my upper thigh, so close to my cock that it makes it twitch in the confinement of my shorts. I reach out and slide my fingers under her chin, slightly tilting her head up so her eyes have nowhere else to go but on mine.

"What's on that dirty, little mind of yours, Little One? I can tell by the look in your eyes that your thoughts are up to no good." I lean closer, blowing my breath on her lips but not touching them, enjoying the whimper that leaves her lips from the teasing.

"Maybe I'm thinking about how badly I want to kiss you," she whispers, her voice barely audible over the crashing waves. I can feel her fingers tracing circles on my thigh, inching closer towards my growing cock. "Maybe I'm wondering what it would feel like to have your hands all over me." Her words send a jolt of electricity through my body, and I can't resist the temptation any longer.

"Fucking Christ," I groan as I capture her lips with mine, feeling her soft breath against my skin as our kiss deepens, my tongue thrusting into her mouth until the tip touches the back of her throat. I grab the back of her neck, digging my fingers into her soft flesh in a way that allows me to hold onto her so I can kiss her exactly how I fucking want to.

The sound of the ocean and the laughter from the group down the beach fade into the background as we become obsessively lost in each other, the taste of salt mixing with the sweetness of her lips. With the sand beneath us, the water splashing all over us, and the stars above, nothing else matters except the two of us, and the endless possibilities of the night... as long as her brother doesn't come and ruin shit.

I pull away from the kiss, panting and staring into Emerson's eyes, a mischievous glint shining in them. "Let's take a ride," I suggest, a sly grin tugging at the corners of my lips.

"A ride?" Her brow raises in question, but she matches my smirk, knowing exactly what I fucking mean.

I wrap my arms around Emerson and pull her onto my lap, sitting her fat, peachy ass right on my cock, while making sure she knows how fucking hard she has made me already. The scattered water droplets glistening on her skin in the moonlight catch my eye, and I find it hard to stop imagining how much better she'd look soaked in water from head to fucking toe.

"I don't want this night to end," she murmurs, her voice barely above a whisper as she leans in and kisses my cheek, slightly rocking back and forth on my lap.

"It doesn't have to," I reply, trailing kisses down her neck, softly and sensually, enough to pull a shudder from her entire body. "Let me corrupt this pussy, Little One," I growl deeply, reaching between her thighs, pushing her drenched bikini bottoms to the side, and giving her soaked cunt a slow, teasing slap with the pads of my fingers.

Emerson's breath hitches as she gazes at me with a mixture of excitement and nervousness in her eyes. She nods slowly, almost imperceptibly, giving me the permission that I was craving. Her lips part as I run my finger along her slit, feeling her warmth and wetness against my touch.

"Mmm, Kane," she moans softly as I continue to tease her, building up the anticipation until she can't take it anymore.

With a fierce hunger in her eyes, she pulls me closer and crashes her lips onto mine, kissing me as if her life depended on it. The urgency in the movements of her pierced, eager tongue ignites a fire in me too, and I know that this move might cost us her brother's trust, but we're in too deep to turn back now, both of us drowning in the desire enveloping us tightly.

The waves continue to crash onto the shore, serenading our bodies entwined in a dance of passion and lust as I hold her hips and rock her roughly back and forth over my cock, desperate to be inside of her. We lose ourselves in each other, exploring the depths of lust, desire, and pleasure that we've been resisting for *so* fucking long.

With the gleaming full moon as our witness, we become part of the ethereal beauty that surrounds us, transcending into a world where only our forbidden connection exists. It's a moment filled with unspoken words, breathy moans, and endless touches—a moment where nothing else fucking matters but us.

Her hands rest on my shoulders, grasping them firmly as she follows my guidance and begins grinding on my cock, slightly bouncing her ass so it slaps against my thighs.

"That's it, Little One." I release my hold on her and let her move freely, watching in pure fascination as she falls into a rhythm that works, not only for her, but for me as well.

"You're *so* damn hard," she gasps, as I thrust my pelvis up into her, pressing my covered cock against her bare pussy.

"And you're *so* fucking wet," I grunt, reaching down to slide my shorts off so my cock springs free, slapping against her needy, wet cunt.

She shivers again, both from the breeze that kisses her wet skin and from the feeling of my bare dick as she rocks feverishly on it. Pulling her puffy bottom lip between her perfect, white teeth, she throws her head onto her shoulders and arches her back, sitting comfortably on my cock while wiggling her hips as a sign she wants me inside of her.

Reaching between her parted thighs, I press on her swollen clit with the rough pads of my fingers, enjoying the way her body jerks from my touch. Gliding them down her slit, I push her pussy lips open and swirl my fingers in her wetness, spreading it all around so her cunt shines like fucking diamonds under the bright glow of the moon.

"Are you going to let Daddy Kane inside this beautiful pussy, Little One?" I ask as I continue to circle her entrance, waiting for permission before I take what I fucking want and then some.

She nods her head, trying to catch her breath as her legs quiver and her body trembles with insatiable need.

"Uh, uh," I click my tongue against the roof of my mouth, leaving my fingers frozen, pressing against her tight, forbidden hole. "You know how to use your fucking words, Emerson. So why don't you be a good little girl, and tell Daddy Kane what the fuck you want?" A deep growl leaves my chest. "Go on and tell me what I want to hear." I wink, raising my brow as the corner of my lip tugs upward, meeting my eyes in a matching devilish grin.

"Ka-" she begins, finally finding her voice, only to be cut off by my finger pressing against her lips to silence her.

"*Daddy Kane*," I remind her sternly, grinning. "Call me Daddy Kane, Little One," I demand, watching her eyes widen and a blush paint her already rosy cheeks as she darts her tongue out and licks my finger.

"I want to fuck you, *Daddy Kane*," she finally admits, her sated eyes searching mine for the right answer. "I want you to make *me* feel good, and most of all, I want to make *you* feel good too." She wiggles her hips again as I reach around with one hand and cup her ass, still keeping my fingers teasing her pussy.

"Good girl, Emerson," I praise her, knowing how fucking bad she's seeking acceptance. "Now lift your ass and let me show you how good I can make you feel. Let me show you how a real man fucks—how I worship a cunt as fucking beautiful as yours." I tap her ass for her to lift it, and when she does, I guide my rock hard cock to her pussy, lining up with her opening.

"Breathe for me, Little One." I swipe my thumb across her lip, feeling her warm breath skate across my hand as I push the tip into her, feeling her tight pussy stretch around my cock.

Fuck, this girl is going to drive me fucking wild. But I'm here for it.

Slowly, she slides down, sinking on my dick, until she's fully seated on my lap and my entire shaft is burrowed tightly between her soaked, pink walls. The feeling of her muscles contracting around me as her pussy gets used to my size makes my toes curl, and a light hiss escapes my throat as she eagerly strangles my cock.

"Fuck, that's my good girl. You take my dick so well, Little One, almost as if it were made. *Just. For. You*," I grunt as my cock pulses in her pussy, her walls gripping me like a fucking vice. "This pretty, forbidden pussy was made for me, wasn't it?"

"Yes... *Oh*, Daddy Kane." Emerson's soft pants fill the air, her chest rising and falling rapidly as she tries to adjust to the fullness of my cock inside her.

I press my hands into the sand beside me, grasping it tightly as I support her movements, enjoying the way she starts to intuitively grind her hips, feeling the friction of her clit against my cock with each rhythm.

The sea breeze tangles in her hair, her eyes closed, and a blissful expression on her face as she bounces on me, the pleasure pulsating through her body as she gets comfortable, amping up her movements. I lift my hips to meet hers, thrusting up into her with unyielding desire, my hands moving from the sand to grip her hips firmly as she picks up the pace. The sounds of our wet skin slapping together and her sweet, seductive moans fill the air, the passion between us becoming almost feverish as she rides me faster—harder, more desperate—lost in the intoxicating sensations that wildly rip through her.

There's no holding back now—our forbidden desire has been ignited like an inferno, and there's no stopping the flames from consuming us both.

As the rest of the world fades into obscurity, Emerson and I lock eyes as she rides me, rocking back and forth desperately and slamming down on my cock over and over, taking me deeper each time.

The waves echo the rhythm of our bodies, the moon casting a silvery glow over us as we become lost in the erotic dance, intoxicated by the all-consuming fire burning rapidly inside of us.

Letting go of her hips, I reach up and cup her throat with my hand, squeezing enough to get her eyes to pop slightly. A serious expression takes over my face as I begin holding her throat and using it to slam her down on my dick, my climax beginning to surface. Her arousal leaks out of her every time she slides up and down, slamming her ass down harder each time, and taking my dick even further until she feels the pressure in her lower belly.

"Christ, Emerson," I groan, entranced heavily as she starts twerking on my dick as if the massive size doesn't bother her anymore. "Ride me, baby. Take my cock and come all over it. I want to see it shine under the stars when I slide out of your pussy."

"Kane... *Daddy Kane*," she whispers, clawing her nails down the front of my body as she shakes, her pussy full and clenching.

As we're both consumed in the madness of overpowering lust, I feel the unmistakable surge of release building up inside me. My grip on her throat tightens, and she gasps for air, her eyes lock onto mine, and I can feel that she's close too.

"Fuck!" she screams, arching her back and slamming down harder, her head thrown back so her eyes are on the shimmering stars.

With one final, powerful thrust, we both reached our climax, our breaths and moans filling the night air as the waves and the moon became the only witnesses to an act—forbidden yet undeniable—unfurling against the backdrop of night. My cum jets into her, my cock throbbing between her tightly clenching walls as she unravels before me, soaking me exactly like I told her to.

"Ahhh," she moans, leaning forward so her face is buried in my chest, her teeth grazing along my skin.

"Good girl. I told you this pussy was mine." I capture her lips as another wave of pleasure rips through us both, rendering us almost useless.

But I'm not done.

Holding her hips one more time, I slam her down even harder, holding her in place as I fuck her from underneath, emptying the last of my cum into her pretty cunt, marking her whether she realizes it or not.

As we collapse on the sand, entwined in a tender embrace, I can't help but smile—the sweet taste of forbidden desire lingering on my lips, and her intoxicating release coating my cock while my cum drips out of her cunt.

Fuck, this is exactly what I've been waiting for.

Fifteen

Botherly Love

Emerson

Soaking in the spacious jet tub in my private bathroom, I lean my head back against the fluffy built-in pillow, letting the soft music sweep me away. The bright sun shines in through the blinds covering the large window, reminding me that it's a brand new day, full of more secrets, desires, and obsessions with forbidden men.

My entire body aches, as if I got hit by a fucking bus, even though Kane let me be in charge last night. Still, the way his massive cock ripped me apart makes me shiver and ache as I continue thinking about it.

Oh, *Emerson*, I sigh aloud, disappointed in myself for sleeping with *not only one* of the men that my father told me to stay away from, *but two of them.*

Even though the guilt is heavy and intense, a small part of me doesn't feel bad at all.

Does that make me a bad person?

I force the filthy thoughts to the back of my cluttered mind, squeezing a glob of soap onto the black loofah in my hand as the pulsating jets in the tub hammer into my back.

Washing every inch of my body, I notice the bruises left by Damon are slowly fading, and a grateful smile curls on my lips. *Finally*.

But just as soon as Damon entered my mind, he was out of it, and Kane and Seven took his place.

I remind myself of the lies I need to tell. The excuses, the stories, to keep my secret life hidden from the people who care about me.

But why should I have to lie? Why can't I just be myself and live without fear of judgment and consequences? Because the truth is, the mystery and danger are what draw me in. The allure of these forbidden men and the adrenaline rush of my double life cloud my judgment and fuel my desires, making me want them even more.

Stepping out of the tub, I wrap myself in a plush robe and pad over to the closet to choose my outfit for the day. As I flick through the clothes, I catch my reflection in the mirror and pause. There's a fire in my eyes—a determination to embrace the thrilling chaos I've created for myself.

Despite the guilt, the fear, and the self-doubt, a part of me revels in the chaos. And as I slip into my jeans and tank top, I feel a surge of confidence.

Maybe I am a bad girl, but does it really matter if I'm enjoying every moment of it?

I shake off the doubt and head out the door, ready to face the day and whatever secrets, desires, and obsessions it brings.

Of course, the first one I see when I enter the kitchen is Eli, sitting alone at the table with a cup of coffee, looking over security footage on his laptop from the club back in Dorchester.

"Morning, Em," he says without looking up, his tone unreadable, making me slightly nervous.

"Morning, Eli," I answer cheerfully as I pour a cup of coffee and join him at the table, the sound of chirping birds creating a symphony just outside the open French doors.

"Sleep well?" He looks at me, raising his pierced eyebrow, a cunning grin on his lips.

"Like a baby." I nod, stretch, and look around, uncomfortable with the silence that follows my words, filling the very foundation of the house. "Where is everyone?"

He sets his cup down and closes his laptop, giving me a once over with a curious look in his blue eyes that eerily resemble mine.

"Well, Stone and Ace rode back to Dorchester to take care of a few things at the club. Kane went for a ride to handle some side business. Nova went home to grab a few things she forgot, and Seven is still upstairs, sleeping, I think." The look he gives me makes me nervous, and I'm heavily wondering if he knows what happened on the beach last night.

"I see the fucking marks that asshole covered you in are fading." Eli moves his eyes over my bare arms, making me feel self conscious.

"Yeah, they're getting there." I take a sip of my coffee to kill the awkward silence, trying to think of something else to say.

"We're gonna fucking get him, baby sis; I promise." He smiles, reaching his arms across the table, covering my hands with his. "No one fucking hurts you—*no one*." I can see his anger begging to be set free, but he does his best to keep it at bay.

"I don't think Damon will be bothering me anymore. I haven't heard from or seen him. I think he got the hint," I say, hopeful but skeptical at the same time.

"That's not the fucking point," he says, raising his voice, making me flinch involuntarily. "Besides, you're here with all of us, so he isn't stupid enough to try anything because he knows we'll fuck his ass up."

I sigh, glancing over his shoulder at the beach, admiring the crystal blue water as the sun hits it. "Don't underestimate him, Eli. Trust me, he's *always* one step ahead."

As Damon keeps getting brought up, my heart thunders maniacally, feeling as if it's about to burst from within my chest. My anxiety begins to rear its ugly head, making me feel like I'm about to have a fucking panic attack the longer we talk about him.

"Emerson, take a deep breath and look at me," my brother says softly, gliding his thumbs along the tops of my hands to try and calm me down.

He knows just how to help me. He knows the cure for my anxiety and panic attacks, and I'm so fucking thankful that he understands.

Finally looking at him, he smiles, reminding me of our father with his charming grin and boyish good looks, which breaks my heart all over again.

"Don't you fucking dare go to that place in your mind."

"What place?" Even though I know what he means, I play stupid, wondering how he's going to prevent it.

"You know, the dark, suffocating place in your mind—in your heart—that always threatens to break you until you're nothing but a shell of the amazing person we all know you are. You deserve to shine, Emerson. You deserve every ounce of light that casts over you, not the darkness and gloom that's controlled you almost all of your adult life."

His words hit me like a fucking punch to the gut, tugging at my heartstrings, and it takes all I can fucking do not to cry on the spot.

Because it's true. My life has been filled with darkness and gloom, secrets and danger, and I feel like I'm suffocating under the weight of it all.

But Eli is right; I deserve better. I deserve to be happy and to live without fear.

I take a deep breath and let it out slowly, nodding at Eli. "You're right, and I'll try. I promise."

He gives my hands a reassuring squeeze and then releases them. "Good. Now, let's finish our coffee and figure out what we're going to do today."

"I think I want to take my bike out for a ride to clear my head." My hands itch as I think about my bike, the one thing I have complete control over—the one place I feel safe and free.

"That might be good for you, Em," he says, giving me a look that tells me there's something else on the tip of his tongue.

"But?" I exhale, pushing my chair out from the table.

"But I think you should take Seven with you. I don't want you out riding alone, especially when we have no fucking clue what Damon is up to."

"Eli," I scold him, knowing he's only looking out for me.

"Listen, I would go with you, but I have some club business I need to handle, and I have a meeting with mom and dad's lawyer a little later today."

"Fine, I'll see if he wants to go, but if he doesn't, I'm still going for a ride," I point out, feeling sick as I think about Damon, and the fact that he still might be stalking me.

But I can't rely on my brother or the guys to protect me forever. I'm a big girl, and as much as Eli doesn't want to hear or admit it, I can take care of myself on my own, regardless of what past events prove.

Even so, knowing I have good days and bad days, some wicked worse than others, all spiraling from the selfish murder of our parents, I can't shake off the feeling that despite everything—the chaos, the fear, and the danger—I feel a tiny glimmer of faith deep within me.

Maybe it's not too late to turn things around and find my way out of the depths of the terrifying shadows that I constantly allow to swallow me whole. But as I hear my thoughts loud and clear, even I know that it'll take a fucking miracle for me to escape the comforting darkness and enter the light where I used to feel so safe and secure.

No longer able to bear the weight of these thoughts, I get up from the table and walk out of the kitchen, stepping onto the back porch and into the hot sun.

My head is spinning with all the confusion and fear that's been gripping me since my parents died. But I'm determined to let go of the pain that I've held for so long.

First, I need to figure out how, though.

Outside, the fresh air hits my skin and the sun warms my face, a wave of peace washing over me as the ocean waves wash against the shore. Maybe taking a bike ride with Seven wouldn't be such a bad idea after all. It's my escape, my way of feeling free—even if just for a little while.

And he is too.

But deep down, I know it won't be easy. The secrets, the danger, and the forbidden allure of men like Kane, Seven, and the others have too tight a grip on me. And knowing that as much as I crave the serenity and the light, the darkness will always have a fucking suffocating hold on me.

But I refuse to let it consume me any longer.

The warm wind rushes through my hair as it blows, and as I gaze at the calm ocean and the slow, rippling water, I smile, thinking about one thing in particular. My bike is calling out to me, and I already know that Seven's soothing presence might bring some peace to my racing mind, and a ride along the coast will bring some clarity to my scattered thoughts.

Right?

SIXTEEN

RIDING THE BIKE & THE BIKER

Seven

While listening to Eli and Emerson talk downstairs, I stand at the top of the hall, rolling my morning blunt. Hearing how broken Emerson is and how worried her brother is crushes me on the inside, but I know they can both overcome it.

I roll the weed into the wrap, lick the edge, and fold it over, making it nice and tight. I tuck the blunt behind my ear and quietly descend the stairs, barely missing Eli on the way in.

Like every other morning, I make a cup of coffee and take it out to the back porch, where Emerson is hunched over the railing, staring at the ocean below. My hungry eyes sweep over her juicy ass as I walk up behind her, stopping only feet away.

Clearing my throat and attempting not to startle her, I watch as she actually stiffens her body and turns around, meeting my smiling face with a nervous grin.

"I figured you were sleeping." She bats her eyes and moves her head, beckoning me to come closer.

So I do.

"I was, but once the sun is up, so am I." Standing beside her, I playfully nudge her arm with mine, and she instantly relaxes in my presence.

I slide the blunt out from behind my ear, light it, and take a rip, holding the smoke in my lungs while she watches. As she goes to speak, I grab her chin between my thumb and pointer finger and press my lips against hers, blowing the thick smoke out of my lungs and deep into hers.

Then she kisses me, wielding her tongue as a weapon with each lash, brush, and stroke she makes against mine.

The fire between us grows brighter and hotter with every passing moment, and I feel a deep, stirring passion rising within me. We pull away, breathless, and I look into her eyes, noticing the turmoil and sadness that still linger. I know I can't fix everything for her, but in this moment, I want to give her some respite from the storm.

"So, how did your night with Kane go?" I ask in a deep tone, watching my words make her body shudder.

"It was... interesting. I had fun," she chuckles, giving me a knowing look that answers every single question I was going to ask her.

"Good, then today you're all mine, aren't you, Princess?" I take another hit off the blunt and expel the smoke into the air, the sun blinding my vision.

"I was going to ask if you wanted to join me on a ride anyway." She takes the blunt from me and hits it, my gaze drawn to her lips and how they seal around the wrap.

"Are you talking about a ride on the bike or the biker?" I wink, inching closer until our chests touch, longing to reach out and hold her.

"Both." She smirks, handing the blunt back to me, taking it upon herself to give me a shotgun this time.

She grabs the back of my neck and pulls my head down, our lips touching as she blows smoke from her mouth into mine. She slips her hand underneath my shirt and runs her nails down my stomach, sensually tracing over my muscles. I groan into her mouth, refusing to pull away until I have tasted as much of her as possible.

But we both know that we have to get ready for the day, as much as we'd rather stay in this moment forever. Pulling away from her, I take a deep breath and smile. "Let's go for a ride then, Princess. I'm all yours today."

Nothing but the hum of our bikes in my ears, the vibrations of the motor piercing my bones, and the warm wind slapping roughly against my body consume me as Emerson and I ride down the strip by ourselves. Every time I squeeze the throttle, she does the same, bringing her bike closer to mine until we are zipping down the nearly empty street in unison. Even with her helmet obscuring her beautiful face, I can tell she's smiling every time I look at her.

I shift gears and rev the engine, slipping in front of her to guide her down a winding backroad away from prying eyes. She stays on my tail, matching every swerve and wheelie I manage to pull off, making me even prouder.

I can feel her energy matching mine, and for that moment, nothing else matters. We are a force to be reckoned with, and the freedom of the open road is ours to conquer. As we round a bend, I notice a hidden path leading into the woods and decide without hesitation to take it.

The overgrown trail is rough and bumpy, but we push on, the rush of adventure coursing through our veins. The canopy of trees overhead casts dappled shadows on the ground, and for a brief moment, it feels as if we have left the world behind. We ride deeper into the forest, our bikes kicking up dirt and leaves along the way.

Finally, we emerge into a small clearing, with the sun shining through the leaves and bathing everything in a warm golden light. I turned off the engine and set my bike on its kickstand, taking in the peaceful stillness of the woods. Emerson does the same, and for a moment, we just stand there, taking it all in.

"Thank you for this," she says, her tone soft and earnest.

I smile, knowing that this is only the beginning of our adventure together. "Anytime," I reply, and in that moment, I realize that this is *exactly* where I'm meant to be.

She removes her helmet and places it on the seat of her bike, gradually coming around to my side. As I remove my helmet, she moves closer, backing me up until my ass hits the seat of my bike.

"What's on your mind, Princess?" I raise my brow and grab her hips, pressing my fingers into her thick waist.

"Do you really need to ask, Seven?" A whisper escapes her lips as she leans in closer, placing her mouth against the side of my neck.

As she sinks her teeth into my flesh and moves her tongue around the area, I shiver against her, my hands sneaking around to her ass and cupping it.

"So, you rode the bike," I grunt, reaching up to grab her throat and pulling her mouth away from my neck. "How about riding the biker now?"

Before I can react, she grabs my waist and pushes me to the ground, straddling me as if I were her bike, which she was about to mount. Pulling her top over her head, I reach around to her back with one hand, unclasping her bra and removing it from her arms. Her tits bounce freely, and the glistening piercings in her nipples make my mouth water.

"Stand up and take your pants off," I demand, removing my clothes the moment she gets to her feet.

I watch as she strips naked, leaving only her pearl necklace on. She licks her lips as her gaze shifts to my cock, the clear beads of moisture around the tip shining in the sun.

"Good girl. Now get back down here and show me how fucking good you are at riding the biker."

She laughs and climbs back onto me, rubbing her warm, wet cunt directly against my cock. "You know how good I ride," she teases, raking her nails down my chest and guiding my cock inside her.

"Fucking prove it then, Princess." I wink, thrusting my hips to meet her cunt as she slams down on me.

I reach up and twist her pearl necklace, choking the shit out of her while she bounces up and down on my cock, her gaze never leaving mine. Her perky, supple tits bounce wildly, begging to be grabbed and sucked on. Pulling her down against me, I suck a nipple into my mouth, nipping and licking hungrily while holding a firm grip on the twisted string of pearls that serves as a choker around her delicate neck.

She rocks and grinds against me, making my cock throb while buried deep in her warm pussy, like a blanket I never want to be out of.

"Seven," she says quietly, her pretty blue eyes rolling back in her head as I thrust my hips to match her rhythm, sinking deeper and deeper into her forbidden cunt.

"What, Princess?" I tighten the pearls, watching her veins pop even more.

But she keeps riding, arching her back to chase my cock, using her knees methodically, and sliding up and down on it in perfect harmony.

"I love you," she whispers again, her eyes closed, as if she is afraid of my reaction to her confession.

I knew she loved me; I just needed her to say so.

"I love you, too, Emerson." I smile and stare at her, waiting for her eyes to open.

The sun sets behind the trees, and we become one with the wild, exploring each other in the golden light. Our passion and desire fuel our every move as we continue to ride the waves of ecstasy deep into the heart of the forest. Our bodies move in perfect harmony, just like our bikes on the open road.

A shy smile spreads across her lips as her eyes finally flutter open, her movements becoming slower as her pussy clenches around me. I let go of her pearls so she can breathe and lift her off of my cock. Getting to my feet, I pull her up, already missing her dripping cunt.

"What ar—"

Cutting her off, I roughly spin her around and bend her over the seat of my bike, kicking her legs open with my foot.

"Don't worry, I'm going to make sure you come." I spit on my hand and wipe it against her pussy before slipping my cock back inside her.

She gasps, digging her nails into the leather seat and pushing her ass against me. I wrap her hair around my hand and yank it, craning her neck backward as I pound into her with relentless, deep strokes, the sound of slapping skin satisfying my every desire.

"Come for me, Princess," I groan, my balls full and slapping against her ass as I pound into her so deeply she can feel my cock in her guts.

As I feel her wetness soak my cock, I groan and let go of her hair, clutching her hips to bring her back to me. Emerson's moans and whimpers reverberate through the forest as I push her to the brink of pleasure, the sun casting an ethereal glow on her gleaming body. She pants and shivers as I repeatedly hit that sweet spot, and I revel in the pure ecstasy of seeing her fall apart beneath me.

Feeling her walls pulsing around my cock, I lean over and bury my face in the crook of her neck, trembling from the intensity of our release. My cum spills into her, spurt after spurt, coating her insides in white. Her loud moans echo. Her entire body shakes uncontrollably. Her pussy grips my cock like a vice, but I smash through the tightening barrier, fucking her with fast, deep strokes that send us both over the edge at the same time.

We stood there for a moment, she still leaning over my bike, and we both tried to catch our breath in the fading light.

As the moonlight begins to shine through the trees, I pull her close to me and press soft, lingering kisses all over her flushed skin. I wrap my arms around her and hold her close, silently promising her that this is only the beginning of our wild and untamed love story.

After getting dressed and concealing the bites and bruises left on our bodies by one another, we sit on the grass and stare at the water, passing a blunt back and forth.

"So, what the fuck are we going to do about your brother?"

•••••••••••

SEVENTEEN

FORBIDDEN THREE

Emerson

After a shower and a change of clothes, I return downstairs, walking into another wild party, music blasting from the surround sound.

Snippets from earlier with Seven flicker in and out of my mind, causing a random smile to curl on my lips as I walk through the room to grab a drink. Kane stands near the table, holding a beer and leaning against the wall, his dark, menacing eyes staring right through me. I turn my head to see where Seven is, noticing him talking to my brother, who doesn't look happy. I ignore it and keep walking, flashing Kane a smile as I approach.

"I haven't seen you all day." He hands me a beer and twists the cap off while his gaze travels the length of my body.

"I went out riding with Seven."

"Riding with Seven, or riding Seven?" he asks, releasing a dark chuckle from his broad chest.

I laugh and step closer, ignoring the possibility that my brother is watching. "Both."

"Do you know how fucking bad I want that pussy again?" he growls, narrowing his eyes to let me know how serious he is.

"But Eli."

Kane presses his finger to my lips, his smile fading as a serious expression washes over his stunningly tanned face.

"I don't give a fuck about your brother. I probably should, but I don't." His voice is deep and daring, brimming with allure and danger. "It was his idea to bring you here with us, and I believe you should do whatever makes you happy, even if that means fucking his best friend... or your father's."

My eyes widen and my heart beats like a bass drum against my ribcage as I realize the gravity of our situation. But Kane's right. Eli can't protect me from every man he doesn't want near me, and I'm getting tired of hiding behind his back. Before I can react, I feel my brother's arm loop around my waist, and he and Seven appear on either side of me.

"What's going on over here?" He looks at me and Kane with curiosity in his eyes, and an awkward silence follows.

"Just talking. I was considering taking Em down to the beach tonight." Kane nods at Seven and smirks as he looks at my brother. "Seven and I were, actually."

"I'm not going to like what's going to happen, am I?" Eli, nervous and slightly angry, shakes his head at his best friend and pulls me closer into his grasp.

"Eli, stop worrying yourself. I'm a big girl," I tell him, trying to stand up to my best friend, my role model.

He shakes his head and steps back, letting go of me. "Do whatever the fuck you want; Ace, Stone, and I are leaving soon."

"Now where are you going?" My question is filled with concern, prompted primarily by the evil look in my brother's eyes.

"To address an issue that should have been resolved a long time ago." He walks away, leaving us with nothing but a cryptic statement and the sensation of my heart slowly breaking.

"He's gonna go try to find Damon," Seven blurts out, pulling me against his body with his arms resting on my hips.

"And we're going down to the beach, so fuck it." Kane puts his beer down and grabs another, snatching my hand and dragging me behind him with Seven clinging to my other hand.

I don't know what is happening or what's on their minds, but the only thing on mine is what Eli is up to. I can't help it. The fact that my brother and his friends are getting involved with dangerous people—Damon, to be exact—is concerning me deeply.

As I'm being led to the beach by Kane and Seven, I can't shake off the feeling that something terrible is about to happen. But as I walk through the sand, feeling it squish between my toes, I realize I need to do what makes me happy, even if it means making decisions that go against my brother's wishes. Although I'm afraid, I'm also eager to break free from the chains that have been holding me back, drowning me, and keeping me from reaching the surface.

I take a sip of my drink and look up at the sky, watching the stars twinkle, feeling Seven and Kane's gaze burn into my body. The music continues to flood out of the house's windows, echoing loudly all around us. I look down, turning to meet Kane's gaze.

"What?" I take another drink and begin to strip, watching the hungry gleam in their eyes as I perform a small show.

"Have you ever sucked a dick under water?" Kane grins as he removes his shirt to reveal his tattooed, rippling muscles, which are perfectly etched into every crevasse of his body.

"No, it seems dangerous." A laugh slips out, and I stumble in the sand, trying to regain my balance.

"Suck it up, Buttercup." Seven strips, then charges at me, chasing me into the cold ocean water, guided by the moonlight.

Kane follows us, ensuring that we stop far enough away to be able to stand, but then they sandwich me between them, their cocks pressing into all of the best parts of my body.

With his hands on my hips and my tits pressed against his chest, Seven leans down and grabs my lips, sucking my tongue into his mouth. Kane's large hands cup my ass, separating my cheeks so he can slide his cock perfectly between them, causing goosebumps to prick painfully across my skin.

As the water splashes around us, I feel a sense of freedom and rebellion. I decide to embrace the joy of spontaneous fun and accept whatever happens next. The strength of these two men around me takes my breath away, and I lose myself in the moment, allowing myself to be consumed by my most primal desires. My heart races faster as I embrace danger and live fearlessly.

Kane grabs my head and turns it, capturing my lips before I can speak. As he kisses me, Seven's hand slips between my thighs and sinks into my pussy with a delicious, slow thrust. I moan into Kane's mouth, my body jolting and instinctively pushing back against him. While our lips are locked and our tongues compete for dominance, Kane gently slides his hand between my ass, pushing two wet fingers inside slowly.

I shuddered, and not just because of the cold water we were in. But the sensation of Seven in my pussy and Kane in my ass, their fingers working like magic as they probe me in a methodical dance that immediately weakens my knees.

"Be a good girl for us, Little One," Kane says breathlessly, pulling his mouth away from mine and turning me to face Seven.

I can feel his cock pushing against my opening below the surface, attempting to move Seven's fingers. When he pulls them out of me, Kane plunges back in, giving me every thick inch of his cock.

"Jesus, the face you make when you're getting fucked, it's.. fucking gorgeous," Seven moans, snatching the pearls around my neck again, twisting tightly until he's choking me.

He kisses me briefly, holding me in place as Kane slowly fucks me from behind, his massive, pierced cock stretching me out in ways that should be fucking illegal. As I push back to match his thrusts, the water makes waves and splashes around us, reminding me of where we are.

The ocean... It's beautiful.

I get lost in the kiss with Seven, twirling my tongue around his in a sensual dance that tells him how much I love him just by the way it moves. My legs start to tremble as he presses against my clit. Kane pumps his hips, slides his cock out to the tip, and then abruptly slams back in.

I gasp into Seven's mouth, and as soon as I do, he shoves me underwater and forces his cock in my mouth. Water slips in before I can seal my lips around him, but I do my best to suck him down my throat just as his cum drips down it. He holds my head, keeping me under the water, while Kane fucks me harder, leaving my pussy throbbing and stinging from the sharpness of his strokes.

Panic sets in, my heart seemingly ready to burst from my chest and my lungs rapidly filling with water. But it is my orgasm that soothes me, making me breathe deliberately while my pussy milks and strangles Kane's cock.

I let myself just stay like this; floating underwater with a hand on top of my head and a cock in my mouth, enjoying being railed by a man twice my age. I know I've fucked up with the things I've been doing lately, but I haven't thought much about my parents, so that's a plus.

Right?

Isn't this what Eli wanted? To be happy and move on? I am happy, but it's because of two men I shouldn't fucking want.

I'm let up, gasping for air as I choke on the rest of Seven's cum as it pours down my throat. He pats my back, pulling me into his arms to comfort me. With Kane behind me, he rotates his hips and draws his cock in and out, pumping every last drop of cum into me that he can.

I feel exposed and vulnerable as I gaze out into the ocean's immense darkness. Despite everything, I can't stop the feelings I have for these men, and I don't think I'd even try.

Eighteen

Completely Unhinged

Emerson

We have been at the beach house for about two weeks now, and every day the confusion increases.

It's not easy.

Fucking confusing.

I was completely wrong to think Damon could not find me where I was. He attempted to run me off the road and pursue me through the woods on a few occasions when I was riding, shooting at me with his .22.

There's been love notes and blue flowers left on my pillow every night, and he's not even ashamed to sign his fucking name.

Every day he spirals further out of control and gets more and more deranged.

Despite their repeated searches, Eli and Stone were unable to locate him. Our entire house is feeling a little tense as a result of th[illegible]

But I can, and I will find him.

"What are you doing out here all alone?" Stone startles me, coming up behind me on the porch as I lounge on the chair and watch the wild waves.

"Reflecting."

"Get Damon out of your head; we have it covered." He settles in and starts to laugh, albeit an irate one.

"If y'all fucking had him, he wouldn't be doing this fucked-up shit, Stone." I roll my eyes, knowing that if I want something done, I'll have to do it myself.

"Don't even think about doing something, Blue Eyes. He is fucking crazy."

I sigh and gaze out at the ocean, where waves crash against the shore. Stone is right; Damon is incredibly unpredictable and dangerous. But I can't just sit back and let him continue to terrorize us.

"I can't just do nothing, Stone. I need to find a way to stop him," I say, determination in my voice.

Stone looks at me with concern, but he knows I won't be swayed. "Your fucking brother would kill us if anything happened to you."

I shake my head, tired of always having to be the one everyone protects—the one who is portrayed as extremely vulnerable. We sit in silence, mulling over our conversation and making silent plans for what to do next. Stone approaches and sits in my chair behind me, pulling me between his parted legs and pressing his groin against my lower back, his arms draping comfortably around me.

Sitting here with him, like this, is soothing in ways that no one else can make me feel. Each guy has something about them that draws me in, making it extremely difficult to choose just one of them.

Stone is protective and more likely to be the one being told what to do in bed.

Ace is a sweetheart, too shy for his own good, but he can perform magic tricks with his fucking tongue.

Kane is dominant, always in control, and he teaches me new things that push me outside of my comfort zone.

Seven is possessive and obsessed with everything about me, and he is not afraid to express it.

Despite the fact that the four of them are so fucking different, they all have one thing in common: they want me and want me to be theirs in every way.

As I sit there, wrapped in Stone's arms, I can feel his steady heartbeat on my back. It's a comforting rhythm, but it can't drown out the fear and determination that are warring inside me.

But at the same time, I'm torn. Torn between four men who have each managed to steal a piece of my heart. They all bring something different to the table, something that I can't ignore. And even in the midst of the chaos and danger, I can't help but feel drawn to each of them in their own way.

"Stop overthinking shit, Blue Eyes," Stone says into my ear in a low, deep growl, licking the shell with his tongue.

He slips his hand down the front of my pants and beneath the band of my thong. "Relax. Let me feel how soaked you are just thinking about the four of us."

I lean back, my eyes closed, as his fingers roll up and down my clit, causing my legs to twitch. I dig my fingers into his thighs, my clit pulsing against the pad of his finger. I bite my lip to avoid moaning and drawing attention to ourselves, and spread my legs to give him more room.

"Mmm," he moans. "This pussy is drowning for me, isn't it?" He runs two fingers down my slit, parting my pussy.

"Yes, don't stop," I plead, curling my toes as he thrusts his fingers inside me, hooking them against the curve of my walls.

"I don't plan on stopping until my hand is soaked in your cum." Sinking his teeth into the side of my neck, right over a pearl-shaped bruise, he pounds harder, scraping his nails against the swollen spot in my pussy that makes my legs quiver with pleasure.

Soft, sensual kisses are sprinkled all over my skin, and the sensation of his lips leaving a burning trail in their wake sets my body on fire. I buck my hips, chasing the depth of his fingers as they fuck my pussy mercilessly.

My mind is whirling.

My clit is aching.

My pussy gushes, and as he adds another finger, he quickens the pace and hammers all three deep inside me in a brutal corkscrew motion.

"Stone, please." A whisper escapes my lips as my body convulses against his, my pussy violently squeezing around his fingers, attempting to fight them off.

Grabbing my head, he turns my head to the side and kisses me, tickling the back of my throat with the barbell in his tongue. He pushes on my lower belly, holding me down so my ass doesn't lift off the chair. And then he fucks me with his fingers like they were his cock, pounding them deep and fast, leaving my pussy soaked.

As the waves continued to crash on the shore, we became lost in our own world, which was much simpler and less confusing than the one outside of our small bubble. Stone's touch was both gentle and rough, creating an ideal combination that drove me insane. But despite the intensity of our connection, I couldn't push away the fears that still lingered in the back of my mind.

Damon's relentless pursuit was still haunting me, and as Stone continued to pleasure me, I couldn't help but think of what I could do about it. Even as I came all over his fingers and soaked his hand like he wanted me to.

The danger piqued my interest.

The risks turned me on.

The fear energized me.

And I knew I was probably as insane as Damon was, if not more.

Nineteen

The Pearl Necklace

Kane

Waiting in the dark alley behind the SSB Club, Eli and I lean against our bikes, passing a blunt laced with dust back and forth. With each hit, we keep our helmets on and allow the smoke to fill the small space, hotboxing it until we open our visors and watch it quickly spill out. We stand silently, coughing through a thick cloud of tainted smoke, looking for the only reason we are back in Dorchester—Damon.

Emerson has been moving forward in a healthy manner, even if she is exploring the fun she can have with the four of us, but Damon continues to hold her back. Between showing up at the beach house and calling her every minute of the night, she is living in fear and can not let go completely.

So we're going to help move shit along.

Eli paces back and forth anxiously, kicking loose rocks on the pavement. "Where the fuck is he?" he seethes, burying his hands in his pockets to keep them occupied.

"He should be here shortly. He thinks he's meeting Emerson, so he shouldn't flake." I shrug and take another hit

from the blunt, feeling the angel dust tingle along my spine and shoulders.

Eli nods, his jaw clenched, as he searches the alley for Damon. I can see the worry and determination in his eyes—the same feelings that are churning inside of me. We can't let Damon continue to hold Emerson back and keep her trapped in this cycle of fear and control.

But as the hairs on the back of my neck stand up, a strange sensation twists inside my stomach.

"I knew I was being fucking played," Damon says, standing behind us as we slowly turn around, an evil, chilling grin on his lips.

Eli charges at him, lowering his head and slamming his helmet against Damon's ribs, causing him to stumble backwards.

"Leave my fucking sister alone, D. Don't make me fucking kill you!" His scream echoes between the buildings, drowning out the faint sound of nearby gunfire.

I just stand here, letting the two of them fight for a few moments before separating them. "That is enough, both of you." I spit at Damon's feet, removing my helmet. "Why the fuck are you here if you already knew it was us?"

He grins wickedly, making me even more uneasy.

Damon reaches into his pocket, licking the blood off his lip from one of Eli's punches, and pulls out a familiar pearl necklace, which makes my fucking blood boil.

"I figured Emerson would want this back; it is her favorite," he laughs, dangling the precious necklace from his fingers.

I snatch it away from him, closing my fingers around it, remembering how Seven choked her with it. Fuck. My cock hardens, straining against the inside of my zipper, making me uncomfortable.

"Damon, stay the fuck out of my house. This is your final fucking warning." I give him one last shove before Eli and I get back on our bikes and ride away, leaving Damon behind, staring at him in my side mirror.

The sound of sirens blares in the distance as we speed through the narrow streets, adrenaline coursing through my veins. Damon's smug expression flashes through my mind as I grip the handlebars tightly, my mind racing with ideas of how to keep Emerson safe from him.

I will fucking kill him.

As we finally arrive at the beach house, I notice Emerson sitting outside, her face streaked with tears. My heart aches at the sight of her, but seeing her with Seven, I know she can't be that heartbroken.

Eli and I quickly dismount our bikes, and I wrap Emerson in a tight hug, whispering reassuring words into her ear as I return her necklace.

As we sit on the porch, Emerson clutches the pearl necklace tightly, her eyes filled with fear and anger. I look at Eli, and we both know we need to take action.

"We got this, Little One. We're not gonna let him scare you anymore," I say firmly, and she looks at us with a glimmer of hope in her eyes.

"Please leave it alone." She sniffles, trying to keep a serious expression despite her tears.

"I don't get why you won't let us fucking help you." Eli becomes angry, raising his arms and running his hands through his hair, making Emerson flinch.

I'm reminded of what she's been through—all the beatings, the assault, the forceful acts. And once again, my blood boils, wanting to kill the motherfucker who did this to her.

"This is my mess. I'll fix it," she says with confidence, no more tears streaming down her face.

Standing up, she walks away, leaving the three of us even more confused than before. We know she means business, but we don't know what she's capable of.

"It's bad enough that you two are fucking my baby sister, but don't you think you should've had my fucking back?"

"Eli, brother, that shit is not fair. We have your back," Seven huffs, attempting to reassure him despite the livid look in his eyes, indicating how annoyed he is.

Eli walks away next, leaving Seven and me alone with our thoughts, trying to figure out what just happened and where we go from here.

We all know that we can't force Emerson to accept our help, but that doesn't mean we can just stand by and watch her suffer.

"This shit is too much. He's never going to stop."

"You're right, Seven, but let's forget about it for tonight. We have a girl with a broken heart who needs some cheering up." I smirk, fantasizing about filling every hole in Emerson's body, fucking every memory of Damon out of her.

It took a while, but Eli and Nova fled, wanting to be alone and away from anyone who wanted to fuck his sister.

Guilt still gnawed at me, knowing that I was destroying my best friend's daughter and claiming her tight, innocent cunt as mine. But the heart wants what it wants, and my cock wants what it wants, so I have to push the guilt *way* the fuck down.

Sitting around the bonfire on the beach, a bottle of Crown Vanilla is passed around among the five of us, with nothing but the crackling flames and splashing waves filling the humid atmosphere.

Each sip relaxes Emerson, and the insatiable look in her eyes soon drives me insane. Locking eyes with her, I lick my lips and pat my lap, rubbing my palm against my cock. Without saying anything, she gets up and walks over, planting her juicy ass exactly where it fucking belongs. Even in front of Seven, Stone, and Ace, she willingly rocks back and forth, making both of us feel good and turned on.

"I want you to do something for me, Little One," I challenge her, winking at the guys around the fire, waiting to see if she will.

"Anything for you, Daddy Kane," she purrs, and my cock jumps under her ass.

"You're going to be a good fucking girl for me, aren't you?" I reach under her ass and pull my cock through the slit in my bathing suit, sensing the desire in her heavily hooded eyes. Pushing her bikini to the side, I rub her cunt with my fingers, spreading her juices around, while the guys stare with fascination and drool on their lips.

"Right now, I am willing to do anything." Taking matters into her own hands, she grabs my cock and guides it to her pussy, sinking on it with a perfect arch in her back that exposes her tits to the guys.

I pull her hair to one side, kissing and biting the exposed skin on the side of her neck, and licking the pearl necklace.

The men gathered around the fire are ecstatic, their gaze fixed on the erotic display in front of them. Emerson's moans blend with the sound of the waves and the crackling of the fire to form a symphony of pleasure.

As we rock back and forth, lost in the ecstasy of the moment, I can't help but feel a rush of adrenaline. I know what we are doing is dangerous, but there is an undeniable thrill to indulging in this forbidden pleasure.

Lost in the moment, alcohol vigorously coursing through her, Emerson bounces up and down on my dick, her cunt swallowing every inch. She doesn't even care that they're watching, it seems to turn her on.

I lean back in my chair, a grin on my face, as I grab her hips and slam her against my cock, feeling her cunt begin to squeeze me.

"Come on me, Little One." *Thrust.* "Come for Stone." *Thrust.* "Come for Ace." *Thrust.* "Come for Seven." *Thrust.*

I keep thrusting my hips up to meet her ass as she repeatedly slams it down, burying my cock so deeply that she feels it in her belly.

She screams, throwing her head back, and her body begins to go limp. I look at Ace and nod him over. He drops to his knees in front of a writhing Emerson and buries his face between her legs as I slide my dick out, lapping up the cum dripping from her cunt as she barrels off the edge. She clings to me as Ace eats her, greedily slurping every drop of her milky release until she's a panting, limp mess.

"Now kiss her," I command, feeling my sack tighten, about to bust.

It's rough and demanding, but as Ace kisses Emerson, spitting her cum into her mouth, the atmosphere changes, getting thick with desire. When he moves away, I push Emerson to the sand on her knees while stroking my cock in her face.

"It is time Daddy Kane gave you his own pearl necklace," I groan as a wave of pleasure rips through me violently, heavily watching my cum spurt out and land in thick globs all around her neck.

She smiles at me, licking her puffy lips as I keep stroking, giving her a pearl necklace, then coating her lips with the rest and smearing it across them.

"Rub them together for me. Use my cum to make your lips shine for us, Little One." I smile, pumping the last few drops from my cock.

She rubs her lips together, smearing my cum like lip gloss, and ends with a smack that elicits a desperate groan from everyone around the fire.

"Fuck, that was hot." She turns to look at Seven, who looks like he's about to fucking pounce on her.

The guys around the fire are mesmerized by the erotic scene, creating a lustful atmosphere. Emerson's eyes sparkle with excitement as she looks around at each of them, her body glistening with sweat and cum, the residue of her intense pleasure.

"Who wants to go next?" she asks in a joking, sultry tone, licking her lips seductively.

The men exchange glances, as if attempting to gauge each other's reactions. Seven steps forward, a hungry expression in his eyes. He approaches her as if in a trance, reaching out to touch her, and a new sense of anticipation fills the air.

"How about everyone?"

TWENTY

WHO GOES WHERE?

Emerson

A soft glow illuminates the room, creating a warm and inviting atmosphere. Bright candle flames flicker in the wind, which filters in through the cracked windows, casting shadows all over the walls. Soft music plays, drowning out the sound of my racing heart and rambling thoughts, providing much-needed distraction.

I sit on the bed, feeling completely exposed in a skimpy bathing suit that barely covers my most intimate areas. Staring down at me as they surround the bed, Ace, Stone, Kane, and Seven all admire what's in front of them—me—giving me a look of pure desire and needy lust as they try to fuck me with their eyes.

"We don't have to do this, Princess," Seven tells me, using his rare sweet voice that makes arousal drip from my pussy into the already wet fabric covering it.

"He's right," Stone begins, stepping closer to Ace. "We're not going to be mad, Blue Eyes. We all fucking want you, but you have to want it as well." He smirks, clutching Ace's ass to elicit a grin, and it works.

"No." I swallow, trying to breathe through my anxiety. "I want to do it. I've never done it before, so you'll have to teach me." I shrug and twirl a lock of hair around my finger, batting my long, dark lashes at Kane, who laughs deeply.

"Oh, we can fucking teach you." He steps forward, grabs the back of my neck, and slams his mouth down on mine, kissing me so roughly that he sucks all of the air out of my lungs and leaves me breathless during the kiss.

I'm pushed onto my back gently, and each man takes part in undressing me, leaving me naked, nervous, and on display for them. They look hungry, staring at every curve, beauty mark, and bruise that collectively covers my skin.

But I'm not shy this time, for some reason.

I feel in control, as if I have the ability to give them what they want. And as they start exploring my body, I realize I want it too. I want to feel their hands on my body, their lips, and their desire.

As they take turns pleasing me, I let go of all my inhibitions and succumb to the overwhelming feelings. Each touch sends shivers down my spine, and I can't help but moan as they bring me to new heights.

Kane and Seven sit down, their hands slipping between my parted legs and going right for my pussy. They both ease two fingers inside me, stretching me out in a new way, thrusting slowly as Stone and Ace watch. Without knowing where to look, I close my eyes and allow their fingers to take me away, pressing deep into my pussy in tandem. Seven sucks my nipple into his mouth and grazes it with his teeth until it becomes hard and tender, giving me painful goosebumps. Kane runs his thick, wet lips over my neck, ghosting them across my collarbone in the most sensual, teasing way I have ever felt.

"Open your eyes, Little One," Kane commands in a gentle and soothing tone, his lips still kissing my burning skin.

I open them, taken aback by the sight in front of me and, to be honest, very turned on.

Stone is at the end of the bed, bent over with Ace behind him, holding his hips and fucking his ass in full view of everyone. Stone's deep, guttural moans turn me on, causing my pussy to drip profusely, soaking Kane and Seven's fingers as they work in a twisted motion between my aching inner walls.

"Slide her down," Stone grunts, pulling his bottom lip between his teeth while Ace pounds into his muscular ass, his gaze fixed on mine.

Kane pushes me to the end of the bed, pausing when Stone's chin rests on the shaved mound between my thighs. Both men are still fucking me with their fingers, curling them deep against the swollen bud that drives me crazy.

"I can fucking smell how turned on you are, Blue Eyes," he says, his chest heaving.

His tongue darts out from between his lips and flicks my sensitive clit, making my back lift off the bed and my hips buck, my pussy rubbing against his mouth.

"Do you like that?" He winks, biting on my clit, until I reach down and begin tugging on his hair, attempting to ride his face while Kane and Seven's fingers remain buried inside me.

"Ye... yes," I pant, struggling to catch my breath.

"Good, because you taste too fucking good to stop." He flattens his tongue and licks the guys' fingers, slurping up my arousal until I am shaking with uncontrollable desire.

As Ace and Stone continue to enjoy each other at the end of the bed, Kane and Seven are fixated on me with intense, primal desire. Their fingers inside me, their lips against my skin—each movement pushed me closer to the edge. I can't contain my moans as they bring me to the brink of release, and I tremble as the overwhelming pleasure overtakes me.

But just as I think I can't take anymore, they slow down and pull away, leaving me panting and needy. I look at them with pleading eyes, silently begging for more, and they exchange a knowing look before returning their attention to me.

"We're not done with you yet, Princess," Seven says with a devilish grin, and my heart races with excitement.

I'm completely under their spell, wanting nothing more than to feel their touch once again.

Without saying anything, Seven lies down on the bed, happily taking my place. With a quick movement and dark, devilish eyes, he grabs me roughly and lifts me onto his lap, transporting me back to the woods the day before.

"Switch with me," Kane says abruptly, a torturous gleam in his hypnotic eyes. "I don't want to hurt her. My cock will fucking rip apart her ass, and I want her to enjoy her first group experience." He winks, sounding cocky, but he's right; his cock is fucking massive, and I'm terribly afraid of how much it'll hurt if he were to fuck me in the ass.

"No matter who fucks me... there, it's going to hurt," I admit softly, my eyes nervously dancing between the four of them. "I've only had... your fingers in there."

All four men grin, causing my pussy to drip onto the soft bedsheet, and as I clench my thighs to relieve the pain, the throbbing in my clit only worsens.

"I promise I'll go nice and easy—nice and slow—until you're ready and begging me to fuck you harder," Seven promises, getting off the bed so Kane can lay down in his place.

On shaky, weak legs, I straddle Kane, putting my needy pussy over his hard cock, feeling his cold piercings graze against my swollen lips.

"Jesus fucking Christ, Little One, you're wetter than I've ever fucking felt." Kane holds my hips and bucks his, pushing his cock against my clit, making my body jerk as Seven gets behind me, kneeling on the bed.

"I want this," I pant softly. "I want this so fucking bad."

"You're going to fucking get it, Princess." Seven let's out a low growl right into my ear, his cock rubbing up and down my ass.

Curious about what Ace and Stone are going to do, I look around, feeling butterflies in my stomach as I watch them stand on the side of the bed, Ace's cock still firmly in Stone's ass as he grabs a belt from the floor. I gulp, slightly panicked on the inside, but as soon as Kane plays with my clit and Seven spits all over my asshole, all of my nerves fly out the open windows, along with everyone else's moans.

"Breathe for me, Princess," Seven says, pushing a few soaked fingers into my ass in an attempt to stretch me for his cock. "And when I put my cock in this tight little hole, try not to tense up."

I nod, my throat dry, basking in the pleasure of his exploring fingers. He fucks my ass with them while everyone watches my face and how I react to the sensation. Kisses are strewn across my back, trailing down my spine as I am pushed against Kane until our chests collide. And then his strong, tattooed arms wrap around me, preventing me from moving.

"Look at me, Little One." He swipes his thumb along my bottom lip, sinking his teeth into his. "I want to see the face you make when Seven fills your ass with his cock."

I meet Kane's gaze, feeling a mix of excitement and nervousness, but also a newfound confidence. I'm ready for this, ready to feel the pleasure of being completely filled by these four men.

Seven lubes up before positioning himself behind me. I focus on Kane's eyes to distract from the pressure and the stinging sensation as Seven pushes into me, ripping through the tight ring of unstretched muscle. I whimper, biting my lip and clenching my eyes shut. But then I feel Kane's lips on mine, his tongue working in sync with the rocking of Seven's hips. It's intense—the simultaneous pleasure and pain—and I lose myself in the sensation. He goes slow, pushing in inch by inch, filling me in ways I never dreamed of.

As soon as Seven is fully inside me, he stops, letting my ass stretch and form around his cock, getting me accustomed to his size. I let out a shaky breath, breathing through the burning pain radiating inside my ass.

"You took my cock so fucking well." Seven praises me, holding my hips and kissing the nape of my neck.

"Now let's see how well you take mine with Seven in your ass." Kane guides me down onto his cock, making me moan into his mouth as they both fill me up. I've never felt so utterly consumed by pleasure, and it's all I can do to hold on to Kane's shoulders as I surrender to the overwhelming sensations that consume my body.

The only sounds in the room are our ragged breaths and the slapping of flesh against flesh as Ace and Stone continue to entwine next to us. I'm lost in the euphoria, my mind and body entwined in the experience, and I revel in every moment of it.

As I go to let out a moan from feeling both men fuck my holes, Stone wraps the belt around my throat and tightens it, quickly shoving his cock between my lips.

"If it's too tight, bite me gently." He smirks, wickedly curling on his lips as he thrusts into my mouth.

Feeling full and overwhelmed, I begin to relax, submitting to the pleasure of being fucked hard and deep, as the pain slowly subsides. I push my palms against Kane's abdomen, bouncing on his cock, while Seven surges his hips into my ass, increasing the pace and depth of his cock.

The belt tightens around my throat, cutting off my air. But I still suck Stone's dick while Ace fucks his ass.

And I still slide up and down on Kane's cock while Seven pounds into my ass, both men only separated by a thin layer of skin inside me.

I SHAKE.

I PANT.

I DROOL

I WRITHE.

I gradually come undone, each hole in my body filled to the brim, and I have never felt more alive.

The pleasure overwhelms me, and I feel every part of my body being consumed by raw, unfiltered desire. It's as if I'm floating in a euphoric haze, my mind and body completely consumed by the sensations. In that moment, I embrace the wild abandonment that has gripped me, giving in to the need, lust, and desire that run through my veins.

The room is filled with the sound of our ragged breaths, grunts, groans, and loud moans, as well as the intense ecstasy of our bodies slapping together. I moan with Stone's dick down my throat, feeling a rush of pure pleasure as Kane and Seven continue to fill me completely, fucking me harder and deeper with everything they have. The sensation is overwhelming, and I enjoy every moment of the experience.

Suddenly, I feel the belt tighten around my throat, and I surrender to the pleasure of being taken so hard and deep that the hot leather begins to cut off my air supply. However, it only intensifies the sensations coursing through my body. As Stone presses his cock against my lips, I obediently begin to suck him gently, still riding Kane's cock as Seven surges into my ass.

The room spins with passion and lust, and I lose control, giving in to the intoxicating pleasure that consumes me. I writhe with ecstasy, feeling alive in ways I never thought possible. Each movement, each touch, propels me to new heights, and I revel in the wild abandon that has overtaken me.

Twenty-One

Admitting Guilt

Seven

My fingers are stained yellow from the nicotine, smoking cigarette after cigarette in hopes that they fucking calm my nerves and suppress my extreme guilt. The air—humid and crisp—washes over me as the heavy wind picks up from off of the ocean, turning the waves wild and daring.

A storm is coming, and not just the one brewing inside of me.

As much as I try to, I can't fucking get Emerson off of my mind; she's all I fucking think about, especially lately. She has woven her way deep into my soul, almost as if she has always been there. I've always wanted her to be mine, but I live by the code, and that code meant that she was absolutely forbidden. Somewhere along the long, torturous road, the lines between loyalty and love blurred, and I was sick of fighting my deepest desires—craving the one girl I could not fucking have.

But the fucking guilt still gets to me, making me feel like a terrible fucking person for betraying my best friend. My

fucked-up logic was that my best friend should be happy for me that I found love for the first time, even if it was with his little sister.

The truth is, I can't keep denying what I feel for Emerson. The way she looks at me, the way she makes me feel alive—it's undeniable. The storm inside me is raging, and I can't hold it back anymore. I need to face the consequences of my feelings and own up to my actions. I need to tell my best friend the truth, and I need to face whatever comes my way.

As warm raindrops begin to sprinkle from the thick, dark clouds floating above me, I release a pent up sigh, my body slightly relaxing. The moment I hang my head and shut my eyes, the door swings open behind me, shutting with a loud slam, but not before a blast of music filters out.

"I was wondering where you were," Kane joins me on the bench by the curb of the bar, clasping his hand around my shoulder.

"I needed some air," I muttered, inhaling another drag off the cancer stick at the same time. "I needed a smoke."

He chuckles, bumping my shoulder with his. "You can't go back there. She asked to be alone."

"I'm not thinking about that, as enticing as it sounds." I raise my head and open my eyes, feeling the guilt start to eat me alive.

"You're not thinking about riding back to the beach house to be alone with Em? You're not thinking about how fucking good it feels to be buried inside of her?" he asks, a mix of shock and teasing laced in his slurred words.

"Fucking stop it, Kane." I crack my knuckles, feeling the urge to hit him just for talking about her and for bringing her up.

Standing up, I drop my cigarette to the ground and step on it, snuffing it out.

"Sit the fuck down, boy. What you about to do?" He stands, puffing his chest out like he's ready to fight.

I'm not, though. I just want to leave.

"I'm not fucking fighting you, Kane. Just... fucking stop talking about her." My voice gets soft as my words begin to trail off, my eyes locking on the person behind him.

"Eli," I mutter, my words cracking. "Let me explain."

"I think I fucking heard enough, Seven." He shakes his head and turns to walk the other way, clutching a beer by his side.

I glare at Kane and shove him away, bolting after my best friend, hoping to salvage the dwindling friendship between us. He doesn't stop and wait for me to catch up, he keeps on walking, ignoring my pleas for him to stop. By the time I make it to him, the bar is well enough behind us to where the music isn't rattling my mind.

"Eli," I growl, grabbing his shoulder and spinning him around. "Fucking stop and let me talk, Goddammit."

"What the fuck is there to talk about, Seven? I'm good on discussing my fucking sister, and that seems to be all you fucking traitors wanna talk about." Glaring at me with a look so deadly, he crouches down and plants his ass on the wet curb, slowly drinking from the bottle in his hand.

Accepting defeat, I sit beside him, ready to get everything off my chest, even if it means losing my best friend. "I'm sorry, brother. I really am."

"For what? Fucking my baby sister, or betraying me worse than anyone else could've?" he laughs, but not because it's funny, but more so because of the unhinged laugh—the laugh of a man about to fucking lose it.

"I'm not sorry I fell in love with Emerson, Eli. I'm sorry, I couldn't keep my feelings in check. I'm sorry I broke a promise to you that I know means everything." A weight lifts off my shoulders as the words spill out of my mouth—a drunken confession long overdue.

"You love her?" he asks, his jaw dropping to the wet concrete our feet are planted on, hard to pick up.

"Yeah, I love her." A smile curls along my lips as I think about her, making my dimples pop.

"You don't fucking love her, Seven!" he laughs even louder, his body shaking through the fit. "You love fucking her; there's a difference."

I shake my head, keeping a straight face as I whisper, "I've been in love with her for years, Eli. It's more than what you're thinking."

Silence falls around us, a thick cloud of tension hanging above, worse than the storm clouds. Eli looks as if I've just slapped him across the fucking face—like I've just killed his favorite pet. Somehow, me admitting I've been in love with Emerson hits him way fucking worse than admitting I love fucking her, and I can't gauge his next move. He stands up, walking in a fast circle as he mutters to himself, anxiously running his hands through his hair. I stand up too, my hands in my pockets, waiting to see what he's going to do.

"You mean to tell me that you've been "secretly" in love with my fucking sister for years? When you were supposed to be my fucking friend? My brother!" He charges at me, knocking me to the ground on my back.

Punches get thrown, and I take them, owning up to my deceit. He wails on me, splitting my lip and turning my eyes blurry and black, but I still don't hit him back.

"Fuck you, Seven!" he screams, his voice pierced with betrayal.

Reaching behind him, he pulls out his pistol from his waistband and presses it to my temple, looking down at me with rage and murder in his eyes. So I pull mine out, putting it to his temple opposite mine, refusing to let him take shit too far.

"Put the fucking gun down, Eli. You wanna fight me like a man, then do it. Real men don't need weapons to settle a fucking score." I shove him off of me, making it to my feet with my gun still pointed at him. But I lower it, tucking it away, and pull out the last cigarette in my pack. Lighting it, I crumble the empty pack up and flick it at him, having enough of this shit.

"You don't want to accept my fucking apology, fine. You can't be happy for me, fine. Leave me the fuck alone." I shove past him, ignoring the gun still pointed at my back.

I did what I could for tonight; he's too drunk and too pissed to think clearly. So, I gather myself and wipe the tears before they can fall down my face, and I rush back to my bike, anxious to go see Emerson.

I need to talk to her and figure out what happens from here—I owe her that much.

She's all I can think about as I kick off the side stand, my engine roaring to life. But as I'm about to leave this fucking storm behind me, I can't help but let my mind drift back to Eli. What happens with us now? In a matter of minutes, I've lost my best friend and betrayed his trust, but I still can't bring myself to regret it. I've found love, something I never thought possible, and I refuse to let it go.

Emerson is the only thing that matters now, and I'm ready to fight for her, no matter what; she deserves someone who will fight for her, *not fight her.*

As I ride back to the beach house, the first hard raindrops start pelting my skin, but it's like nothing compared to the storm that's still raging inside me.

••••••••••••

TWENTY-TWO

FEELING ALIVE

Emerson

Walking down the desolate beach, barefoot in only a t-shirt long enough to cover my ass, I welcome the rain as it drenches me, making me feel alive.

Somewhat alive.

With a blunt in one hand and a bottle in the other, I dig my toes into the sand with each step, trying to breathe through the overwhelming stress that's seeped into my bones. I take a hit, then a swig, trying to numb the parts of me that hurt, not wanting to feel anything anymore.

I thought I'd never leave Damon, *but I did.*

I thought I'd never get over Damon, *but I did.*

I thought I'd never find anyone I loved as much as him, *but I did.*

But at what expense? I've come between my brother and his best friend. I've come between my brother and the man he looks up to as a father. I've come between the men in the club and my brother. I've ruined his life all while trying to make mine better. But as much as I've hurt Eli, I can't

get those men off my mind, and it makes me a shitty fucking person—a shitty sister to the only family I've got.

I shiver from a ransom chill, not from the rain or the whipping wind, but from the unsettling feeling of someone watching me. Nervously, I turn around, slowly looking everywhere I can, but I don't see anyone. Immediately, my mind goes to Damon, and suddenly everything else doesn't seem as bad as it did.

My heart is racing as I continue to walk along the beach, the rain pouring down around me. I can't shake the feeling that Damon is still out there, somewhere, watching me. But for now, all I can do is keep walking, hoping that the rain will wash away some of the pain and confusion inside of me.

Approaching the lit-up part of the beach from the stream of light from our backyard, I see a dark figure standing in the distance, and alarm bells start going off inside my head. I swallow slowly, taking another hit and another sip, forcing my feet to keep moving. But as I move, the figure doesn't, leaving me confused. Is it Damon? Wouldn't he have chased me down by now? I wonder, but the fact that he likes to watch and torment me from afar makes me think it isn't him, and a wave of relief washes over me.

Getting closer and closer, I let out the breath I've been holding when the light illuminates Seven's bruised, bloody face, thankful that it isn't Damon. I run the rest of the way to him, jumping into his arms and knocking him down onto the sand. I bury my face in the crook of his neck, letting my tears soak into his skin as he protectively wraps his arms around me, holding me firmly on top of him.

"What are you doing out here all alone, Princess?" he asks, sounding worried but relieved at the same time.

"I needed to think," I admit, finally drawing back to look at him and running my fingers gently over the marks on his face. "Eli?"

"Yeah, we got into it at the bar once I told him how I felt about you, like how I really fucking felt." Seven smiles, his split lip leaking blood as the scab breaks.

I sit up straight on him, my hands on his stomach, while he reaches around and holds my ass, his touch giving me goosebumps.

"And how do you really feel?" I ask nervously, my voice strained and soft.

"I fucking love you, Emerson," he admits, his teary eyes glistening under the glow of the light. "I've loved you for *so* fucking long, and I'm tired of trying to fight it."

I feel a mixture of emotions overwhelm me—shock, fear, and a glimmer of hope all at once. "Seven, I... I don't know what to say," I whisper, feeling the weight of his confession.

But before I can process it, he leans in and gently kisses me, his lips soft against mine, tasting of blood and rain.

"I love you," I blurt out, so fast I couldn't take it back if I wanted to. But that's the thing—I don't want to.

Seven smiles, his black, swollen eyes glimmering under the dim light, as they pierce into mine, searching deep within my soul. He cups my cheek, his soft hand holding me protectively as the calloused pad of his thumb glides with ease across my bottom lip, smearing the mixture of our spit around.

"You love me, huh?" He jokes, sinking his teeth into his lip as I rock against him, leaning my cheek against his palm for even more of his touch.

"Yes, I love you, Seven. I know I shouldn't. I know my brother is going to be fucking pissed, but at the same time, I need to do what makes me happy, and loving you is at the top of my fucking list." I dart my tongue out from between my lips and lick his thumb sensually, watching dark lust flash in his eyes.

He smirks, holds my throat tighter, and casually pushes his thumb into my mouth. Instinctively, I seal my lips around it and stroke it with my tongue, feeling his cock jump under my ass as his eyes grow hooded and dark. I suck on it like I would his cock, feeling him thrust further into my mouth, slightly pressing down on my tongue.

"*Shit*," he groans, biting his lip again while his eyes do the majority of the talking. "That's my good fucking girl," he sweetly whispers, easing his thumb out of my mouth. And with all the spit soaking it, he smears it all over my lips, looking hungry as fuck... *for me.*

I shiver from the look he gives me, not knowing how to fucking respond. It's silent, all but the angry, crashing waves, rattling thunder, and pelting rain against our bodies. We entwine on the beach, not moving, enveloped in a fucking beautiful blanket of darkness that wraps tightly around us, giving off a light that's only meant for us.

There's something oddly satisfying about being corrupted by darkness, like it's where we were meant to be, meant to prevail. I'd rather delve into the darkness with Seven, than be trapped in the light all alone.

It's funny, you see, I was never afraid of the shadows that haunted me—*I welcomed them.* But I grew afraid of Damon lurking in them over time; I feared him, and still do.

I was never afraid to be broken into pieces—*I craved the challenge of trying to put myself back together again.* But when my heart, body, and soul became broken beyond repair, I wished for someone to fix me because I couldn't fathom doing it all by myself.

I was never afraid of death—*I accepted the fact that we were all going to die one day; it's the natural order of things.* But when my parents were callously murdered, I couldn't understand it—I couldn't accept it.

Somehow, being here at the beach with the guys who helped put the shattered pieces of me back together again has allowed me to heal in the most unexpected ways, and I am fucking loving the person I am gradually becoming.

Embracing the gloom and despair, we stay here—together—as the storm rages on around us, and for the first time, as Seven smiled up at me, I felt a sense of peace and clarity that I had been desperately fucking craving.

I knew it wouldn't be easy, and that there would be consequences, but in that moment, with the two of us becoming one with the storm, I didn't fucking care.

••••••••••••

Twenty-Three

A Darker Side of Me

Seven

Sitting on top of me, running her nails up and down my chest, Emerson looks so innocent. She's not, though. She looks curious as fuck too as she licks her plump, shiny lips when I run my hand up and down her back, forgetting about all of the bullshit from earlier.

"You look fucking perfect, Em."

"Thank you, Sev." She blushes, and her cheeks turn a lighter shade of red than her shirt—*my shirt.*

The glow of the moon hits her blue eyes and makes them fucking sparkle as I get lost in the deep, forbidden abyss.

She has that shy, innocent look on her face, and it tugs on the strings of my heart that I didn't even know I fucking had. My eyes move around her face and slowly make their way to her neck, noticing the bruises from last night that she attempted to fucking cover with make-up; I can still see what the fuck we did, though.

All of the fucking plans I had for us tonight flew out the damn window the second I walked down the beach and saw her in my shirt, so short it showed off her perfect, peachy ass.

I wanted to annihilate her tonight. I wanted to make her pussy sore. I wanted to punish her for her fucking brother's bullshit, and I wanted to show her a glimpse of the darker side of me.

However, all I want to do now is lay down and have her ride my fucking cock and show me how she likes it—show me what it takes to make her come. Tonight I'll take it easy with my princess, sort of, anyway.

"This is gorgeous here at this time of night," she says as we stare out at the water and the crashing waves as the storm intensifies.

"Not as fucking gorgeous as you, Emerson."

"You look fucking sexy too, Seven, especially in all black... I'm having a hard time keeping my hands off of you."

"We look good together, don't we?" I ask her, reaching up to glide my finger over her lips.

"We absolutely fucking do."

I take her tiny hand in mine and bring it to my mouth, gently kissing her knuckles and gliding my tongue across her vanilla-scented skin. My cock is already fucking hard, and I know she can feel it poking into her ass while sitting on top of me.

She smiles, bites her bottom lip, and blushes again when she looks at me. “Let's walk.”

Getting up from the wet sand, I take her hand in mine and pull her along with me. We walk down the beach as giant waves crash against the shore, spraying droplets of water all over us, the rain pouring down and soaking every inch of our aching, burning skin.

"I am going to make you mine, Emerson; every fucking part of you will belong to me, if you can take it... "Can you handle it, Princess?"

"I don't know; we'll have to wait and see, Seven." She raises her brow and smirks, making me fucking crazy.

We reach a secluded, dark spot on the beach and pause to watch large bolts of lightning illuminate the dark sky.

"Sit with me?" she asks, taking a seat on the sand beneath an array of trees that flank the beach.

I sit beside her, but yank her roughly back onto my lap, wrapping one arm around her tiny waist and the other tangled in her luscious hair, twirling her long, silky brown strands around my finger and gently tugging to make her moan.

I kiss the back of her neck and watch as goosebumps appear on her bronze skin from the touch of my lips. She wiggles her fucking ass in my lap, rubbing her plump cheeks against my throbbing cock, making it grow quickly and harder beneath her.

"Mmm, is that a gun in your pocket, or are you just excited to see me?" She laughs as I reach into my waistband for my Glock and show it to her with a sadistic, sinful smile on my lips, causing her body to tremble against mine.

I fucking love the reactions I get from her—all of them.

Little does she fucking know the pleasure I can bring her, just by using my gun on her.

"I told you, Princess, I don't go any fucking where without my gun... and you'll see why soon."

"I'm intrigued, Seven..." She winks, leaning in so that our mouths are inches apart, her breath hot against my tingling lips.

I grab the back of her neck, gently this time, and pull her down closer to me, shoving my other hand up the bottom of her shirt. I find her bare pussy right away and pinch her pierced clit with my thumb and forefinger, causing her fucking legs to tremble as I flick and twist it, begging me to fuck her.

I can smell how fucking aroused she is for me, and when I swipe my fingers along her slit, I can feel how soaked she is; they glide between her pussy lips with blissful ease. I dip two fingers inside her tight, sopping cunt, and push them in so far that my fucking knuckles disappear.

She reaches back with her hands free, and grips my thighs so tight, that she pinches my fucking skin through my pants, sending jolts of pleasure to my cock and making it twitch under her ass as I drive my fingers deeper into her.

"Mhmm, yess, baby; I *love* this..." she moans, her body shaking with need.

"What do you love, Princess? Tell me what you love." I finger fuck her hard and fast, making her pussy lips swell with every thrust of my fingers, probing her and parting them within her tight little pussy while she squirms around on my lap.

"I love when you touch me, Seven."

"Do you like when my fingers are fucking with your little pussy? Do you like when I stretch you the fuck out with them, and when I bury them deep inside your tight little hole?"

"Yes, fucking, yes," she whimpers, clinging to me for dear life.

I yank them out just as quickly as I push them in, and then thrust them into her mouth for her to lick clean. And when she does, leaving them coated in her cum and spit, I yank them out of her mouth and suck them into mine, craving her taste on my tongue like a fucking fiend.

As much as I want to continue to fuck her tight, wet pussy with my fingers, my cock needs to be inside of her more. She rocks her hips as she straddles me, grinding her bare pussy against my black pants, soaking me with her juices, but I couldn't give a fuck right now what my fucking pants look like.

"I need to be inside of you, Emerson. I need you to ride my fucking dick the way you like it—show me how you like to ride a fucking dick," I hiss through gritted teeth, my jaw tightly clenched.

"Mhm." She lifts her shirt over the plump curve of her ass, exposing her bare, forbidden territory to the goddamn world—she's fucking lucky no one else but me and her are here, and I'm the only one who can see it.

I unzip my pants and pull my cock out, giving it a few, firm strokes before letting it spring free and stand up straight, resting against the wet, glistening slit of her cunt.

"I want to come in your mouth tonight, Em; I want you to fucking choke on it—gargle it like it's mouthwash—and when I've done that, I want to cover you in it. I can't wait to see how fucking gorgeous you look with my cum all over your lips." A deep growl leaves my throat as I whisper, "sit the fuck on my cock, Princess; take me deep in that cunt in *one fucking try.*"

She puts her hands on my chest and lifts her hips, wiggling them a little to get the tip of my cock aligned with her soaking wet entrance, ready to fucking sink on it. "I fucking love that dirty mouth, Sev," she moans, flashing me a wink that makes my balls ache.

She lowers herself slowly onto my cock, making it disappear into her pussy as her lips swallow me and strangle me in a good way. When she's seated on me completely, I grab her hips hard and dig my fingers into them, rocking her back and forth so her tingling clit gets some friction too.

I reach my hand behind her back and slip it under her shirt, finding her ass immediately. I cup it with both hands and squeeze with all my might, spreading her cheeks apart as she rides my cock like a fucking cowgirl.

I take my finger, lick it generously, and then graze it along the crack of her ass, soaking her forbidden hole and rubbing the tight skin with my thumb, making her ride me harder and faster as I give her a sensation that she fucking loves.

"Do you like when I play with your tight little ass, Emerson?"

"Fuck, yes. Please don't stop," she begs, bouncing on my cock as I finger fuck her ass ruthlessly.

I slip my bandanna out of the pocket of my pants, ball it up, and fucking shove it into her mouth. I smile at her as I watch her eyes go fucking wide, but she still twerks her juicy ass on my cock, slamming down on me over and over again with such fucking hunger like she's desperate for fucking more; she's desperate for me to fill her up.

My finger moves faster, rubbing and teasing her back entrance as I thrust my hips up and slam my cock deep into her tight little cunt, hitting her so deep that she feels it in her lower belly and rocks viciously against me, begging me with her eyes to give her everything I fucking have.

"Don't worry, Princess; I'll take it out when I'm about to cum so I can empty myself down your tight little throat." I reach for my gun, a wild idea floating around in my head.

Pulling out my fingers, I push the muzzle of the gun against her puckered ass, pushing in slowly while watching her hypnotic eyes slightly widen in fear. Still, she continues to slam her ass down on my fucking cock as I ease my gun into her ass.

She shudders, arching her back and bracing herself as I push my gun further in, watching a satisfied smirk tug at the corners of her lips. She lifts her hips and slides me out of her tight walls, so just the tip is inside of her as she bounces her ass in the fucking air. Then, she aggressively slams back down, her pussy swallowing my throbbing, pulsating dick and making it disappear like she's a fucking goddamn magician.

"I'm about to come," she whispers, riding both my dick and my gun as if it's something she can't get enough of, and I smile in absolute delight. Emerson mumbles with the gag inside of her mouth and rocks her pussy desperately against me. Soon, I can feel her gripping my massive cock with her tight walls, soaking the veiny steel rod she keeps sitting on.

Feeling my climax rushing through me fast, I rip the bandanna out of her mouth and push her off of me, my gun falling from her ass. I shove her head down and guide her mouth on my cock roughly, making her swallow all ten inches of me as I jet my heaping, warm load into her mouth and down her throat, glazing it generously with my cum. She sucks me with those perfect, pouty lips, and I grab her hair and yank it as my body spasms through another intense wave of pleasure.

She deep throats me and lets me finish emptying myself right into her stomach as she looks me in the eye, looking like a good-fucking girl with my hard dick between her lips. I pull myself out of her mouth at the last second and smack the tip of my cock against her lips, watching my cum shoot out and cover her face in a sticky, white mess. I watch it drip down her cheek and down her lip as it falls on her shirt.

When I shudder through the last wave of pleasure, Emerson takes me back into her mouth and sucks around the tip of my cock like a fucking jolly rancher. She swirls her tongue around in methodic circles to lick the last of my salty cum away before she lifts her head and licks her swollen, red lips.

"All done, Seven?" she asks with a sly smile.

I smirk back, still feeling the thrills of the climax, but there's definitely more I want to do, and I can see that she's not done either. "Get on your knees," I order, my voice surprisingly soft considering the forceful command.

We are getting deep into the act, making her give me exactly what she wants. And I want to take it. I shove my fingers into her mouth again and spread my cum around in it just to mark my territory, while squeezing her throat so tight that her beautiful face turns fucking red.

I need her to trust me and love *only* me. She's mine now—all fucking mine. And in time, she will know that.

I want her to ask. To beg. I seek to add to the long list of reasons why she can never even dream of fucking leaving.

Her eyes sting with tears, knowing which hand plays with her body as we re-enter our private world of pain and pleasure. I'll tie her up at some point if I still feel that she needs extra incentive. But, for now, I'm just going to keep my knee on her back until I make sure she never forgets.

I need to see her cry when she's on the brink, and her tears have been making her cunt so much wetter.

In this world, it's about me and her. I'm going to make sure she knows that and she'll love me for it in the end. I reach to take a little special memento from my pocket—*her pearl necklace.*

She knows its purpose. She knows it because we've done this before. It's her sign. Her permission to let me do what I like with her body. While we're here and until we decide that it's time to leave, I'm in control, and Emerson knows it. She needs me to be in control. Not because she wants to be controlled, but because she *gives* me the power to take control of her.

And I'll make sure she's fucking mine forever.

Twenty-Four

Drowning

Kane

The sound of happy birds chirping their bullshit right outside the window is the first fucking thing I hear before I'm even fully awake. Never mind them, but the bright sun fucking blinds me the very second I crack my eyelids open, burning the shit out of my irises. To top it all off, the splitting pain spreading inside my head, making my brain thump against my skull, grows worse and worse every time I fucking breathe.

I don't know what or how much I drank last night, but fuck, I have a killer hangover from hell. I'm not in my twenties anymore, but I could still keep up with the kids—not anymore.

Finally pushing through the immense pain, I force my eyes open and sit up, whipping my pillow at the window to scare the fucking birds, just needing them to shut the fuck up.

My body aches, my throat is dry, and I have the worst case of cottonmouth I've ever fucking had. If this is what growing old feels like, I'm fucking over it already.

Groaning in utter fucking agony, I stumble out of bed and make my way to the bathroom across the hall, hoping some water and painkillers will help ease the throbbing in my head. As I splash cold water on my face, I catch a glimpse of myself in the mirror. The lines on my face seem deeper, the bags under my eyes are more pronounced, and my silver-streaked hair is more noticeable. I guess this is what they mean by "the morning after hitting harder as you get older," but why the fuck am I just feeling it today for the first time?

What in the ever-living fuck did I do last night?

After brushing my teeth and gulping down some much-needed water, I shuffle to the kitchen to brew a strong pot of coffee. As the aroma fills the room, I realize that maybe I need to start taking it easier, especially when it comes to alcohol.

And maybe invest in some better fucking blinds for the goddamn birds.

Instead of being met by the smooth, clapping ocean waves as soon as I step onto the back porch, angry yelling and thick commotion pierce my fucking ears. I nurse my coffee like it's my fucking lifeline, and curiously make my way down the back steps, seeing everyone gathered near the firepit, freaking the fuck out.

Eli has the phone pressed against his ear, pacing maniacally until his feet dig into the soft, white sand underneath them.

Seven is on the phone too, but working diligently on his laptop with a baffled expression, consuming the features on his face.

Ace is talking to a few other club members, who didn't come with us on this trip, making me nervous about what's actually going on.

Peeking over his shoulder, I see Stone scanning his laptop screen intensely, carefully watching video feed from inside and outside of the bar.

"What the fuck is going on, son?" I ask with a mouthful of steaming hot coffee, noticing the time, and how it's earlier than usual for these fuckers to be up.

"We had a fucking attack at the bar last night," he seethes, and I can feel the anger radiating off of his body as he speaks. "Five of our members were targeted while on routine runs, and a drive-by nabbed a few more—nothing deadly. Destroyed the fucking bar too." He turns to look at me, confusion written all over his face, even though a tiny glint of realization swirls in his hazel eyes.

"What the fuck? Was anything stolen?"

"Yeah, whatever cash and product the guys were carrying, but nothing from inside the bar."

"Shit, any idea who fucking did it?" I ask, feeling the anger beginning to bubble up inside of me.

"Nothing solid. I don't get it," Stone begins, shaking his head as he stands up. "We don't have beef with anyone right now, so it can't be other bikers."

I look around, suddenly realizing that Emerson is nowhere in sight, and panic begins to flood my veins. "Wait, where the fuck is Emerson?"

"In the water. She's having a rough morning too, but I don't think she knows about what happened." He gazes down at the beach, and I follow his line of sight, my eyes landing on Emerson floating in the water on her back, just letting the waves take her out to sea.

"Then why is she having a rough morning?" I take the last gulp of my coffee, noticing the throbbing in my head slowly easing.

"No fucking clue. She wouldn't say shit to any of us; just ran out the damn house like it was on fucking fire." He shrugs, unable to pull his focus off of her.

But I can't seem to either.

I pat my son on the back and walk away in the direction of a frantic Eli, still on the damn phone. When he sees me approaching, he ends the call abruptly and lights another cigarette.

"Stone filled me in. What do you want me to tackle?" I offer my assistance since the club is my baby, but Eli just shakes his head, nervously glancing back at his sister.

"Nah, we're good on that end, but I need you to do something else for me, Kane." His voice drops to a hushed tone, as if he's trying to make sure that nobody hears him.

Following his lead, I whisper back, "okay, name it, E."

Torture flicks in his eyes and a quick frown curls on his lips before he recovers, his lips making a firm, straight line across his face.

"I need you to go down to the water and try to talk to Emerson. I have to know what's bothering her." He runs his hand through his hair, sighing painfully. "I've never seen her this upset before, Kane, and I'm fucking worried."

I nod, giving him a sympathetic smile. "Sure thing, kid."

He flashes a small but grateful smile before pulling out his phone again, obviously ready to get back go what he was doing.

With my eyes fixed on Emerson, still floating in the water, I make my way down to the beach and walk into the bitter cold water without stopping. The water submerges my body all the way up to my chin, by the time I reach Emerson, shivering from the cold with her eyes squeezed shut. I cautiously reach out and graze my fingers along her cheek, getting her to open her eyes.

"What's wrong, Little One?"

She doesn't answer—won't even talk—but quickly gets off her back and swims right into my arms, locking her legs around my waist and looping her arms over my shoulders. I don't protest. I hold her as tight as I can, sensing she just needs the comfort, the safety that I bring her. Silently, she rests her forehead against mine and looks into my eyes. Before I can say or do anything, she crashes her lips down on mine and thrusts her tongue into my mouth, kissing me with an extreme sense of hunger that I've never seen, but I fucking love.

Caving to every craving, every desire I have for her, I kiss her back even rougher, using dominating lashes that have her tongue eagerly dancing around mine. She holds my face in her hands, keeping our mouths fused as the kiss turns ravenous and possessive. I slide my hand around to the back of her neck, squeezing tightly to hold her in place too, shoving my tongue deep down her throat, toying with the back of it.

She moves her hips, grinding against my cock as we float toward the shallow water, and I know right then exactly what she fucking wants.

"Tell me what you want, Little One," I order, pulling away from her mouth.

She just looks at me, heavily panting, trying to catch her breath.

"You want my cock? You want me to fuck you? Then you need to own that shit and fucking tell me." My upper lip curls, but my eyes darken, feeling the need for control taking over.

"I want you to fuck me," she admits, huffing. "I *need* you to fuck me, Daddy Kane." She bites her lip and flutters her lashes at me, knowing she just poked the fucking bear.

"You need me to fuck you?" I growl teasingly, roughly ripping her bikini bottoms to the side.

I take out my cock and position her over it, lining it up perfectly with her needy little cunt. And then I drive into her with a brutal, deep thrust that has her scratching her nails deeply into my back.

"Tell me why you need me to fuck this pretty little cunt, huh?" I lick the shell of her ear as she bounces up and down, making the water splash roughly around us.

"I just fucking need you, Daddy," she whimpers, craning her neck back as I begin surging my hips forward rapidly, plunging over and over into her cunt.

I can feel her squeezing my cock with a vice grip, desperation in every move she makes. So when she goes to kiss me again, probably to stop all the talking, I kiss her back, exploring every inch of her mouth. Sliding my hand up her back, I tangle it in her wet hair, grabbing a handful and pulling it roughly. She cries out, but the sound slips into my mouth since she refuses to stop kissing.

I relentlessly pound into her, feeling her walls tighten around me as she screams out in ecstasy. Our bodies move in perfect tandem, sharing the same urgency and hunger, seeking release and fulfillment. The pressure builds inside of us, ready to explode. Gasping for air, Emerson breathes out a long, needy moan, looking up at me with her eyes glazed over with a raw, primal need.

"Drown me, Kane," she begs. "Hold me under the water and fuck me until I come."

A little shocked by her request, I raise a brow and smirk, pushing her off of my cock and spinning her around so her back is against my chest. Standing on the bottom of the ocean, the water up to my midriff, I spread Emerson's ass and guide my dick back to her pussy, sliding back in with a full-body thrust. She gasps, leaning forward as I hold her hips and fuck her wildly, holding nothing back.

"You sure this is what you want, Little One?" One more time, I ask her, just to be sure before I push her under the water and hold her there.

"Yes, it's what I fucking want. Now fucking drown me, Daddy."

As soon as the words leave her lips, I push her head underwater, holding firmly at the back of her neck. I slam into her, fucking her needy cunt with deep, vicious strokes. I can feel my orgasm building in my core, and I know Emerson is even closer. As her pussy clenches around me, I drill in deeper and harder, bottoming out inside of her. One final slam, and she's rapidly squeezing my cock, soaking it with her cum as I bust, jetting white ropes deep into her cunt. We come together, trembling from the same frantic sensations, even as she's held under water for longer than usual.

She doesn't fight me for air, which begins to worry me. So as soon as I finish filling her up with my cum, I fist her hair and yank her out of the water, into my arms.

"I needed that, Kane," she whispers against my lips, her voice heavy with desire and shaking with fear.

I press my forehead to hers, feeling her heart thundering in sync with mine. "I know, Little One. I know." I hold her close, cherishing the way she feels in my arms. "Let's get dried off, because, like it or not, you're going to tell me what's bothering you."

She rolls her eyes, but a small smile finally plays on her purple lips, but it doesn't stay for long. Keeping her hand in mine, I lead her out of the water and onto the sand, the sun's burning rays beating down on us.

I can tell she's struggling as we walk toward the house, trying to find the right words to say. I can't tell if she's ashamed, upset, or scared, and that fucking worries the fuck out of me.

"Come on, baby, tell me, please." I bring her hand to my mouth and kiss her knuckles, grateful when she doesn't pull it away.

"Things with Damon are *escalating*; he's getting worse," she finally admits in a pain-filled voice.

My veins bubble with rage as murder and violence course through them.

"He's filming me, and he's leaving the videos for me to watch."

"That's gonna stop real fucking quick. I'm done playing this motherfucker's game." I promise myself that I'm going to end it, no matter what it fucking takes.

"Kane, it's not that simple. He wants me, and he's not going to fucking stop until I come back." She begins to sniffle, visibly shaking and terrified to her core.

I spin her around to face me, my hands holding onto her shoulders. "What the fuck did he do that has you so fucking spooked?"

She pauses, trying to catch her breath and steady her racing heart before responding. "He filmed me and Seven on the beach last night... together, and he fucking lost it. He filmed the whole thing, then sent it to me, along with a message from him."

"You're not fucking going back," I snap, feeling adrenaline coursing through my veins.

She pulls away from me, clearly upset and torn about what she should do. I chase after her, refusing to give up on something so important.

"Emerson, did you fucking hear me. You're never fucking going back to that bitch."

"I have to, Kane! I don't have a fucking choice!" she screams at me, the tears streaming down her puffy cheeks, making them even puffier.

"You always have a cho-"

"No, not this time, I don't. If I don't go back to Damon, he's going to kill... he's going to kill everyone I love." She chokes on her words as if they're poison and her body is trying to fight them out.

"Who do you think shot up the club and put five of the guys in the hospital? It was Damon, he sent me a video of him doing it. He told me if I didn't come back to him, then he'd start killing y'all and film it... then he'd make me watch the video."

I pull her into a tight hug, securely wrapping my arms around her shivering body as she sobs in the crook of my armpit. I stroke her wet hair, trying to soothe her as best as I can while trying to remain calm about the shit she just blurted out.

"You know there are other ways to handle him without having to go back to him." I bite my tongue as soon as the words leave my lips, knowing I've already pissed her off by bringing it up.

She yanks out of my grasp, wipes her tears, and lifts her chin in defiance, trying to prove that she's got shit handled.

"I'm taking care of it, Kane," she seethes, anger dripping off of her as she balls her fists down by her sides.

And then she walks off, kicking up sand with the heels of her feet. I don't yell her name or chase after her, knowing it'll only push her further away. If she says she can handle it, she'll handle it, and I have to be able to put my trust in her to do so.

Well, fuck. That could've gone better.

Twenty-Five

The Escape Artist

Emerson

Confused, broken, and angry, I bolted away from Kane, not wanting him to see how unraveled I truly was. I tried convincing him that I had a handle on Damon—that I could take care of shit on my own. But truth be told, I had no fucking idea if I could or not. Damon was losing his fucking mind, and not only me, but the ones I loved were caught in the crossfire. It was my fault the guys were hurt. My fault the bar got shot up. All of it was my fault. All because I fucking left him. Luckily, I'm motivated by doubt, and there was plenty of it going around the beach house, so a small part of me knew that whatever I decided to do, I'd be able to put a stop to Damon and his madness.

But what was I going to do?

I didn't want to get back with him, for fucks sake. The last year of our relationship was toxic as fuck, and I had gotten to a point where I gave up on myself, allowing him to put his hands on me. I wasn't myself. I was drowning in misery and daily beatings, and I was so afraid that if I didn't leave, I'd end up drowning to death at Damon's hands. Walking

away from him—my first love—was one of the hardest things I'd ever had to do, but I knew it had to happen.

As I thought about all the ways I had let my brother and everyone down, I kept running, flying past everyone gathered down by the porch. And much like I did with Kane, I ignored them as they called my name, rushing into the safety of the house.

I took the stairs two at a time, panting and out of breath by the time I walked into my room and slammed the door, locking it to keep everyone out. Just as I was about to drop to my knees and break down, my phone went off, immediately sending uneasy chills down my spine. I didn't feel good about it, but curiosity had me checking to see who it was and what the fuck they wanted.

I instantly regretted it, sank to the floor with my back against the door, and did my best to keep the bile from rising in my throat.

Don't cry, baby. I did all of this for you—*for us.*

You shouldn't have left me, Emerson. You shouldn't have walked the fuck away.

I shivered reading Damon's text, doing all I could to not look out the windows to see where he was. He was out there watching me, for sure, but I was too much of a pussy to find out where. I tried to ignore him and the messages, but they kept coming, putting me in a tough spot.

You can ignore me all you want, but I'm never going away.

Oh, I left something for you; check your top drawer.

I froze as I read the last message, feeling fear and dread seep into every bone in my body. I didn't want to get up, but I knew I had to.

My shaky legs carried me to my dresser, and with each step, I felt the bile rise a little more each time. Breathing in and out slowly, I curled my fingers around the knobs and pulled the drawer open, feeling the life drain from my body as my eyes landed on six bullets, all neatly lined up in a row on top of the new underwear I had to buy because of Damon stealing every pair that I owned.

Before I could really take in what was in front of me, my phone went off again, and I angrily reached down to snatch it off the floor.

Pick them up and look at them, Emerson.

I put my phone on top of the dresser and reached into the drawer, pulling a bullet out with trembling fingers. Carefully inspecting it, I felt my heart stop as I figured out what he was talking about, growing more fearful by the second. I dropped the bullet and picked up another, then another, and another, until I cautiously looked at all six.

Not only were there six bullets in my drawer, but carved into each one was a name.

ELI. SEVEN. ACE. KANE. STONE. EMERSON.

I dropped the bullet and slammed the drawer shut, feeling more enraged than anything. I picked up my phone and tapped the phone icon, wanting Damon to hear me loud and clear. Of course, he answered on the first ring, a laugh in his voice as he spoke my name.

"Emerson, baby, I take it, you saw my gift?"

"It's not fucking funny, Damon. Leave me the fuck alone, and leave the guys alone, too."

"Or what, Em? Huh? What the fuck are *you* going to do about it?"

"Just *please*, stop this."

"You made your fucking bed, now you have to lie in it. I told you what you needed to do, so if you don't want to see the people you love drop dead one by one, I suggest you pack your shit and come back to where you fucking belong. You know where to find me."

He hangs up, not giving me a chance to plead my case, but he was never going to. And I knew that.

So, I rushed to my closet, found my backpack, and dumped its contents out, knowing exactly what I needed to pack. I grabbed my gun case and unlocked it, removing my pistol from the cushion and putting it into the empty bag along with an extra full clip and a change of clothes. And then I zipped it shut and got dressed in my usual riding outfit, ignoring the penetrating chill that relentlessly wracked my body.

Even dressed in tight black jeans and a black cropped sweatshirt, I was fucking shivering, hearing my teeth chatter from the fear gripping my body. I slid my knife into the ankle sheath under my pants and tried to compose myself, trying to not look like a hot mess. But fuck, it was impossible not to.

There was nothing left for me here if the guys were gone, nothing left in this life that I wanted other than my peace and safety and the peace and safety of the men I loved. I refused to sit back and watch, so I started to slide the backpack over my shoulder as I decided there was only one thing left to do—I had to go back to Damon. He was right, it was my fault and my problem, and if it was the last thing I ever did, I had a plan to make it right.

I popped Zanex like they were candy, washing them down with the rest of the water in the bottle on my nightstand, hoping I wouldn't have a panic attack before they kicked in.

With one last deep breath, I slipped out of my bedroom and made my way back to the gathering on the porch, walking out with all eyes on me.

"What's going on?" My brother asked, concern pinching his brow.

"I have to go," I said as I pushed my way through the crowd, my eyes searching for Kane, who met them with anger and worry that mirrored my own.

"Where the fuck are you going?" Seven interjected, stepping in my path to try and block me from leaving.

"I have to go," is all I said, forcing my way past them, knowing I wouldn't have much of a head start if I didn't hurry my ass out of there.

They were all wicked protective over me, and although I loved it, at times it annoyed me. And today was one of those times. I needed to take care of this on my own. I needed closure, and I only knew of one way to get exactly what I was looking for.

Stepping out of the house and into the darkness of the night, facing my fears and my demons, I climbed on my bike and quickly started it, putting my helmet on just as the guys ran around the corner to get onto theirs.

I took off at a high rate of speed, pushing the speedometer past one hundred in a matter of seconds. The wind whipped angrily against my body, trying hard to knock me off my bike, but I held onto the handlebars tightly and made the throttle my best friend, pushing limits and breaking boundaries as I tried to get far enough away from them.

But they were right behind me before I knew it, trying to box me in, so I had nowhere to go and nothing else to do but stop. I turned and looked to my right, seeing Seven on his bike right beside me. To my left, Kane was there, trying to keep up with me as my brother, Ace, and Stone stayed behind me, the six of us zooming down the winding road along the beach that led back to Boston.

All I could think about as I pushed my bike harder than ever was the six bullets with each of their names carved into them, and it gave me a surge of adrenaline that I desperately needed. I don't know how, but I managed to gain more speed, inching away from the group as I smiled under my helmet. The rush was intense, and as my bike vibrated between my legs, sending pleasurable hums throughout my body, I couldn't help feeling turned on.

Was it the risk of them catching me? Or the climbing speeds past 160 mph? I didn't know what it was that made me feel the way I did, but I fucking loved it. I focused on that feeling and lowered my chest against my bike to fight the forceful winds as each man faded into the distance behind me one by one. The only bike I heard roaring in my ears was mine. I had finally lost them. I couldn't help but smirk, knowing that I had smoked their asses in a race. Sure, it wasn't what I had in mind when I thought about racing them, but I did it regardless. And even though I knew they were pissed at me for taking off, I also knew that they were proud of me for holding my own.

I still had no fucking clue what I was going to do, but I had to figure it out soon. I had to face Damon again and put an end to this shit.

Gritting my teeth, I continued to speed down the road, feeling a mix of fear and excitement as I willingly headed straight back into the lion's den.

The sad thing was, I was prepared to not make it out of there alive.

TWENTY-SIX

THE SAME GIRL

Ace

"So does it feel weird for you that you and your father are fucking the same girl?" I ask Stone out of the blue, sliding his cock out of my mouth.

Looking at the road with one hand on the steering wheel, he huffs and shakes his head. "Nah, as long as my dick isn't anywhere near his, I'm golden," he laughs, quickly looking down at me and flashing me a wink.

The rain beat down on the car as we cruised down familiar roads back in Dorchester, searching for any signs of Emerson.

As soon as we lost her, it started raining, and within minutes, it got so bad that we switched out our bikes for our cars. With everyone paired off, we've been scouring the city high and low, hoping to find her. But the fucking rain is making it harder, of course.

"Fuck, where would she have gone?" Stone looks around frantically, at a loss, like the rest of us.

Trying to get him to relax, I pick up where I left off, seal my lips around his thick cock, and slide them all the way

down to the base. He grunts like his fucking soul is leaving his body as I cradle his balls and massage them, working him deeper into my mouth until my throat squeezes around the tip. When he puts his hand on my head and pushes me down, I shiver from the sensation and suck him even faster. My head bobs up and down as my lips roll smoothly over his shaft, feeling the bulging vein gliding against my lips.

"Fuck, Ace," he moans, leaning the back of his head against the headrest.

Groaning with pleasure, Stone tightens his grip on the steering wheel as the rain continues to pour down. His breath quickens, and I keep my pace steady, my eyes lifting to meet his as he watches me with a desperate hunger in his eyes.

His balls grow heavy in my hand. His cock twitches and throbs against my tongue as I swirl it around him. And as I widen my jaw and deep-throat him, the familiar taste of pre-cum lingers on my tongue, letting me know that he's fucking close.

I increase the suction and speed, determined to take him over the edge as I continue to bob my head with fervor. Suddenly, his body tenses and his hips lift off the seat, driving himself deeper into my mouth as he releases with a guttural moan. I swallow every drop, not wanting to waste a single bit of it.

Breathless and satisfied, Stone looks at me with a dazed smile as he catches his breath. "Damn, Ace. You always know how to calm me down," he says, brushing a strand of hair away from my face.

Sitting up, I wipe my mouth and lean back in my seat, a small smile playing on my lips. "Let's keep searching. We'll find her," I reassure him before turning my attention back to the road ahead, hoping to God I was fucking right.

We spent hours in the car searching for Emerson, but we didn't have any luck finding her. Needing a break from the rain and tired eyes, the group agreed to meet at the SSB bar. I didn't want to see the damage from the drive-by, but I knew it was inevitable.

The bar was a second home for me; I basically grew up there. With my father being the president, we spent more time at the bar than we did at home. And when my mother eventually ended up leaving, we fucking started sleeping there. She left because of my father and the type of life he wanted to live. She didn't want this for me. She wanted me to do better.

But I didn't.

I followed in my father's footsteps and bought my first bike when I turned 15, joining the SSB the moment I was able. The club was my life, my family, and I knew I could count on my brothers no matter what. After graduating high school, I chose to become a full-time club member, and kissed any dreams of going to college goodbye. Especially when I went to prison for manslaughter. But I moved past that, and I had every one of my brothers by my side through every step.

The bar had become something special to me, so the fact that it wasn't as safe as I thought it was bothered me a lot.

The bar is also where I met Emerson for the first time, and I knew then that she'd become trouble—in the good way, of course. We bonded over our shared passion for music and our shared hatred for algebra. After school, she would come to the club to see her father, and his ass would always have her do her homework, refusing to let her interact with us or us with her.

She was off-limits... forbidden, and we were fucking warned to stay away from her. So naturally, him forbidding it only made us want her ten times more.

But none of us made a move on his baby girl. We kept our promise until he was murdered, then she was fair game.

If he were alive to see this—his daughter not only fucking one member of the club but four—his ass would fucking croak.

Seven and them have their own reasons why they're obsessed with her, or in love with her—same thing. And I have mine.

I used to watch her while she sat at the bar and did her homework. I was able to count all the freckles I saw on her face and remember exactly where they were. I was infatuated with the way she'd lick her lips, completely unsuspecting. I obsessed over the way she'd stretch when she sat too long, and the little moan that slipped from her throat. I was obsessed with everything about her, but I never fucking told her.

So when we pulled up to the bar and parked the car, my heart sank when I saw the guys standing outside looking at all the bullet holes in the building—without Emerson.

"You didn't find her?" They shake their heads when I ask, looking defeated in every sense of the fucking word.

The bullet holes didn't bother me anymore. I was too worried about Emerson and where the fuck she could be. The bar could be fixed. But depending on where Em was and what happened, she might not.

Flicking his cigarette into a puddle near the curb, Eli turns around and walks inside, his shoulders slumped from the weight and pressure that were stacking on top of them with each passing second.

I hurried through the doors of the bar to follow him, and I was greeted by the familiar smell of cigarette smoke and whiskey. The music seemed to relax my racing nerves, but with each glance at Eli, my anxiety worsened. Emerson was everything to him—the only family he had left. He was supposed to protect her, and he fucking failed. We all did. But obviously, Eli was taking it the hardest because it was more personal to him than any other problem he had in the past.

The four of us slide into our usual booth in the back and have drinks placed in front of us before we can speak.

"Y'all checked Damon's place, right?" Everyone in the booth gives Stone a dumbfounded look, the tension growing thicker.

"Yes, we fucking looked there, Stone. Neither of them were there." Seven looks like he wants to fight someone, but he does his best to keep his temper in check.

"Seven, can't you track her or some shit through her phone?" Kane blurts out, looking hopeful.

"Yeah, but I can't get her pin unless she takes or makes a call."

"Then let's call her until she picks up."

"I tried calling her, but she isn't answering. She isn't answering any of our texts or calls. It's like she's fucking vanished into thin air," Eli says, signaling to the bartender for another drink.

"We need to keep fucking trying," I whispered, knowing we couldn't just give the fuck up.

The feeling of helplessness was suffocating. I didn't want to lose Emerson, not now. Not ever. We all sat in silence, not knowing what to do next, and fearing the worst. The thought of never seeing her again was unbearable. We had to find her.

Our club was our world, and Emerson was a part of that world. We fucking had to get her back.

Twenty-Seven

Russian Roulette

Emerson

Tightly knotted rope digs into my wrists, chaffing my skin and making it bleed each time I move. But I still try to break free from the restraints.

Sprawled out on a bed, my legs are spread, and my ankles are bound with thick leather straps to the bed posts, preventing me from going anywhere. A pair of my underwear that Damon had stolen are bunched up into my mouth to muffle my screams, held in place by a thick belt looped around my head. The only part of me that's free is my eyes, but I'm forced to look at nothing but darkness as it swallows every inch of the room.

I'm fucked.

The random rainstorm had derailed my plans and gotten me hemmed up, making things go fucking easy as shit for Damon. I wasn't even off my bike for a minute before he came up from behind and hit me with something hard in the back of my head. I collapsed in the parking lot of the bar, so fucking close to finally ending this shit. But Damon was watching me—behind me every step of the way. So when I

stopped at the bar because I couldn't see through the intense rain, he saw an opening and took it, catching me completely off guard.

I had to think fast. My mind raced as I tried to come up with a plan. But with my hands and feet bound, it seemed impossible. I closed my eyes and took a deep breath, trying to calm the fear and panic that threatened to overwhelm me.

I had to stay strong. I couldn't let Damon win. As I lay there, I focused on the sound of the rain outside, the only familiar comfort in the darkness. My mind searched for any possible escape route, any weakness in Damon's plan. And then, an idea began to form. It was risky, but it was the only chance I had.

After moving my head around so much that the belt ended up sliding down to my chin, I began to work on the restraints, trying to loosen the knots with my teeth, straining against the pain in my wrists. It took what felt like hours, but finally, I felt the rope loosen. With a surge of hope and trembling hands, I began to work on the straps around my ankles.

Finally, I broke free. I removed the gag from my mouth and the belt from around my neck, and I scanned the room for any sign of Damon. But he was nowhere to be seen. I knew I didn't have much time. I had to get out of here before he came back. Struggling to regain my composure and push the fear to the back of my mind, I climbed off the bed and snatched my backpack up off the floor, bolting for the bedroom door.

I dialed my brother's number and swung open the door. There, waiting for me on the other side, was Damon, wearing a devilish smirk on his face as he dangled a revolver between his fingers.

"Going somewhere?" His smirk never falters; if anything, it gets even more twisted, making me cringe.

"Leaving," I whisper in a hoarse voice, my throat sore and dry from screaming.

"Nice fucking try," he laughs, backing me up into the room I was trying to get out of.

The lock on the door clicks, and all hope drains from my body. Damon shoves me toward the bed, causing my phone and backpack to fall from my grasp to the floor. He hovers over me, pushing the gun between my lips as he tears at my pants to pull them down.

"Damon, please let me go," I plead with him, hoping that a part of him still has a shred of remorse left.

"I give you props for breaking free, but I still can't let you leave." He shoves my pants down to below my knees and grasps my thong, violently ripping it off of me, cutting my delicate skin with the sharpness of the lacy fabric. I whimper, and he laughs with nothing but evil dripping from his lingering tone.

"Now, you're going to listen to what I tell you to do, or I'm going to pull the trigger." He cocks the gun and winks, letting me know how fucking unhinged he really is.

"Give me your fucking hand," he orders, keeping the gun on me while taking out a pair of leather cuffs, securing one to the post near the headboard.

Swallowing hard and even slower, I raise my arm for him to take, wincing as he tightly secures the other cuff around it, making sure I can't move.

"Alright, now the other one." He grabs a pair of cuffs already attached to the post at the bottom of the bed, waiting for my other hand.

But I refuse to give it to him, knowing what's about to happen when I do.

"Give me your fucking hand, Emerson." Spit sprays all over my face as he hisses, growing angrier by the second.

"No, Damon." I refuse, gripping the blanket under me in my hand, trying to stay grounded to the bed.

Without saying anything, his frown turns into another twisted grin, making me feel wicked uneasy. He sighs and shoves the gun further into my mouth until the muzzle hits the back of my throat and makes me gag.

And then he pulls the trigger, the sound of the empty click echoing in my ears.

I breathe heavily, feeling panic surging through me as little beads of sweat form on my brow.

He tried to shoot me. I mean, fuck, he shot me, but there wasn't a bullet in there.

"I told you that I'd pull the trigger if you didn't listen. Did you think I was fucking joking?" He brushes his lips across my cheek and presses his cock into my stomach, slowly easing the gun out of my mouth.

He opens the gun and spins it, showing me that, in fact, there are bullets in the gun—two, to be exact.

"You wanna play a little Russian roulette, I see. Well, baby, I'm fucking game," he laughs coldly, putting the gun back between my lips. "Now give me your fucking hand." He glares at me, his eyes dark and diabolical.

Fearing him, I comply, giving him my hand so he can secure it to the post.

I squeeze my eyes shut as he works his pants off, feeling his naked body against mine. He violently rips my thighs open as much as he can since my pants are still half on, and he maneuvers between them, guiding his cock to my pussy. I squirm, trying to fight him off, but he slides the gun out of my mouth and hits me across the forehead, drawing blood immediately.

"You wanna play another round?"

"No, Damon," I cry, refusing to look at him. "Please don't do this."

"It's too late for all of this begging shit. You're fucking mine, Emerson, not Seven's, not Kane's, *no one's.*" He licks the blood dripping from my forehead, groaning in satisfaction. "You know what's funny?" he asks, and I can tell I'm not going to like the answer just from the tone of his voice. "I had no idea that it was me who hit and killed your parents until I watched my dash cam footage the next morning." He forcefully thrusts into me, painfully ripping through my pussy.

My jaw drops, and my entire body stiffens, tears filling my eyes until everything I look at is blurry. I ignore the fact that he's inside of me, taking what he wants. I focus on his admission, feeling my heart shatter all over again.

He was the hit-and-run. He was the drunk driver who ran into them, killed them, and then took off. It was Damon.

I gasped in shock and disbelief, feeling sick to my stomach at the revelation. All this time, the person I had been in love with was the person responsible for my parents' deaths. The intense hatred I felt towards Damon welled up inside me, intensifying with every thrust he made.

But at the same time, I knew I had to play this smart. I had to get through this and lull him into a false sense of security.

Damon continued his sickening assault, the weight of his body pressing down on me, taunting me with his cruel laughter. My mind raced with possibilities, each second feeling like an hour. As if sensing my hesitation, Damon tightened his grip on the gun, pressing it into me even harder, a twisted smirk dancing on his lips.

Despite the fear coursing through my veins, I knew I had to be strong. I couldn't let him break me. I had to find a way out of this, no matter what it took.

So with a gun to my head and my wrists tightly bound to the bed, I just laid there while he ruined me, praying through every vicious thrust he delivered that an opportunity would come for me to escape.

TWENTY-EIGHT

MISSING POSTERS

Seven

"I've got her!" Eli screams, running over to us as we gather in the back of the bar, still trying to track down a lead on Emerson's whereabouts.

I look up from my laptop, my heart thundering against my ribs. "Where?" I ask, my shaky hands trying to rest on the keyboard.

"I don't know. She called me, though; it's still connected," he says winded, out of breath as he hands me his phone so I can start a trace on it.

Working diligently to find a ping that'll tell us where she's at. There's nothing but silence on the other end, but the call is still connected, so I focus even harder. While the program does its job to triangulate her location, I fiddle with my hands in my lap as everyone gathers around me and holds their breath.

"How fucking long does it take?" A frustrated Eli growls behind me as he paces with lead feet.

"Try to relax, brother. This shit takes time, but it'll work." I force a smile as I turn around to face him, trying hard to believe my own words.

"I'm finished with the missing posters," Ace speaks softly, his voice full of worry and concern.

"Just hold off. Let's see if we can find her with Seven's program."

The tension in the bar is heavy and palpable as we wait for any indication of Emerson's location. After what feels like an eternity, the program finally comes up with a result. "Got it!" I exclaim, relief flooding through me as I relay the coordinates to the rest of the group.

Without a moment to lose, we all spring into action, racing out of the bar and piling into our cars. We speed through the streets, following the directions provided by the GPS, until we finally reach a rundown apartment building deep in the ghetto of Southie.

"What the fuck is this place?" Parking the car at the curb, I look around, taking in the gloom of the desolate area, getting an unsettling chill along the curve of my spine.

"No fucking clue. This isn't where Damon lives." Eli pushes the passenger door open and hops out, making a beeline for the building as we all run to catch up behind him.

The building looms in front of us, dark and foreboding. As we make our way up the steps, I can feel the tension growing among us. We reach the top floor and stop in front of the apartment that the GPS coordinates led us to. Without a word, Eli kicks the door in, and we rush inside, our hearts pounding in our chests.

The apartment is empty, and a feeling of dread washes over me as I realize that we might be too late. We split up, searching every inch of the place, but there's no sign of Emerson.

Suddenly, Stone calls out from the other room. "Guys, you need to see this."

We all gather in the room, my breath catching in my throat as I see what's on the wall. It's a map, covered in red string and pictures, all connected in a web that leads to a single name written in the center: Emerson.

On the single bed, leather bindings dangle from the rusty posts, slowly swaying back and forth—we just missed her. My mind reels at the thought of what might've happened on the bed, and bile starts rising in my throat, burning the lining of my esophagus. As I roam my eyes around the room, I spot a light coming from underneath the bed. Crouching down, I reach my hand under the bedframe and feel around for the source. My hand hits an object, and I pull it out, my heart sinking to the fucking floor when I notice that it's Emerson's phone, still connected to the call with Eli. I stand up and end the call, reaching out to my best friend.

"Eli, look," I whisper, sadness coating my voice in an obvious way.

"Motherfucker!" Eli roars, kicking a wooden chair in front of him, on the verge of a severe breakdown. "Send out a mass text with the missing flyers you made of Em," he tells Ace, his eyes fixated on the wall of horror and mystery.

And then he bolts, running out of the room without as much as another glance behind him to see if we're following.

The rest of us all exchanged worried looks before hurrying after him, not willing to let him face whatever lies ahead alone. As we race down the stairs and out into the street, I can't shake the feeling of impending doom. My heart aches for my friend, and I can't imagine what he must be going through. It aches even more for Emerson, though. But we can't give up.

We reach the street just in time to see Eli jump into my car and speed off, leaving us in a cloud of dust and exhaust fumes. Without a second thought, we all pile into the remaining vehicles and follow him, determined to find Emerson and bring her home.

The drive is a blur of anxiety and desperation; hope is quickly dwindling, and I can feel the weight of the situation pressing down on all of us. As we speed through the city's wet streets, I know that time is running out. But we won't stop until we find her, no matter what.

The sound of sirens fills the air as we race through the city, our hearts pounding in our chests. The minutes feel like hours as we scan the streets, looking for any sign of Emerson, but there is none that we can see.

Arriving back at the bar, we get out of the car to head back inside, our breath coming out in visible puffs in the cold night air. Eli is already out of the car and running towards the entrance. Ace and Stone run inside after him while Kane and I hang back, chain-smoking the fuck out of our Marlboros. He looks miserable, pain flitting across his face, but he doesn't talk about it. None of us talk about it.

Emerson being missing is fucking torture, eating me up on the inside because I feel like I let her down. I should've stopped her. I should've put more effort into stopping her before she left the fucking house, but I wasn't thinking that something like this would happen to her.

Leaning against the building, I hang my head in shame, my chest aching from the smoke infiltrating my lungs. This can't be fucking happening. I waited so fucking long to tell Emerson how I felt about her and things just started progressing, and now she's gone, and I'm terrified she isn't coming back.

My love for her is like the darkness that's followed me all of my life; it consumes every part of me in a delicious way.

It pierced my bones and weaved its way into my body.

It wrapped itself comfortably around my tortured soul and put life back into my dying heart. And although I can live without it—without her—I don't fucking want to.

Emerson is a part of me—the part that makes me a somewhat decent human being.

I'm a fucking addict for her love—her body—and a desperate fiend when I can't have her.

She does something to me that no one ever has, and I want her to keep doing it.

She fucking owns me—controls me—and she doesn't even fucking know it, but because it's Emerson, I'll give her every fucking part of me, and I'll do it without a second thought.

The sound of footsteps approaching pulls me out of my thoughts, and I look up to see Kane standing in front of me, an expression of concern on his face. I forgot that he was even out here.

"You good, Seven?" he asks quietly, his voice a low rumble in the cold air.

I nod, unable to voice the storm of emotions raging inside of me. "Yeah, I'm good," I mutter, flicking the end of my cigarette onto the ground and stomping it out with my boot. "Let's get back inside."

"I promise, Sev, we're gonna find her," he assures me, trying so fucking hard to believe his own promise.

But I can see the doubt swirling in his dark eyes and a glint of fear lurking in his dilated pupils. Big and bad Kane is even fucking worried, which makes the worry coursing through me spread like a damn wildfire.

As we head back into the bar, I know that our search for Emerson is far from over. This is just the beginning of a long and dangerous journey, but I'll be damned if I let anything happen to her. I owe her that, and so much fucking more.

And I'll do whatever it fucking takes to bring her home, safe and sound, with me, with us... No matter the cost.

Back inside, we gather around the bar, the flickering neon lights casting an eerie glow over the grim faces of the guys. But in our eyes, I see determination and resilience.

As the rain picks back up, pelting against the bar's roof, and the night stretches on with the hours slipping away into oblivion, we carefully strategize and plan our next move. We'll leave no stone unturned, no lead left unexplored. The thought of Emerson out there, alone and in danger, is fucking unbearable—gut-wrenching, even.

But we won't give up fucking hope. She's out there somewhere, praying, and waiting for us to come save her... and that's exactly what we're gonna fucking do.

•••••••••••

Twenty-Nine

A Promise to Myself

Emerson

Everything on and inside of me fucking hurts. I feel broken—mind, body, and soul. And I know that as long as I'm trapped here with Damon, this shit is never going to end. In fact, it's going to get a lot worse. He's raped me, beaten me, cut me, choked me until I passed out and raped me while I was unconscious, and kept me bound to another bed more securely this time, making sure I couldn't escape.

Once he found out that I had called my brother, he took me away from the first place and brought me to another, now held up somewhere else. I have no phone to use for help. No clue where I fucking am. And with each passing second, hour, and day, the little bit of hope I tried to hold onto is fading.

I've accepted the fact that I might be here forever—that I might die here, but I don't want to. It's been at least two days since I've been missing, and I know my brother and the guys are probably freaking the fuck out. I miss them all, and thinking about them is the only thing keeping me going.

To stay alive, I play the game that Damon wants. He tells me to get on my knees and give him head, so I do. But he still taunts me with the gun and the single bullet that terrifies me every time he pulls the trigger. I've been lucky so far, and haven't been shot yet, but I fear my luck is running out.

I still pray, to God, to my dead parents, even to the fucking devil—anyone I can think of, and all I can do is hope that someone somewhere is fucking listening.

I refuse to give up. I refuse to let him break me completely. I'll keep fighting, keep waiting for the right moment to make my escape. I have to believe that there's a way out of this nightmare. Whether it's through my own strength or the help of someone else, I won't stop hoping for the chance to break free from this house of horrors.

I'll keep playing his sick game until the moment is right, no matter how much it eats away at me. And maybe, just maybe, someone is listening. Someone will come to save me. I have to hold onto that belief, or I'm truly lost.

I never imagined that the boy that I fell in love with would turn out to be a fucking monster... but there had been signs. Unfortunately for me, I didn't see any of them until it was too late. Now I've gotten myself in this twisted, fucked up mess—a tangled, dangerous web that Damon has weaved, and for me right now, there's no fucking way out in sight. Not when he keeps me tied up and chained. He hardly feeds me, says he likes it that I'm so fucking weak that I can't fight back. But I've been saving my strength—what little bit I have—and I'm determined to find a way out of this nightmare of horrors.

I don't know how much longer I can hold on, but I have to keep trying. I can't let Damon win. With each day that passes, I'm filled with more and more desperation. I have to find a way to escape. But the thought of what he might do to me if I fail, terrifies me to my fucking core.

But I can't give up.

I won't give up.

I have to stay strong and focused, even though the pain and fear consume me every moment of every day. I know that I can't let the darkness take over.

Not while there's still a glimmer of hope left in me. And even if it seems like no one is coming to save me, I have to hold onto the belief that someone, somewhere, will fucking find me, or that the opportunity will come when I'll be able to break free of this filthy prison of torture, humiliation, and pain.

And when that moment comes—cus it will—I won't just make a run for it.

No.

I'm going to summon every ounce of evil I have buried deep inside of me, and I'll fucking unleash it.

I'll make him fucking pay for everything that he's done to me.

I'll show Damon that he can't break me, that he can't control me any longer. I'll take back my power and make sure he never has the chance to hurt anyone else ever again.

I refuse to be a victim. It's time for me to become the hero of my own story, no matter what it fucking takes.

I *will* survive this horror, and I'll make damn sure that Damon fucking pays for every moment of agony he's fucking put me through.

My strength will be my salvation. And I'll never stop believing that freedom is within my reach, even in the darkest of moments.

With a smile on my face and revenge in my eyes, I'm going to fucking kill him.

I'll make sure it hurts him much worse than he's ever hurt me.

Because I refuse to cower. I refuse to let him win. I'll find a way out of this nightmare even if I die trying...

I have to.

Thirty

Bloody Payback

Emerson

Something hard and shockingly cold is slammed against me, causing blinding pain to immediately shoot through my entire body. Waking out of a deep, drug-induced sleep, my eyes fling open, filled with fear, and frantically search the space around me for the cause.

"Wake the fuck up, captive," Damon demands, his voice chilling and deep as he hits me again with the unknown object across my kneecaps.

He hovers over me, a sadistic grin curling on his lips—lips I used to love kissing. Grabbing me by my throat, he pulls me up into a sitting position, proudly showing off an aluminum bat he's got clutched in his other hand. As I get a decent view of the room I'm in since he has the light on, I notice my belongings in a heap in the corner by the door, my knife gleaming on top of the pile.

I'm in a room with no windows and soundproof padding covering every inch of the walls. But I try not to let it frighten me more than I already am.

"You having fun yet?" He winks, making my entire body cringe.

"Tons," I snicker, trying hard to keep my mouth shut so I don't get hit again. "When are you going to let me shower?"

"You don't need to. I'll be back tonight to give you a bath." He brushes my bloody, sweat-soaked hair out of my face, matting it to my head.

And then he does something I wasn't expecting. He undoes the restraints around my ankles, freeing my legs from the uncomfortable position they've been stuck in. And then he uncuffs my wrists, allowing me to be free for the first time since he took me. I breathe a relieved sigh, holding in the tears that so desperately want to fall. But I don't say a word, in fear that I might unknowingly set him off again.

"Don't get comfortable because after I'm done with you, the cuffs are going back on," Damon laughs, his eyes dark and foreboding.

"Thank you." I force a smile and pretend to be grateful, playing the game in order to survive.

He says nothing as he gets up and leaves the room, closing the door behind him, but keeping it open a crack which is not like him.

I know I won't be able to make a run for it, especially not knowing the layout of this place or even where I am. I have to play it smart.

Looking at my knife, I gather all the courage I have inside of me, ignore the radiating pain shooting throughout my body, and manage to get off the bed to grab it. Once I have it, I hurry back to the bed, slipping the knife under the pillow so it's close for when I need it.

And then I wait for him to come back, trying to come up with a plan in my head that I hope to fucking God works.

I hear footsteps approaching the door, and I tense up, readying myself for whatever is to come. As the door creaks open, I pretend to be asleep, my heart pounding with anticipation. I can feel Damon's presence in the room, his heavy breathing, and the sound of him moving closer.

"I know you're not fucking sleeping." Suddenly, he grabs my arm and pulls me up forcefully, laughing as he sees the fear in my eyes. But as he moves to restrain me again, I grab his hand and cover it with mine, giving him a look that I know he can't say no to.

"Please, don't put them back on just yet," I beg him, knowing how much he likes it when I do. "I want you to fuck me with my hands free so I can touch you." I gag on the words as they fall from my cracked, bloody lips, but my fake smile never falters.

"You're finally coming around, I see." His lips sweep across mine as he positions himself over my body.

"I think so." Even though I have to fight to lift my arms, and the thought of touching him makes me want to throw up, I reach around his body and rake my nails down his back.

He shudders against me, letting out a low groan with his face buried in the crook of my neck. He pumps his hips, rubbing his cock against the inside of my thighs, not paying attention.

This is it...

Subtly reaching under the pillow with one hand, my other still rubbing his back, I retrieve my knife and grip the handle tightly, trying to prepare myself for what I'm about to do.

You've got this, Emerson. I tell myself.

And while his head is still buried and he's grinding on top of me, I hold the knife steady and plunge the blade deep into the side of his neck.

His eyes widen in surprise as he lifts his head, and for a split second, I see fear flicker through them. "What the fuck did you do?" He roars angrily, looking shocked more than anything.

But then his expression hardens as he puts his hand over the wound and grabs for the bat, ready to strike. Without hesitation, I lunge forward with the knife, catching him off guard and stabbing him in the chest, blood spurting everywhere.

He lets out a roar of pain and stumbles back, clutching his chest as blood pours from both wounds. With him on his back, I straddled him, wielding the knife with a crazed look in my eyes.

"Fuck you, Damon!" Tears streaming down my face, I begin stabbing him all over, slicing every part of his body that I can. Blood soaks into the bedsheet, turning the white a dark crimson from the multiple gashes on his body.

But I keep going, losing myself with each thrust of the blade. He doesn't move, but he's still breathing, his eyes wide in shock as they follow my every move, every slice—every stab. Putting the knife down, I climb off of him and pick up his bat, making sure to hold it tightly so it can't slip from my blood-soaked hands. And then I swing, connecting with the bones in his body, the crunch echoing in my ears.

He groans in agony, and his body begins to shake, bringing a smile to my face.

But what finally brings me the peace and closure I've been searching for is when I pick up the knife and put it to his throat. I can feel a genuine smile spread across my lips as I swipe the blade, digging it into his flesh and making a deep gash from ear to ear, finally ending the torment.

The room is filled with an eerie silence as I stare down at his lifeless body, finally feeling a sense of relief as I realize that I'm finally free from his captivity. The sight of his bloodied corpse sends a chill down my spine, but at the same time, it fills me with a sense of triumph and liberation.

Right now, in this blood-soaked room, I feel like I've finally reclaimed my life.

Now I just need to figure out how the fuck I find my way out of here.

Thirty-One
Ironic Epiphany

Emerson

I wanted so badly to be out of this dungeon, but I haven't been able to bring myself to leave. Even with Damon's lifeless corpse in the other room growing stiff and his tainted, velvety blood coating my skin, I can't seem to take a few steps to the front door. Instead, I pluck a cigarette out of his pack and light it, feeling the rush from the invasion of cancerous smoke filter through my entire body.

The throbbing pain in my bones hasn't stopped, but I've learned to ignore it. The horrific memories of his vile torment still linger in the depths of my mind, but I refuse to let them define me. With each second that I stand here, staring at the dinghy front door, I can feel his blood start to dry on my skin, making me extremely itchy.

I need to shower.

Finding the bathroom in his little one-bedroom apartment isn't hard. Walking past the bedroom where he lies dead on the floor is.

But I force myself to do it. The apartment feels so small and suffocating as I walk down the small hallway, forcing myself not to look in the bedroom.

I reach the bathroom and flip on the flickering light, stripping off my bloodstained clothes and stepping into the hot, steaming water. The warmth soothes my itching skin, and I scrub furiously, trying to rid myself of any remaining traces of him. It doesn't even phase me that I'm scrubbing my skin raw.

As I stand under the water, I think about what I'm going to tell my brother and the rest of the guys. Why do they need to know about what happened here? About what I did in retaliation. I don't want their pity. Looking down as the scalding water cascades over me, I get lost in the swirl of the bloody water as the drain sucks it down, a never-ending whirlpool of red.

I stand here until the water turns cold and clear, knowing for certain that every spec of Damon's blood is washed away from my body, but I still don't feel clean.

Stepping out of the shower, I dress in the extra set of clean clothes I packed, shoving the bloody ones into a bag to burn before I head home.

I gather my belongings and make my way to the front door, taking one last look at the room where I endured so much horror. Flashbacks of my time bound to the bed attack my mind, threatening to send me into a spiral, but I force them down as far as they'll go, refusing to let Damon and his evil corrupt me any longer.

I'll move past this shit, just like anything else I've had to overcome. I know it won't be easy. I know it won't be overnight. But I'm determined to fight for my peace of mind, no matter how fucking hard it is. No matter how long it takes.

On my way out, I grab a bottle of vodka sitting on the small kitchen counter and pocket what's left of the cigarettes I'd been smoking, needing something to fill the void inside of me.

With a deep breath, I turn the doorknob and step out into the fresh air, leaving the darkness of the dungeon behind me.

Finally, I am free.

I notice my bike parked beside his building, and relief floods through me. The itch to ride is overwhelming; I just want to feel the wind in my hair. I walk over, dropping my bloody clothes in a cheaply made burn pit, and dousing them in the vodka I grabbed before striking a match. As my clothes erupt into flames, I lean against my bike and watch the fire, the crackling echoing in my ears. I stay until there's nothing left but ash, feeling like a piece of my soul was sucked out of my body and burned along with it.

Finally, it's time to leave this place behind and forget about what went on here. I take a deep breath and swing my leg over my bike, revving the engine and feeling the familiar rush of freedom and safety wash over me.

As I speed away from Damon's mysterious apartment, I can feel the weight of his torment and manipulation slowly slipping away. The wind whips through my hair like I've been craving, and for the first time in what feels like forever, I feel the anxiety I've been carrying for so long dissipate from my body.

I ride freely as the storm clouds roll across the velvety sky, the open, winding road stretching out before me. As the clouds turn dark and angry, I realize that I'm finally ready to face the truth of what happened and seek the help I need to move forward.

Not just the truth about what Damon put me through, but the truth about how much my parents' murders affected me.

I didn't want to admit that I was as broken as I was. I tried to put on a brave facade, but even I could see right through it.

I was fucking weak.

I didn't want to deal with the internal pain of losing them, so I pretended that I was okay even though I wasn't.

I was the furthest thing from okay there was.

I was miserable. I was lost. I was self-destructive.

I felt like no one would ever love me like my parents did. Of course, no one would love me like they did.

But I didn't even want anyone to love me, because I was terrified that I was incapable of loving anyone back.

But Seven helped me break the chains that kept me heavily guarded. He showed me how much I was loved—how much he loved me. He made me realize that I truly loved him back, but I was too fucking afraid to admit it.

Kane helped me realize that it was okay to open up and allow myself to seek comfort in someone who would guide me through the tough times like my father used to. He helped me see that I didn't only think of him as someone I could look up to, but someone I could trust to take care of me in ways that I never had—ways I'd never allow.

Ace showed me what it was like to love unconditionally, to be proud and unashamed, and to fight for what and who I wanted no matter who thought it was wrong or forbidden.

And Stone, Stone showed me how to let down my guard and break the walls around my heart, showing me that it was okay to love your friends more than just a friend. Sometimes, a friendship is just a cover for something really beautiful, something worth risking a friendship over because it might just be what you'd always hoped for.

Most importantly, they all showed me that I could stop hiding in the darkness and letting the scars control me; that it's time to confront the demons and reclaim my life.

With a newfound love, confidence, and determination, I ride into the eye of the storm with a smile on my face as the ice starts melting from around my heart, leaving behind the traumas and horrors of the past and embracing the promise of a brighter future where I know that I'll be okay.

Thirty-Two

Bruised Blue Eyes

Stone

As Eli and my father continue their search for Emerson, Ace, Seven, and I sit around the fire on the beach, feeling utterly useless and defeated. We scoured the city for the last three days she's been missing, looking in abandoned buildings where we know she hangs out—her and Eli's house, Seven's tattoo shop, Damon's apartment, the bar, even the cemetery where her parents are buried—nothing. We've never felt more powerless. Since we have her phone, there's no way for us to track her anymore. She hasn't called or tried to reach out, which is unsettling to say the least.

This summer was supposed to be a chance for her to move past the trauma and grief she'd been carrying since her parents' murders. And although she was making immense progress, I feel like whatever has happened is just going to make her recovery even worse. But we're not giving up.

As we sit together, the flames casting a warm glow over us, I know that no matter what challenges we may face, we will always be there for each other, through thick and thin, good and bad—ride or fucking die.

The sound of the crashing waves against the shore feels like a soothing balm to our frazzled nerves. As the flames from the fire crackle and dance, I can't help but feel a surge of determination rising within me. We can't give up on Emerson, not now, not ever.

Just as I open my mouth to suggest another avenue of search, a distant, rumbling sound catches my ear. The three of us look at each other, curious and hopeful, turning our heads to look behind us with a view of the long driveway that loops around to the back of the house.

"Who the fuck is that?" Ace asks, his words soft and slurred from one too many shots.

"I think it's Emerson. That sounds just like her fucking bike," Seven points out, sounding and looking hopeful.

"It's... it can't be." I stumble over my words as they fly out of my mouth, standing up to get a better look at who's pulling down the driveway.

As a blue glow from headlights on a bike flicker in our eyes before the engine gets killed and everything goes dark, my heart pumps rapidly, praying that it is, in fact, Emerson.

I know the sound of her bike from any fucking place.

Seven, Ace, and I watch intently, following the dark figure's every move as they dismount their bike.

"Well, fuck. I'll be damned," I mutter, breathing a sigh of relief, still riddled with complete confusion.

It's Emerson, stumbling out from the shadows of the trees, disheveled and exhausted. Relief floods through me as we rush to her side, engulfing her in a tight embrace.

"Thank goodness you're okay," I whisper, my voice choking with emotion as I smooth out her wet hair, her body shaking terribly against mine.

Seven and Ace pull back, giving her a careful once over to see if she's okay, but the darkness surrounding us prevents them from being able to tell.

Emerson looks up at me with tear-stained eyes, nervously glances at the guys, and nods. "I'm so sorry," she manages to say, her voice hoarse and trembling.

"Where have you been?" Seven asks, choking back the tremble in his tone, trying to put on a brave facade that, regardless, we can see right through.

Emerson stares at the beach, taking in the crashing waves, relishing the sound as they connect with the shoreline.

"I don't want to talk about it right now," she says flatly. "I'm fine, though." A forced smile lets us all know that she's not fine, but we don't push the issue—*yet, anyway.*

"Have you talked to your brother?" Ace asks, unable to rip his eyes off of her, in fear that she'll disappear again.

She shakes her head, not removing her eyes from the water. "No, I don't have my phone."

"We have it, Blue Eyes. We found it when we were out looking for you," I admit softly, pulling it out of my pocket and handing it to her.

She snatches it out of my hand and pockets it, turning around with her back to us. "I'm going to take a shower, but I'll be down to join you." She walks off without uttering another word, leaving the three of us confused, shocked, and definitely feeling like we're fucking missing something—something big.

"That was fucking strange." Seven's eyes follow her all the way into the house, where the bathroom light upstairs flips on within seconds. "Call Eli."

I nodded in agreement, pulling out my phone and dialing Eli's number.

"She's back. She's here," I say, not bothering to hide the relief in my voice.

We hear a string of curses on the other end of the line before Eli responds, "I'm on my way back. Don't let her out of your fucking sight."

"We won't," I promise before ending the call.

As Seven and Ace look at me with relief and concern intermingled in their eyes, I know that the next few hours or days are going to be difficult. But we have to know where the fuck she's been and what the fuck happened.

As we walk away from the beach and back up to the house, the sound of the shower running from the bathroom, flowing out through the open window, fills the air, and I can't help but wonder what kind of hell Emerson went through these past few days. But for now, all that matters is that she's back and she's safe. And that's all we could have hoped for.

Seven crouches down as we reach the back driveway, pointing his phone's flashlight under Emerson's bike.

"What are you doing?" I crouch down, asking in a whisper in case she's curiously peeking out the window above us.

"Eli had me put a tracker on her bike when she first got it, so he always knew where she was," he says, feeling around near the back tire. "If it's still here, we'll be able to tell where the fuck she's been." His fingers dance in the dark around her bike until they find what they're looking for, and Seven pulls out a mini GPS tracker, showing it off with a winning grin on his face.

The three of us slip in the back door of the garage, grabbing a cold beer from the fridge before collapsing on the leather couch.

"Stone, go keep her some company. Make sure she doesn't come down here." I nod as Seven plugs the USB drive into his laptop, trying not to show my excitement at the thought of having her all to myself.

"Text me when you're done," I tell him, slipping into the house, a little too anxious to climb the stairs to her.

As I reached the top step, I noticed the bathroom door open and the light off. Looking down the hall as I walked softly and slowly, I noticed light peeking out from under her closed bedroom door, Sleep Token blasting from beyond it, so loud it reverberated through the walls and shook the upstairs.

Judging by her choice in music, I knew she was going through some shit, and deep down, I felt lucky to be the first one to try to comfort her.

But would she let me? Would she let me in, not only to her bedroom but to her heart and mind as well? There was only one way for me to find out, and I was fucking dreading it. More so, dreading the fact that she might push me out and away as far as she could. But fuck, it was Emerson, and I had to fucking try. She wasn't the type of girl you'd give up on, no matter fucking what. I never even thought about giving up on her, and shit, I wasn't going to start now.

Taking a deep breath, I squared my shoulders and knocked gently on her bedroom door. "Emerson, it's Stone," I called through the door, hoping she would hear me over the sound of the music. After a moment, the music was turned down and the door slowly opened, revealing her tear-stained, bruised face, my jaw falling to the floor.

"Stone," she said softly, her voice filled with a mix of surprise and exhaustion. "What are you doing here?" She casts her eyes downward, almost as if she were trying to hide her beautiful face from me.

But I could still see everything—the bruises, welts, and cuts, and I was beyond fucking pissed—not at her, of course, but at the motherfucker who did it to her. Deep down, I knew who it was, but I needed her to tell me herself, not make my own assumptions.

"I just wanted to check on you, Blue Eyes," I replied, trying to keep my tone gentle and reassuring. "I know things have been tough lately, and I want to be here for you."

Emerson hesitated for a moment before stepping aside and allowing me to enter her room, closing the door behind us to keep the rest of the world out. As I sat down on the edge of her bed, she collapsed into the chair at her desk, looking at me with a mixture of sadness, shame, and a slight hint of gratitude, definitely trying to put some distance between us, which I fucking hated. All I wanted to do was hold her and never let go, but I knew I couldn't push it. She'd have to come to me when she was ready, and I'd be patiently waiting for that very moment.

"I don't know if I can handle this," she suddenly admitted, her voice barely above a whisper as her swollen, bruised eyes danced around the room, looking everywhere but at me.

"You don't have to handle it alone," I said, reaching out to take her hand, gently tugging her up from the chair and over to me, where she sat nervously on my lap. "I'm here for you, Emerson. I care about you more than you fucking know."

For a moment, we sat in silence, the only sound being the faint hum of the music still playing from her speakers. Then, slowly, Emerson leaned into me, resting her head on my shoulder. And in that moment, I knew that no matter how difficult things got, I would always be there for her. Because she was worth it. She was worth fucking *everything.*

I really wanted to ask where she had been for the last three days, if she was okay, which I knew she wasn't, and if I needed to kill anyone for her. But I didn't. I didn't want to push her away just when I had gotten her to lower her guard a little.

I just held her close, feeling her shake with silent sobs. All I could do was be there for her, and that's exactly what I intended to do. So I stayed there, holding her, until her breathing evened out and she finally fell asleep in my arms. And as I lay there with her clinging to me as if I were her safety net, I knew that I would do anything to protect her, no matter what the cost. Not only because I wanted to, but because I fucking loved her, and I had for a long, long fucking time.

••••••••••••

Thirty-Three

Secrets Unveiled

Seven

The good thing about the tracker Eli put on his sister's bike was that it gave us every fucking address where her bike went these last few days.

The bad thing? We had to go track them all down to find out what she had been up to. But lucky for us, there weren't that many, and most of them we recognized, but there were a few we didn't.

After having the data sent to my phone and plugging in the first address, I finish my beer and reluctantly get off the couch. Eli and Kane rush in through the back door to the garage, worry washing over their exhausted faces.

Out of breath, Eli gasps, "Where is she?"

"Upstairs with Stone while we looked through the tracker data from her bike." I wave the USB drive in the air before slipping it into my pocket.

"Has she said anything?" Kane asks, sounding like he's trying hard not to run up there and check on her.

After pulling my black hoodie over my head, I shake it, feeling slightly deflated, but knowing we're the fucking

close to finding out the mystery we've been struggling with for three fucking days now. "Nah, but she wasn't in the mood to open up when she got home, so we didn't want to push it and trigger her without knowing it."

"At least she's fucking home. Everything else will fall into place," Eli mumbles, still looking hurt and worried for his sister.

But he wasn't the only one who felt like that.

"Who's riding with me?" I asked, grabbing my bike keys and heading for the back door.

"You three go," Kane suggests. "I'll stay here with my boy and Emerson."

Eli and I exchange a look before nodding and heading out the door with Ace, Emerson on my mind with each step. The night air is cool and refreshing as we hop on our bikes and start the engines. I take the lead, with the tracker data guiding us to the first unfamiliar address. The streets are quiet as we ride, our headlights cutting through the darkness to guide our way into the unknown. One by one, we check all of the places she was, not finding a clue as to why she was there or what happened.

Finally, as we pull up to the last address, we see a small, run-down apartment building and Damon's Mustang parked in the driveway, looking like it's out of place, especially for this area. Eli, Ace, and I exchange another look before dismounting our bikes and approaching the entrance. I notice a tire track in the mud that leads to beside the building, and a sinking feeling settles in the pit of my stomach.

The door is unlocked, so we pull it open and walk inside the dark, desolate building, chills trickling down my spine.

"Something ain't right," Ace whispers as we follow the GPS that leads us to the only door on the hall, dim, flickering lights hopping around in my vision.

Stopping at the cracked open door, I pause, turning to make sure they're ready to see what, if anything, is waiting for us inside. "I don't like it either, but this is the last stop and our last chance to find out what Emerson was doing for the last three days."

"Open it," Eli demands, shoving his twitching hands into his pants pockets.

I push the door open the rest of the way, drawing my gun, and prepared to use it. The pungent smell of death overwhelms our senses, causing us to gag, pulling our sweatshirts up over our noses to block the stench. Fear seeps into my bones with each step, and my heart thunders inside my chest, pulsing loudly in my ears. A trail of dried blood on the floor puts the fear of God in me, and I do my best to brace myself for whatever we're about to find. Ace leans against the front door, shaking his head as he hunches over.

"You go. I can't stomach the fucking smell," he gags, every ounce of color draining from his face.

Eli and I continue to follow the blood trail, stopping as we get to the bedroom, gloom following us like a shadow. As I flip the light on, my fucking jaw drops to the floor as I take in the bloody sight in front of us.

There, lying on the floor, is Damon, covered in blood from all of the stab wounds all over his body. Flies are heavily swarming around him. My eyes scan the room, and I instantly feel sick to my stomach, but not because of the stiff, dead body in front of us. Attached to the bed are handcuffs and leather straps, which are obviously used to restrain someone. Polaroids are scattered on the floor at the end of the bed, and as I walk over and bend down to pick one up, I freeze when I see Emerson posed in different positions, both awake and unconscious.

"What are those?" Eli asks, stepping over Damon's body as he walks over.

I quickly stand up and drop the picture, trying to keep him back so he doesn't see his baby sister like that. "No, Eli. Trust me, you don't need to see them."

His nostrils flare, his sharp jaw clenches, and for a moment, it feels like he's about to fight me over the pictures. But he relaxes eventually, turning back around to look at Damon and letting out a chillingly dark chuckle that makes my nerves uneasy.

"She fucking killed him, Seven. She killed him, and she didn't want us to find out." He takes his gun out and cocks it, then fires, the sound of recoil echoing loudly in my ears. He doesn't stop, either. Eli stands steady and empties the clip into Damon's corpse, getting his revenge even though his sister beat him to it.

But I don't stop him. He needs this, mostly to feel like he's protecting his sister, even though, by the looks of it, she doesn't need it.

And then he breaks down, his strong exterior crumbling as he collapses against me, thinking about the horror and torture

Emerson went through. I hold him and let him sob, trying to hold back tears of my own, but I can't.

I glance up at Ace, who has managed to compose himself in the doorway, still pale and on the verge of barfing. He nods at me, his eyes filled with a mix of sympathy and understanding. With Eli still leaning on me for support, we eventually leave the apartment, knowing that the nightmare is far from over.

Getting home well after two am, Ace goes right upstairs to his room, desperate to shower, hoping it'll wash away the stench of death still clinging to him—to us. Eli is still silent, not knowing what to say or how to process the horrific scene seared into our minds.

He walks like a zombie to the dark kitchen, his shoulders slumped, a distant look consuming his murderous eyes, obsessively fixated on a bottle of Jägermeister that he snatches off the top of the refrigerator. Without speaking, he walks straight out the back door, taking the entire bottle with him.

The quiet tapping of footsteps descending the stairs grabs my attention, and I turn around to see Stone coming toward me, rubbing his bloodshot, tired eyes with a grim expression on his face.

"How is she?" I whisper, glancing up at the top of the stairs, making sure Emerson didn't follow him.

He shakes his head and walks into the kitchen to grab a bottle of water, chugging half of it before he speaks. "Not good. She's struggling, but still won't open up just yet."

"I'm not surprised," I admit, shaking my head as I stare blankly out the kitchen window at the waves, bile rising in my throat. "She fucking killed him."

He chokes on the water, looking at me with bulging eyes and his mouth slightly ajar. "Wait, what?"

"Yeah, we found him mutilated on the floor of some apartment, lying in a pool of dried blood." I shudder just thinking about it as the images from the pictures flash in my mind. "He put her through hell, so I don't blame her."

"Fuck, I don't even know what to say." Stone just stares at me, almost as if he's waiting for me to say, 'Just kidding'. But those words never come out of my mouth.

"She's afraid to face us, and I don't blame her," I whisper, bowing my head as I squeeze the bridge of my nose, trying to hold back the onslaught of emotions overwhelming me. "Eli's about to hit a very dark place."

Stone nods, a grim understanding overshadowing his face with dark, hooded eyes. "We're all in one, grim company, but he and Emerson are facing the worst of it."

"Yeah, and all we can do is be there for them. But we need to clean ourselves up and figure out what's next. We can't live in this fucking mess forever," I scoff, still trying to grasp the severity of the situation.

He reaches into the drawer, pulling out two cigarettes that he lights, handing one to me before puffing on the other himself. "She's going to need all the help and support she can get."

"We're all going to need a lot more than that," I mutter, realizing that this was only the beginning of something we never saw coming our way.

••••••••••••

Thirty-Four

Lingering Nightmares

Emerson

Bloody, brutal nightmares tortured me all fucking night, making me fear sleep every time I tried to close my eyes. I knew I was safe at the beach house—safe with the guys—but I couldn't handle the flashbacks, nor could I forget what had happened to me. It had only been less than twenty-four hours since I killed Damon and managed to escape his house of horrors, but I wanted to be fixed right away.

I wanted to forget. But I couldn't, no matter how much I smoked or how many Xanax or Ambien I took. Even having Stone sleep in bed with me didn't help, but fuck, did I want it to. While he slept, I stayed awake, staring into the darkness that surrounded me, flinching at every little noise I heard.

I was becoming paranoid, and for no fucking reason either. Damon couldn't hurt me anymore. I fucking made sure of it, but the traumatic memories of what he did to me lingered long after I slit his throat.

I needed to find a way to move on—to heal from the trauma that was consuming me. Stone tried to comfort me, but I could see the worry in his eyes. I didn't want to burden him with my demons, but I knew I couldn't face them alone. The nightmares had left me exhausted, and I longed for a sense of normalcy that seemed to be so fucking far out of reach.

But I felt a glimmer of hope in the darkness. I knew I needed to talk to someone who could guide me through the pain and help me find my way back to myself. The thought of opening up to my brother or any of the guys was daunting, but I knew I couldn't continue to suffer in silence. Still, I refused to tell them what Damon did to me, even more than what I did to him. I didn't want their pity or for them to look at me differently. I wanted to spend the rest of my time here having fun, exploring each new relationship I had gained with the guys, and focusing on moving forward. I was determined as fuck to make all of that happen.

So, I felt that if I could keep it from them for as long as I could, living with myself would become easier, and I'd eventually move on one way or another.

But would they let it go, no questions asked? Knowing them and how fucking protective they were over me, they'd figure out a way to find out what happened, and that's the last fucking thing that I wanted.

After lying in bed, wide awake, until I had composed myself as best as I could, I finally forced myself to get up and carry on like nothing ever happened. With Stone still sleeping, I crept to the bathroom in my room and shut the door, gasping the moment I saw my reflection in the mirror.

Fuck, the bruises.

I had forgotten about the fact that Damon had used me as his personal punching bag, leaving me with an assortment of ugly, colored marks to prove it. Panicking, I spent the next twenty minutes painting my face with more make-up than I had ever worn, just to try and cover every reminder of his torture, even going so far as curling my hair to try and draw attention away from my face. I pulled a hoodie on and brushed my teeth, hoping I did a good enough job where no one mentioned anything.

Stone had seen my face and some of the marks last night, but no one else had. As I snuck out of the bathroom and quietly slipped out my bedroom door, I prayed hard that he hadn't opened his mouth and told anyone.

My body ached with every anxious step I took, but I breathed through the pain and brushed it off, grasping onto the only sense of normalcy I had left. The kitchen was empty when I walked in, and immediately I breathed a sigh of relief, knowing I'd be able to have my coffee in peace. I made myself a mug of the steaming vanilla-flavored beverage and quickly rolled up a small joint, moving to the back porch when I was finished.

Summer was coming to an end and I could feel it in the air as a gentle breeze blew, giving me a chill. The sun was shining brightly, casting a warm glow of its rays right on me. With the first break in the wind, I quickly lit the joint and greedily inhaled a long, hard rip, holding the potent smoke deep in my lungs until I couldn't breathe. As I exhaled, the wind blew again, taking the smoke and the scent of MaryJane with it. If the guys weren't up, they sure as fuck would be now, especially with the delicious aroma of the weed wafting all around them, most likely in through their open windows.

I didn't worry about them, though. Instead, I nursed my coffee and toked on the joint as I stared at the beautiful, yet rough ocean waves crashing against the seawall, due to high tide rolling in. I welcomed the serene environment and the peace and silence I'd been yearning for, trying to soak as much of it in as possible before everyone else woke up.

Once I had finished my joint and my mug of coffee, I prepared myself to face the day that lay ahead. I knew that sooner or later, I would have to confront the demons that were haunting me—owning me—but for now, I just wanted to enjoy the calm before the storm, because I knew that what was coming, wasn't a usual storm; this one was about to roll in like a fucking hurricane and wreak havoc on everything and everyone in its path of destruction. I selfishly hoped that it wouldn't be as bad as it was in my head, but only time would be able to give me an answer, unfortunately.

As the sun continued to rise and the beaming rays burned brighter and hotter, I sat there on the back porch, feeling the gentle warmth of the morning sun, trying to find the strength to face my reality.

My body still ached, the emotional and physical pain consuming every inch of my being, wrapping like a blanket around my tortured soul. But the lingering sense of normalcy that the morning had brought, made me feel like *maybe* things would get better.

Maybe...

Or at the very least, give me some desperately needed silence in my head to mask the violent thoughts trying their hardest to take over.

Even though I felt like it, I knew that I wasn't alone in this battle. But reaching out for any kind of help was a hard pass for me. I took a deep breath and closed my eyes, determined to find a way to move forward and heal from the trauma that had gripped me harder than Damon's hold over me.

After some time, the bright sun is blocked by a shadow looming over me; even with my eyes closed, I can feel someone. I don't rush to open them, fearing who might be there.

"You come home and don't say shit?" Eli says, his words slurred and laced with anger.

Slowly, I open my eyes and slide my shades over them, blocking out the sun, and trying to hide the bruises on my face even though the layers of make-up covering them are doing a decent job. He leans against the railing, a bottle of vodka dangling by his side.

"Eli, are you drunk?" A sense of shock hits me, knowing that it's still morning, and before noon at that.

"Yeah, cus that's what everyone wants to know: if I'm fucking drunk or not," he scoffs, blatantly taking a generous swig while his glassy eyes remain on mine. "I want to know where the fuck you've been for the last three days, Emerson, and I wa-"

"Eli, brother," Stone interjects, walking over with his father, both of them giving my brother a guilty, knowing look that sends a rush of panic flooding through my body. "I hate to interrupt this... reunion, but I need to talk to you right away." Stone smiled at me as he put his arm around Eli, helping to steady him on his feet while leading him away.

"We're not done here, Em," he spits, sadness swirling in his eyes as he gives me one last glance.

I watch them leave and drop my head into my hands, breathing a sigh of relief. Part of me knows that I can't avoid the inevitable conversation that needs to be had, but for now, I'll welcome a moment of peace and quiet before the storm arrives.

Kane sits down beside me, cautiously curling his arm around my back. He then gently tugs me against his body, putting my crippling anxiety slightly at ease.

"I don't want to talk about it," I tell him, my tone coming out more as a matter of fact than anything else.

He sighs, tightens his hold, and just sits there, being there for me even in silence. I hear the waves crashing against the shore and the birds singing their annoying melody that pierces my ears as they fly above me. And if I listen close enough, I can hear the rapid thumping of Kane's heart clear in my ears. His presence soothes my overworked mind, and for that moment, I find solace in the comfort of his embrace. The storm may be coming, but for the time being, I'm grateful for this little pocket of peace.

"Wanna go for a ride?" he asks out of nowhere, his voice coming out dangerously low and seductively thick, sort of like molasses.

We turn to look at each other at the same time, and heat immediately engulfs me, putting me in a position where nothing fucking matters, and all I really want is... *him.*

As long as we don't have to talk about what happened, I'm fine.

"Yeah," I smirk, twisting my lips in a devious way that makes him obviously squirm in his seat. "Let's go for a ride."

We stare off intensely until he growls, "get the fuck up then, Little One. Show me that you can handle yourself against me."

Even though we both knew that we were still deeply affected by everything that had happened, there was a mutual understanding between us—that we would take things one step at a time and carve our *own* path back to healing.

Getting up, I gave Kane a sly smile and swayed my hips methodically before heading off to the garage, ready and willing to escape with him, even for just a short while. If it meant I could get away from the stares of anger and pity and the suffocating reminder of the elephant in the room, then I wanted to do it.

I knew that everyone healed and dealt with their trauma differently, and this was my fucking way. I didn't care who liked it or who didn't.

As Kane entered the garage right behind me, his black cut-off tee clinging to his tight, sculpted body, he slapped my ass as I swung my leg over my bike, cupping it firmly.

"Shit, I want you to straddle me the way you straddle your bike." He winked, putting his helmet on at the same time as me.

"I know just the place." I nodded, smirking under my helmet, walking my bike out before him.

The sun pelted down over us, igniting the already burning flames of desire that stuck to us like our shadows, but I ignored it.

I craved the feeling of the open road washing away my stress. I longed for the soothing rumble of my bike as I pushed it past its limits, setting every nerve ending in my fucking body on fire.

And looking over at Kane, I could tell that he knew *exactly* how I was fucking feeling. So we took off, eager, like kids leaving school on the last day to begin their summer. And even though ours was coming to an end, I could tell that today was the beginning of *something—I just didn't know what.*

The loud revving of the engine felt like freedom, and as we sped off down the empty roads, it felt like we were leaving our troubles behind, if only for a little while. For now, we would take what we could get, and make the best of it.

And just for that moment, it was all we needed.

Thirty-Five

Reckless Coping

Kane

Inch by inch, Emerson crept ahead of me, her legs tightly hugging her bike as she rode with both hands held high in the air above her head.

She never looked freer.

Holding the handlebars with one hand, I took out my phone with the other and began to record her, wanting to remember this moment long after it was over. For a brief moment, she was herself again, and fuck, I missed seeing her like that. I snapped a couple stills as the camera recorded, not knowing if she knew what I was doing or not.

Her long brown hair that usually hung down the middle of her back was now flying behind her in the wind, and the way she handled her bike effortlessly with every curve just turned me on even more. Usually in a crop top that accentuated her perky tits and toned stomach, she was now covered by a black, fitted hoodie that left so much to the imagination.

But I knew why, and I didn't bother saying anything.

No matter what Emerson wore, she was *fucking beautiful.* Her showing off her perfect body was just a plus.

I knew what she was battling—for the most part—but she didn't know that I knew, and that part fucking killed me inside.

So we rode in denial, just enjoying each other's company as the afternoon passed us by. The blue skies that hovered over us eventually turned dark, filled with gorgeous hues of orange and pink blended together like a picture on a postcard.

But it wasn't the sight above me that took my breath away; it was the one right beside me of Emerson on her bike with her hair blowing in the wind that fucking did it.

The way the setting sun reflected off her delicate features was enough to make me forget about everything else. For those few moments, it was just the two of us, lost in the world of our own making.

But as the sun continued its descent, reality crept back in. I knew that eventually we would have to face the demons that haunted us both—the ones that threatened to tear us apart.

But for now—*in this fleeting moment*—I pushed the thought from my mind and focused on the feeling of freedom as we rode side by side. The wind in my hair and her laughter in the air. Because for now, it was just us and the comfort of the open road that welcomed us with open arms.

Pulling off a familiar side street that led to a secluded part of the beach, miles away from the house, I followed Emerson until she came to a stop and parked her bike. My legs were numb and shaky when I climbed off mine, taking in the rough waves in front of us that the bright moon bounced off of as I walked toward her.

"It's fucking beautiful," she said, sighing contentedly as I walked up behind her and wrapped her in my embrace.

"It sure the fuck is," I whispered in her ear as she wiggled her ass against my cock, making it harder and making the urge to bend her over the seawall and fuck her under the stars even more intense.

But I didn't want to make a move. I didn't want to push her to do something when she was still so fucking fragile. I was content with just holding her in my arms like this.

But she wasn't. She wanted more.

She spun around and grasped my waistband, tugging me against her tiny frame. I took my helmet off, dying to have my lips on hers, then took hers off and dropped them both to the ground. As she clung to my pants, I grabbed her face and seized her pouty lips like I was fucking fiending for them—like an addict needing their next fix. Her hand slipped down my pants as we lowered ourselves to the ground, and she stroked my dick from the base to the tip to see how I liked it.

"Fuck," I mumbled against her mouth as she pushed my pants down with one hand, never messing up her stroking rhythm.

As soon as the air hit my balls, they tightened, and my cock throbbed angrily against her palm. I pulled my mouth away from hers and leaned back, admiring the way her eyes glimmered in the light. She willingly took her pants off, making a show of sliding down her tiny black thong until she was naked from the waist down. It was dark, but I could still see her.

Tugging on her sweatshirt, my lips curled up into a smirk that met my hooded eyes, silently urging her to take it off. But she climbed on me instead, rubbing her dripping cunt over my cock until it was slippery and soaked in her arousal.

"Take this off for me," I demanded, but she shook her head with a firm look on her face that told me she wasn't going to. So I dropped the topic, letting her take complete control of the situation.

"Put this on, Daddy," she whispered in a tone that made my cock jump against her pussy lips as she picked up my helmet and handed it to me.

"You want me to wear my helmet while you ride me?" I asked, taking it from her.

"Yes." She nodded and playfully bit her lip as she picked up her helmet and put it on. "I want us *both* to wear them."

This was new, but I wasn't going to make a fuss out of it. She needed to feel like she was safe by hiding herself, and in the end, that's exactly how I wanted to make her feel. I was fucking pissed that I couldn't kiss her while she bounced on my dick, but I also knew that her lips weren't going anywhere and that when this was over, I could kiss her for as long as I fucking wanted. Getting to kiss her while I was buried deep inside her cunt was just another bonus that came along with her.

"Now fuck me, *Daddy*," she begged in a domineering tone as she swiftly climbed off my lap, positioning herself on all fours.

I wasted no time getting on my knees behind her, fitting her perfect, peachy ass against my pelvis while I guided my cock to her dripping entrance. A breathy moan flew from her mouth as I rubbed the tip around her clit, making her body jerk against mine. She shook with need as I slowly slid into her, feeling her tight, pussy walls stretching around my cock until I bottomed out inside of her. Balancing herself on one hand, she reached behind her with the other and took my hand in hers, guiding it to the front of her body and to her throat, desperately wanting me to hold it.

So I did.

"Tighter," she begged, arching her back perfectly as my hips began to move and my cock slid inside of her.

"Like this?" I asked, clasping my hand around her throat until the veins in the side of her neck pulsed against the pads of my fingers.

She nodded, unable to speak due to the pressure I applied around her throat. My other hand slipped under her sweatshirt and swept across her back as my fingers danced soothingly along her spine, making her shiver as I fucked her.

Soon, we were lost in each other's rhythm, moving together in sync as the waves crashed and the stars shone down on us like a fucking spotlight. She slammed her ass back as my hips surged forward, my cock driving between her clenching walls. Our breathing and moans filled the air, and even though I had her, all I could think about was Emerson: her beautiful body, her vulnerability, and the way she needed me. *And, fuck, she needed me.*

I could feel her whole body trembling as my cock owned her cunt, and the sound of my name escaping her lips was all I needed to know that she was mine. Completely, utterly mine; at least, in that moment. She dropped her head and pushed her ass out, her fingers gliding over the pearls draped around her neck. As I clutched them and twisted, choking her with them, she shuddered hard, squeezing my cock in a vice grip.

She was using sex as a coping mechanism, needing and wanting to take her mind off of what had happened with Damon. I knew we were playing a dangerous game and fucking with her emotions, but if she wanted something to think about other than the hell she overcame, then fuck, I was going to give her something to think about.

I choked her even harder, feeling her body shaking against mine as she struggled to breathe.

But I wasn't done.

Feeling my orgasm on the verge of barreling through me, without warning, I pulled out of her pussy and thrust into her ass in a single, brutal stroke that made her entire body tense up and a loud gasp slip from her throat.

"Kane!" she screamed, taking every thrust without resistance.

"Say it again, Little One," I grunted, sweat dripping from my forehead onto her sweatshirt as I pounded into her ass without mercy. "Say my fucking name again."

Her body loosened up as my cock plunged deeply into her, and she sang my fucking name at the top of her lungs as if it were the only word she knew. It didn't take long for my cum to start spilling into her, and as it did, I leaned back while I fucked her, watching thick, white ropes drip out as I slid back, trickling down her shaky inner thighs.

It was a fucking stunning masterpiece I was creating—my cum on her skin, glistening like the fucking dancing stars under the gleam of the crescent moon.

She reached under her and pushed her fingers into her pussy, but I smacked them away, grinning at the desperate whimper that left her parted lips.

"Daddy," she begged, giving me the final push I needed to send me crashing over the edge the rest of the way.

I knew she needed to come, but I wasn't going to let her. She wanted something to think about—something to distract her—so that's exactly what I was going to give her, *even if it left her pissed at me in the end.*

"You don't get to come right now, Little One," I laughed, fucking her tight little ass even harder and deeper than I was, filling and coating her forbidden hole with every drop of cum I had in me.

And then I pulled out of her, ripped my helmet off, dropped my head, and spread her ass cheeks apart. She shook like fucking crazy as I put my mouth to her gaping hole and dipped my tongue inside her, greedily sucking my cum back out. As I held it in my mouth, I flipped her onto her back and pulled her helmet off.

She had no fucking idea what I was doing, which made it even better.

Squeezing her cheeks with the tips of my fingers, I forced her mouth open and slammed my lips onto hers, spitting my cum between them until it covered her tongue.

With my hand around her throat, twisting her pearls until she couldn't breathe, I kissed her for the second time that night.

She tried to swallow my cum and kiss me back, but the force from the pearls choking her wouldn't allow it. So we swished it back and forth urgently in each other's mouths with each thrust of our tongues. I dominated her mouth with my tongue, unbothered by the salty, bitter taste of my sperm. She gasped for air, letting gooey strings drip from her lips, but she still kissed me back, trying her best to keep up with the fierce movements I teased her with.

I could tell how much she fucking enjoyed it, and shit, I was enjoying it just as much, if not more.

Swept up in the passion igniting between us and the overwhelming desire that coursed quickly through my veins, I twisted and tugged on her pearls so hard that they broke, *finally* giving her the blast of air that she'd been fucking craving. And then, like a good fucking girl—*my good girl*—she swallowed *every* drop of my cum... then *angrily* shoved me off of her, feeling around her reddened neck in a panic for her pearls that were now scattered in the sand beneath us.

"What the fuck, Kane?!" The angry scream that followed pierced my ears, leaving a ring behind and shattering my fucking heart.

"Shit. I'm *so* sorry, Little One." I shook my head and got to my feet, taking a step back so I was no longer blocking the light that she needed so she could see.

I didn't mean to break them. I knew how fucking special they were to her. It was an unfortunate accident, but Emerson wasn't seeing it that way.

As expected, she fucking lost it on me, her facade finally crumbling as she dropped to her knees in a panic and felt around for the loose pearls, trying to find every single one.

I grabbed her and pulled her up on her feet, holding her shoulders firmly to keep her grounded. I wanted so badly for her to look at me, but she refused for the first time ever. Instead, her teary, wild eyes frantically searched the sand for the ones she knew she still hadn't found.

"I'll find them and I'll fix it for you. I promise," I reassured her, but she wasn't listening to me anymore. Everything I was saying to try and diffuse the situation went in one ear and quickly out the other. There was no fucking talking to her.

Tears fell down her cheeks as she ripped herself out of my grasp, dropping back to the ground in a frantic attempt to find every last pearl. As I listened to her heartbreaking sobs, it fucking dawned on me; it wasn't just about me breaking her necklace.

No, of course it fucking wasn't.

Everything from the last few days was finally hitting her—hard and unforgiving—and she had no idea now how to channel her emotions or deal with the shitty hand that she'd been dealt.

She fucking snapped.

All I could do was stand there and watch as Emerson was engulfed by her emotions, and as much as I wanted to fix things, I knew I fucking couldn't. I didn't know how to fix it. But I had to try to help her, even though what I had done pushed her over the fucking edge.

When she finally found and collected every last pearl from the broken necklace, she stood up and just stared at me with bloodshot, angry eyes. I wanted to say something—anything—to fix things, but the look on her face just silenced me. I felt like a fucking idiot, and I was too busy kicking myself on the inside to even realize that I should be focused on helping her. I'd ruined the little bit of happiness that we had found on this beach, and I knew I would have to find a way to make it up to her if I ever stood a chance of fixing things.

But the look in her eyes told me that she wasn't ready for that. Not fucking yet, anyway.

So I just stood there, swallowing my pride and my embarrassment, as I watched her storm off in the direction of our bikes, leaving me alone on the beach. The moon provided little light, but she was able to find her way.

She didn't fucking look back, not even once, and it fucking hurt; it broke me.

I stood there for a few moments, just watching her go, feeling like an absolute asshole. I wanted to call after her, to run after her and beg for her forgiveness, but I knew that it wouldn't help. There was nothing I could say that would make the situation better; all I could do was pray that she'd come around eventually and that she wouldn't hate me for the rest of our lives.

If I had fucking lost her, then shit, I would be lost too.

So I stood alone on the beach, listening to the sound of her bike as she sped away, feeling the weight of my actions settle over me like a leaden cloak. It was like an anchor sinking me into the sand, leaving me just standing there with no course of action to take.

I needed to give Emerson the space to feel her emotions and to work through them on her own, but it was fucking tearing me apart knowing that she was suffering because of me. I'd fucked up—big time.

I felt bad enough to deny her an orgasm, but breaking her pearl necklace really took the fucking cake. I felt low as fuck—like a total piece of shit.

I didn't know the story behind the necklace and why it was so damn important, but I needed to know—*especially now.*

But I was determined as fuck to find out the significance and more than fucking willing to do *whatever* the hell it took for her to forgive me.

••••••••••••

Thirty-Six

Fiery Passion

Seven

While Kane and Emerson were off doing their own thing, me, Ace, and Stone spent the day trying to get Eli to calm the fuck down. Dealing with his stubborn ass was hard enough, but add in the fact that he'd been drinking vodka like it was water since he got out of bed, and it made it even harder.

Emerson had returned home after being missing for three days, not wanting to talk about where she had been or what had happened. And fuck, it bothered her brother more than we thought it would.

We had all agreed to keep the knowledge of Damon's abuse and murder to ourselves until Emerson was ready to open up to us about it. But for Eli, it was absolute torture. He wanted to be there for his baby sister. He wanted to fix her and take all her pain away, but felt completely powerless when she made it clear that she didn't want to talk about it and that she didn't want help from anyone.

We knew that she'd eventually come to us and trust us with her deepest, darkest secret, so we didn't push. But Eli

wasn't having it, and because of her silence, he drowned his emotions with liquor... which was the worst thing he could've fucking done. He was getting aggressive, starting fights with anyone who looked at him the wrong way. Ace and I tried our best to keep him in line, but it was a losing battle. We had to come together and support him, just like we knew we would eventually need to do for Emerson. But first, we had to get Eli to understand that drowning his sorrows in alcohol wasn't the answer.

But shit, he wasn't willing to listen to any of us, so we didn't push him.

Waiting for Emerson to get back, I rolled a blunt and sprinkled it with little crumbs of coke to hype up the somber mood of everyone in the house, and then took it down to the beach, where I posted up around a roaring fire. Ace and Stone stayed inside, taking turns watching over Eli to make sure he didn't do anything stupid.

As I relaxed by the fire alone, I twirled the blunt in my fingers, anxious to light it, but I was trying to wait for Em before I did.

When I heard the rumble of her bike, I stared hard at the back of the house, just waiting to see her pull down the driveway with Kane. However, I was shocked to see that it was just Emerson, who bolted off her fucking bike as if it were on fire and then ran straight into the house. Kane wasn't anywhere in sight.

Okay then...

I got up from my seat and walked back to the house, curiosity filling the voids in my mind. Just as I reached the steps to climb the back porch, Kane rode in on his bike, looking rough as shit as he pulled off his helmet and whipped it to the pavement with all of his strength.

Kane wasn't one to mess with when he was fucking angry. I'd seen him almost beat a motherfucker to death, all because earlier that night the Patriots had lost to the Cowboys; poor bastard accidentally bumped into Kane in the bar, and he pummeled him until he broke his fucking wrist... then he resorted to kicking. I didn't want to be on the receiving end of Kane's diabolical wrath—none of us did.

"Uh oh," I began, walking towards him with extreme caution as he made his way to the back door of the garage. "What happened out there?"

"I ruined her fucking night by accident, and now I think she's spiraling even worse, and much quicker than we anticipated." He shakes his head, clearly pissed at himself, and barges in the back door.

I follow him, needing to know more before I try approaching Emerson. He grabs a Bud Light from the fridge, twists off the cap, and collapses onto the couch, sucking down the icy-cold brew without stopping for air.

Grabbing myself a beer, I sink into the cushion beside him. "What did you do?"

He looks at me and shakes his head, muttering, "I accidentally broke her necklace."

My jaw drops, and a pained sigh leaves my throat as I turn to him to explain why she freaked the fuck out. "Her father gave her that the day he let her join the club."

"Fuck me," he huffs, hanging his head in shame.

"It'll be alright, trust me. She just needs some time, Kane," I assure him, trying to make the guilt building inside of him easier to deal with. "We'll fix it."

Looking blankly across the garage, he remains silent, clearly needing some time to sort through the shit in his head. I stand up and give him a friendly pat on the back of his shoulder, but he doesn't even acknowledge it.

"I'm going to check on her, but if you want to talk later, then I'm all ears, brother."

He nods and motions me away, wanting to be alone for now.

I quietly made my way to Emerson's room, bracing myself for the storm that was sure to come. When I found her, she was sitting on her bed, clutching the broken necklace in her hand. Her eyes were red and puffy, and I could see the pain etched into her face. Due to her tears, I was able to see the bruises on her face from where her makeup had washed off, and it fucking enraged me. It took everything in me not to fucking say something to her, but somehow I managed to push it to the back of my mind with a mental note to bring it up at a later time. Instead, I sat down beside her and wrapped my arm around her, trying my best to offer some comfort, which had always worked for me before.

Emerson and I had a special bond, one unlike any of the others she had with the guys. It gave me hope that I'd be able to pull her out of her funk, soothe her sadness, and finally put a fucking smile back on her beautiful face.

"It's okay, Em. We'll fix it. I promise," I said softly, staring at the pearls clutched protectively in her shaky hand.

She didn't say anything, just continued to stare at the broken necklace for a while as we sat closely, silence looming over us. And then finally, she got off the bed and went to her dresser for her bottle of Xanax, pouring a few into the palm of her hand. Washing them down with my beer that she snatched out of my hand, a smile *finally* crept across her lips as her eyes landed on the blunt tucked behind my ear, and her mood switched just like that.

"Have you been waiting for me to smoke that?" She grins, her dimples popping, defining her already perfect cheeks.

"Indeed, I have." I match her grin and remove the blunt, pulling my zippo out of my pocket to light it.

"Not here," she states, grabbing my hand and pulling me to my feet. Then she grabs a bottle of liquor off her nightstand and drags me out of her room and down the stairs, leading me straight out the open back doors that take us to the beach.

She sits on my lap when I take my seat around the fire, making herself comfortable as I spark the blunt and take the first rip, feeling the cocaine numb my lips immediately.

"It's got coke on it," I advise her, making sure she knows ahead of time what she's getting into.

"Perfect." She nods, her blue eyes sparkling from the lingering tears coating them.

With a deep inhale, she holds the blunt in her fingers and breathes out a cloud of smoke, her eyes twinkling like the stars in the sky, dancing around the moon. I can feel the weight lifting from her shoulders as we pass the blunt back and forth and drink from the bottle, and I can't help but smile as she visibly begins to relax.

The darkness that had been clouding the house seemed to dissipate as Emerson and I sat there together, watching the flames happily dance in front of us, reminding us what it felt like to not have a single fucking care in the world. I held her close and so fucking tight, afraid to release her, my breath sweetly kissing her skin as my lips ghosted across the side of her neck.

I fucking *loved* being with her; it didn't matter where we were. There was always something about Emerson that captivated me, and I was determined to hold onto the feeling.

As I began to sensually pepper her neck with kisses, she sighed deeply and leaned into my touch.

"Seven," she moaned quietly, her eyes big and dark from the drugs and alcohol streaming through her veins.

"What is it, Princess?" I held onto her hip and gently rocked her back and forth on my lap, feeling my cock grow under her ass.

She leaned her head back and rested it on my shoulder, swiftly rocking against my cock on her own. It was almost as if she was silently giving me a fucking sign or something. Like she wanted to fuck, but without all the talking.

That was the thing about the two of us; I always knew what she wanted—what she needed—and she trusted me to give it to her. Her guard was never up with me, like it was with some of the other guys, and for that, it brought us closer, especially in desperate times of need.

After a few, quiet moans and a full-body shiver that hit her randomly, she says, "I need to come, Seven." She rolls her hips and pushes her ass even harder against my cock. "Kane didn't let me."

I brush her hair to one shoulder and lick a teasing line across the side of her neck. "Is my princess needy?" I ask, reaching my hand between her thighs and rubbing her pussy over her pants.

"Fuck... *very*," she pants, tightly gripping the side of my thigh while frantically grinding against me, desperately trying to chase the intense friction from my fingers as they continue to tease her. "Make me come, Seven," she demands in a fiery tone that lets me know she isn't fucking around. "*Please*, make me come—make me feel so fucking good that I forget about all the bullshit I'm struggling with."

"For you, my Princess, I'll fucking do *anything.*" Sliding my hand up to her waist, I unbutton her pants and pull them open, just enough to push my hand down them and cup her needy, soaked cunt. "I'll make you feel *so* fucking good that you'll forget your name, not just the bullshit. *This pussy...*" I growl. "Is. Fucking. *Mine*, Emerson, and I know *exactly* how to make her drip for me—how to make her fucking come for me—and, Em, you fucking know I ain't lying either," I hiss through gritted teeth, my palm rubbing her soaked cunt.

Emerson spreads her legs, inviting me in as my eager fingers skate down her bare pussy until they slip between her lips.

"You're fucking drenched, Princess; ain't that right?" She nods, tugging her bottom lip between her teeth, desperately wanting—needing—so much fucking more.

"So fucking needy *and* desperate for my fingers," I tell her, knowing I'm right.

"Yes, Seven... *Yes, I'm so fucking needy for you.*" She trembles, her voice cracking, trying to catch her breath just from my filthy words alone.

I nip at her earlobe and roughly sink my teeth into it, making her tremble as I dip my fingers into her cunt.

She melts into me as my fingers work their magic, thrusting deeply in a corkscrew-like motion, gliding sensually against her slippery pussy walls.

"*Harder*, Seven," she pleads, her breath heavy and ragged while her chest heaves deeply.

I oblige, feeling her body quiver with pleasure. The flames from the fire reflect in her dark eyes, and I watch as they dilate with desire.

It was wrong; I knew that, but there was something addicting about her that made me lose all control. And at that moment, I didn't fucking care.

All I wanted was to see her come apart in my fucking arms. And with each long, deep thrust of my fingers, she was getting closer and closer to that edge... *because of me.*

"I killed him," she blurts out, only realizing what she had said *after* it had involuntarily slipped from her mouth.

She tries to get off my lap—to run away, of course—but I hold her down and keep fucking her with my fingers, knowing it'll distract her from wanting to bolt.

"Seven," she moans, but there's a hidden tone in her voice that I can tell she's trying to mask.

She didn't want to open up, but shit, for me, I knew she would.

Instead of letting her run and just forgetting what she said, I force her to stay, using my fingers to take her mind to a different place.

"I know, Princess," I whisper, feeling her pussy clamp around my fingers as I drive them even deeper, her arousal squishing around like music to my fucking ears as she gets even wetter. "And it's okay."

"I... I..." she stutters, unable to find the right words for what she wants to say, mainly due to the pleasure clouding her mind.

So I help her out, knowing just how to get her to talk freely. "Tell me again," I whispered, adding a third digit into her soaked pussy, feeling her back immediately lift off of my chest as she started to ride my fingers like she was riding my cock.

But she didn't say anything, which prompted me to keep pushing, knowing that I could get her to break.

"Emerson, fucking say that shit again for me, or you won't be coming on my fingers either," I threatened, knowing how fucking close she was to breaking her silence just from the way her body was reacting to my touch.

"Sev... ah," she moaned into my ear, her head still resting against my shoulder as my soaked fingers slid in and out of her cunt knuckle deep, purposely driving her to the brink.

"What did you do, Princess?" Using the pad of my thumb, I press down on her sensitive clit and roll circles over it, watching intense spasms rock her tiny body.

When she doesn't answer, I stop thrusting and rubbing, letting her know that I'm serious about not letting her come. In a desire-filled panic, she reaches between her legs and pushes my fingers back inside of her, holding her hand against mine to keep them right where she wanted them the most.

"*Don't stop*," she begs in a sexy moan that makes my cock twitch under her ass.

"Then fucking tell me again what you did," I growl, sinking my teeth into the side of her neck.

"I killed him!" she screams, watching the flames and riding my fingers desperately until I slowly start moving them again. "I killed Damon," she finally admits, going limp against my body, her pussy walls constricting around my quickly moving fingers.

I finger-fuck her needy cunt faster, harder, and deeper, ripping seductive moans from her dry throat that echo in my ears. "Good girl, Emerson."

As she reaches her peak, her moans turn into high-pitched cries, and I hold her close, relishing in the sound of the pleasure ripping from her throat.

She shook frantically, riding my fingers as I drilled them relentlessly into her until her pussy gushed all over my fingers and hand. She came hard, clinging to me to the point where it was becoming painful as her nails dug into my flesh and broke through. But I kept going, fucking her with my fingers through her entire orgasm, wet, squishy noises singing from her pussy.

I wanted all of it—all of her juices I had coaxed from her cunt and the symphony of moans and cries I made her scream with just three fingers buried so deep inside of her that she felt them in her lower belly.

And I had gotten it all—every fucking thing that I wanted, and then some.

We were lost in the moment, bonding over her secret that she finally came off of. The world around us was forgotten as we chased the fiery passion and the release that we both desperately needed. And when it was over, we were left breathless, tangled in each other's arms as we watched the embers of the fire slowly fade into the night, feeling something passing between us that was deeper than anything either of us had experienced before.

But I knew we had only scratched the surface of the darkness Emerson was carrying, and I was ready to go to hell and back for her. Because when it came down to it, I would fucking do anything for her.

Unfortunately, that loyalty might just be my fucking downfall.

Thirty-Seven

Knee-High Socks & Vans

Ace

After a few days of sun, humidity, and brutal heat, thunder and lightning decided to make another appearance, bringing fierce winds and buckets of warm rain along with them and forcing us inside. But Emerson, shit, she isn't phased in the slightest. Braving the storm, she stands alone on the back porch and watches the catastrophe unfold, her body swaying back and forth in perfect rhythm to the music filtering through the open French doors. Angry waves ripple across the ocean in the relentless wind, and quick flashes of lightning brighten the dark sky seconds before loud booms of thunder rumble in the distance, creating a hypnotic symphony of destruction from the storm.

Sitting around the table in the back room with the guys, immersed in an intense game of spades, buried flashbacks of the years I spent in prison start to force their way to the front of my mind. But just as I feel myself slipping into the darkness of my past, Stone's foot softly rubs against my shin, quickly snapping me back to the moment. Looking up, my eyes meet his across the table, making the corners of my mouth tug upward into a flirtatious smirk.

"Your turn," he says, licking his lips with an insatiable glint in his eyes that makes it hard to focus.

Between his ass and Emerson, the growing desire coursing through me makes it hard as fuck to focus.

"Hold up," his father says, standing up with his cards in his hand. "Let me grab another beer. Anyone need one?" Kane quickly glances at Emerson and then shifts his focus back to us.

"Yeah, one for everyone," Seven answers, pouring the rest of his into his mouth.

Finishing off my beer, I look at Emerson again, wondering if I should go check on her. But I decide to wait until after the game, knowing that she's still trying to come to terms with what Damon put her through. It's been a few days now since she came back, but she still hasn't spoken to us about it. She did admit to Seven that she killed him, so it's just a matter of time before she let's the rest of us in and opens up.

With Kane back at the table, handing out cold beers, and the storm intensifying by the second, I adjust in my seat and turn my focus back to my cards.

Papercut by 'Linkin Park' fills the room, the high-end speaker system amplifying the sound. My foot instinctively taps along with the beat on the smooth, hardwood floor, feeling the pulsating bass reverberating through the entire house and relaxing my body. Looking at the cards in my hand, I hum the words softly, trying to decide what my next move is as Stone's foot continues to rub up and down my leg.

I can't fucking concentrate, though.

Just as I'm about to make a move, the power cuts out, plunging the room into complete darkness. The thunder and lightning outside grow louder and more intense, and for a moment, everything is obscured by the black of night. I feel Stone's foot slip between my thighs and gently massage my cock. Even over my pants, his touch grounds me in the chaos of the storm.

"Well, fuck," Seven spits, dropping his cards on the table before pushing out his chair and standing up. "I guess that's the game."

"Let's go dig out the candles and shit," Kane orders, motioning for Stone and Seven to join him. With Eli spending the night with Nova, we have to find everything on our own.

Leaving me alone, the three of them disappear into the darkness, giving me the opportunity to go check on Emerson.

Walking out onto the porch, I'm drenched immediately and hit with a hard gust of wind, a shiver wracking my body. Emerson never moves, keeping her eyes locked on the treacherous waves in front of us. I slowly approach her, hoping she doesn't push me away even more. We're not as close as she is with the others, mainly because I haven't been around as long.

Growing up, Stone and I were inseparable, bonding over our struggles with our sexuality, among other things. I spent most of my time at his house, especially after my parents kicked me out the first time I got arrested. I was closer to his family than my own.

I had an abusive father who drank as much as he fucking breathed and an absent mother who preferred standing on street corners, seeking the validation of every man she could find. She'd come home when she needed something or when she was trying to hide from someone, and my father allowed it. He was always too drunk to care about what she was doing or who she was with but when she did come home, they fought like fucking cats and dogs. The only time they wanted anything to do with each other, was when their food stamps and social security hit; then they couldn't get enough of each other. But when the money was gone, the endless cycle would start all over again, and it got worse every time.

I fucking hated it and I hated them.

Being around Stone and his family saved me, in more ways than one. It was them who pushed me to get my shit together and helped me stay out of prison for good. Kane treated me like I was his son, and even after Stone's mother left, he never gave up on me. Bringing me into the club, he gave me a second chance, and to this day, he still hasn't given up on me.

Emerson and I grew close as time passed. I was put in charge of keeping an eye on her while her father and Kane had business to take care of, and during then is when I developed feelings for her. I didn't want to lose the respect I'd earned from the guys, so I never acted on them, but buried them instead. However, things can only stay hidden for so long, and eventually, I told her how I felt.

But through it all, I've always had Emerson's back, even before we all formed our little family here.

Reaching Emerson, I stand beside her and let the storm rage around us. She finally turns her head to look at me, her eyes glistening with unshed tears and something else I can't quite place.

"Hey, Brat," I say softly through a grin, hesitating before placing my hand on her shoulder. "You wanna come in?"

Her eyes search mine for a moment before she shakes her head, a small, almost imperceptible, movement. But it's enough for me to know that she's slowly starting to come around.

We stand there together, watching the destruction with a sense of understanding between us, and I know that even though the storm may be fierce, she's fucking stronger than she thinks.

Taking it upon herself, Emerson reaches for my hand and laces her fingers tightly in mine. She smiles as if everything's okay, but the turmoil raging within her eyes tells a different story, and I'm anxious as fuck to find out what it is.

"Wanna go for a walk?" she asks in a hopeful voice, keeping her smile strong.

"Yeah, why not?" I shrug, offering her a playful smile as we descend the slippery steps with caution.

The rain shows no sign of letting up, but we walk anyway, embracing the storm together. A few times, she looks at me, but nothing is said for a while. It's not until we get halfway down the flooded beach and turn around to walk back that she finally speaks.

"Eli hates me, doesn't he?" she blurts out, her smile slowly fading.

I squeeze her hand, giving her a silent reassurance. "He doesn't hate you, Emerson, he's just having a hard time. You know how your brother is," I scoff, a hint of a chuckle in my tone. "He's beating himself up because he couldn't help you. He feels like he failed you."

"But he didn't. None of y'all did." She sounds fucking defeated, looking down at her feet as she walks.

Ascending the steps, she stops at the door, pausing before going in.

"It's not easy to talk about, Ace, especially when it comes to Eli."

"I know," I say, standing beside her. "But you need to realize that it's okay to let your guard down. And besides, you don't have to tell him every fucking detail." Taking the lead, I pull her into the house, and out of the rain, the music still blaring through the speakers. Everyone must have gone to bed because downstairs is empty, with only the entryway light guiding us through the darkness. With our hands still entwined, we climb the stairs together, leaving a trail of water behind us as it drips off our bodies. Expecting me to come into her room with her, her face falls when I try to walk toward mine.

"Where are you going? You're not coming in?" She pouts, her shiny lips and her beautiful lashes flutter, and fuck, it's one of the sexiest things she fucking does.

Chuckling, I tell her, "I'm just going to change into some dry clothes, Brat. If you want me to come back, you know I fucking will." I wink, watching an obvious breath hitch in her throat as I tug my bottom lip between my teeth and drag my finger teasingly down the front of her body.

"Do me a favor, be a good boy for me, and put on those gray sweats that I love." The words roll seductively off the tip of her pierced tongue as she boldly reaches out and cups the bulge growing in my soaked pants, making my body jump in reaction to her touch.

Fuck, what a damn tease.

"I can do that, Brat, but you need to do something for me," I whisper, leaning in close so my mouth is inches away from her ear and my breath dances across her bronze skin.

"And what's that?" she whispers back, swallowing hard.

"Put those blue knee-high socks on, your tiny black thong, and your black Vans on, and wait for me on your bed... *wearing nothing else." I* don't give her the chance to respond before I walk off, knowing how needy and wet I've left her.

I return to my room and quickly change into a pair of my dry gray sweats, feeling the sexual tension building between Emerson and me.

This would be our first time alone, and the thought has me fucking anxious. But I want her. I fucking need her, and I'll be fucking damned if this shit doesn't happen.

After taking more than a few minutes, I eagerly make my way to her room, and as I approach her door, I can hear 'Deep' by Nine Inch Nails playing from inside, the soft sound of rain still pouring outside creating a soothing background melody. I push the door open and she's there, just as I fucking asked.

She lays on her bed, her incredible body clothed in nothing but her tiny black thong that hardly covers her pussy, the knee-high socks, and her Vans, her eyes dark with carnal desire. Her tattoos and piercings are on perfect display for me and her long brown hair fans out across the pillow, looking like a halo above her head.

"What are you waiting for, Ace? A fucking invitation," she laughs playfully, her hungry eyes roaming over my bare chest, taking in the unique beauty of my tattoos

I step into the room, locking the door behind me, before making my way over to the bed.

"Fucking breathtaking and such a good fucking girl for following directions," I praise her as I hover over her body and cup her tit, giving it a deep but gentle massage before moving to the other one.

Emerson reaches between the small gap of our bodies and rubs my cock over my sweats, staring deeply into my eyes. My hand travels further down her body, tracing the beautifully intricate tattoos covering her soft skin, all the way down to the thin band of her tiny black thong. She rubs my cock harder as I rub her pussy over the lacy fabric, feeling her wetness soak the palm of my hand through the material. Lifting her head off the pillow, she presses her mouth to mine and dips her tongue between my lips, keeping her lustful, blue eyes open during the kiss.

"Jesus, Brat," I grunt, lowering my body onto hers as I pull her supple bottom lip between my teeth.

Her hands find their way to my hair, and she runs her fingers through it, sensually moving her body in sync with mine as I grind my pelvis into hers.

"Ace." A desperate, breathy moan escapes from her throat while my teeth are still clamped onto her lip, refusing to let go.

"What is it, Brat? Tell me what you want."

"You, Ace." Her hooded eyes roll back as I grind harder, feeling the heat from her dripping pussy through my pants. "I want you to fuck me, now," she pleads, writhing beneath me.

"Oh, I'm definitely gonna fuck you. I'll give your pretty pussy exactly what she needs," I promise, my chest rumbling against hers as I chuckle. "But I have something else in mind first." Releasing her puffy lip, I push off her body and stand at the end of her bed, feeding off the confused look on her face.

Pushing my sweats down with my boxer briefs, I kick them both off and immediately begin stroking my cock while she watches.

"Get rid of those fucking underwear, baby girl, and play with your pussy for me." Through the devious grin curling on my lips, I demand, feeling my heartbeat increase rapidly.

Without hesitation, she hooks her thumbs under the thin band and lifts her ass off the bed, sliding her thong all the way off. Before she can drop it, I snatch it out of her hand and wrap the soaked fabric around my cock like a blanket.

"Really?" Her eyes widen as she laughs, still clueless as to what my plan is.

"Really." I nod, keeping a straight face through every pleasurable stroke. "Now stop being a fucking brat and spread your legs. I want to watch your fingers disappear inside of you."

Smirking, she glides her fingers around her pussy lips and eases them inside her, thrusting to her own rhythm.

Fuck, I can't take my fucking eyes off her.

Every thrust, moan, and move she makes, only intensifies my strokes as I jerk off with her underwear.

Feeling the tension in the room grow thicker, my strokes become more erratic as I watch her pleasure herself with her fingers, two at first, then another, and another, until she has four of them twisting knuckle-deep in and out of her pussy. Her moans fill the air, making me ache to be inside her, filling her with every inch of me and every drop of my cum. But we've barely fucking started, and it's already getting hard as shit to focus.

I can feel my climax rip through me as I jerk off even faster, her hips bucking as she rides her fingers while plunging them as deep as she can. I watch as her thumb rolls around her clit and presses down, her body spasming from the sensation. I can tell she's going to come, so I reach out and yank her hand away, pulling her soaked fingers out of her cunt. But I never stop stroking.

"Ace!" she gasps, her brows pinching together as she quickly sits up, trying to catch her breath. "Why did you do that? I was about to-"

"I know." I grin, my body trembling and my legs tensing painfully as hot cum jets into her underwear.

I grunt and groan through gritted teeth, my jaw clenching hard from the raging waves of pleasure coursing through me. She watches intently as I pump my hand frantically up and down my dick, squeezing the tip with intense pressure until every drop of my cum is emptied into her thong.

"Fuck, that felt good." My cock still throbs, not having nearly enough of what it desperately wants.

"That wasn't fair," she pouts, clearly needing to come.

As the tension builds between us, I drop the cute act and bunch her soaked panties in my hand, standing at the edge of the bed with my cock in the other.

"Enough," I growl, shoving them into her mouth as a gag to silence her, wanting to watch as she sucks my cum out of the lace.

She looks at me, shocked, not knowing how to react, and all it does is turn me on even more. Crawling over her and pushing her flat on her back, I speak softly, knowing what she wants to hear. "It's my turn to take care of you, Brat."

With that, I position myself between her legs and enter her with a firm thrust, feeling the flood of her wetness coating me. She gasps, her underwear muffling the sweet sound, arching into my touch as her hands claw desperately at the sheets beneath her.

"Be a good girl for me and suck my cum off your thong." I raise my brow and fuck her roughly, shaking the bed with my wild movements.

The feeling of being inside her, the warm, velvety grip of her pussy, is almost too much to handle. I give into the fevered pace building inside me and ravage her with everything I have, claiming her with every rough thrust as my hand finds its place around her throat.

She meets my rhythm, matching my fervor with her own, her moans catching in her throat as she reaches the edge of release. I admire every sound, look, and feeling I coax from her, falling in love with her a little more with each thrust.

With a feral cry, she unravels, her body convulsing beneath me as I ride out her orgasm, my own release teetering on the edge. Her cunt squeezes my cock as she soaks it, bucking her hips into mine while trying to chase the feeling of me ripping through her tight, clenching walls.

As she comes, writhing and shaking from her high, I let go again, finding my own release deep inside her, filling her with everything I have left to give.

With every touch, kiss, and twist of our bodies, we let go of the past and embrace the fierce desire drawing us together. In each other's arms, we find refuge from the turbulent storm building outside, as we lose ourselves in each other.

Collapsing on top of her, I pull her underwear out of her mouth. Desperately, I catch my breath as I roll to the side, pulling her to my chest and wrapping her in my arms. And under the relentless symphony of thunder and lightning, our passion ignites, bringing us closer in ways that neither of us have ever experienced before.

And I fucking love it.

Thirty-Eight

Admitting It

Emerson

Clutching my phone in my hand and occasionally peeking at the time, I work diligently, trying to control my breathing, knowing that what I'm about to do is going to be absolutely terrifying.

But I can't back down now—I fucking won't—not when I've already prepared myself for it. Not when I've finally admitted—regardless of how fucking hard it was—that I needed help, and most importantly, that I fucking wanted it, too.

Admitting that you're powerless is a hard step, of course. But the hardest step of them all—to me—is to openly admit that you're willing and ready to ask for and accept help.

Strolling along the deserted beach, feeling the soft sand caressing my painted toes, a gentle breeze envelops me in a comforting embrace. Yet, it fails to soothe the anxiety consuming me. The only time my mind is blank and I'm not dwelling on my trauma is literally when I'm being fucking railed six ways from Sunday.

I've had more sex this week alone than I have in the last fucking year, but it's the only thing that silences the harsh reminders of what happened. And it's fucked. I know.

The scars on the inside may not have healed, but the bruises on the outside of my body have, and I'm slowly starting to feel like myself again.

Every so often as I walk, I glance toward the house, catching a glimpse of the guys in the backyard setting up for the BBQ we're having to celebrate the end of summer. Remembering that I'm in a bikini for the first time in weeks, I get nervous when I catch them looking at me, but I force it down, trying to push through the awkwardness.

This isn't me. This was never me. And fuck, I refuse to allow myself to become this timid person all because the devil took my power and confidence away. I've come too far to let that happen.

As I continue to walk along the shore with a light bounce in my step, the sound of the waves crashing against the sand brings a sense of serenity to my troubled soul. I take a deep breath and blow it out, trying to focus only on the good. Like how close Seven and I have become, or Ace and I, even with Kane and Stone. And even though I've pushed them away lately, and am still kind of keeping them at arms length, each man has helped me grow and heal in their own way.

The vibration of my phone kind of pulls me out of my head, only making me a bit more nervous than I originally was. Glancing at the screen, a lump forms in my throat when I see the name blinking, taunting me almost.

You can do it. I tell myself, slowly swiping up the green phone icon to answer the call.

Putting the phone to my ear, I clear my throat and manage to find the simple word, "hello?"

"Good afternoon. May I please speak to Emerson Cole?" A chipper voice booms through the phone, surprisingly putting my nerves at ease.

"This is her," I reply, my voice calm and steady.

"Great! This is Dr. Ana Murphy. We have our first therapy session today; is now a good time?"

"Now is perfect," I tell her, a genuine smile spreading across my lips as I continue my walk down the beach.

For the first time in my life, I feel hopeful about starting therapy. I know it's going to take a while for me to be myself again, if I even get there, but I have to try.

Walking into the backyard an hour later, I feel refreshed yet broken at the same time. With my past brought up front and center in my mind and my emotions on my sleeve, I'm not sure what to think or how to feel. I didn't want to talk about certain things, but Dr. Ana told me it was part of the process. Luckily, we didn't get into anything too deep since it was the first session, but what we did get into fucking shattered me.

All I need right now is to relax and enjoy the company of my friends, to push away the dark thoughts and memories that are still lingering in the back of my mind. Plus, the smell of

BBQ in the air, the catchy music, and the laughter of everyone around me are a much-needed distraction.

I take a deep breath and make my way over to Seven, who wraps me in a comforting hug. "Where did you disappear to?" he asks, concern evident in his eyes.

"I needed some air, so I went for a walk," I reply, not wanting to burden him with my troubles.

Reaching into the cooler for a beer, I spot Kane, Ace, and Stone near the fire, while my brother sits by himself on the seawall, his legs dangling over the edge.

"I know what you're thinking, Princess," Seven whispers in my ear, hugging me from behind. "Go."

"What?" I ask, not taking my eyes off of Eli, my heart breaking from the pain surrounding him.

"Go talk to him; it'll be good for both of you." He trails soft kisses along the nape of my neck, giving me a gentle shove toward my brother.

I turn around, looking at Seven, and he gives me a nod of encouragement as I flash a grateful smile. As sad as it is, I needed a little push to finally talk to my brother. It never was this way between us before. Eli and I were always each other's best friend. But when Damon came into the picture, things slowly started changing, mainly because he purposely did his best to pull us apart. He tried to isolate me from everyone, but my brother wouldn't let that happen. Because of his persistence, Damon ended up moving in with me and that's when everything went downhill

Thinking back on all of the good and bad we went through, I make my way over to Eli, settling down next to him on the wall.

"Hey," I say softly, not wanting to startle him. He looks over at me and just nods. We sit in silence for a few moments, and then I gather my courage. "I know we haven't really talked lately, but I just want you to know that I'm sorry for the way I've been handling everything lately."

He reaches over and puts his hand on top of mine, letting out a deep breath that sounds almost agonizing as it leaves his mouth. "You don't need to apologize, Emerson. I'm just glad that... I've missed you," he says, smiling as his eyes glisten from the water filling them.

Wrapping his arm around my shoulders, I lean in and rest my head on him, the soft thumping of his heart soothing me into a blissful state, and I've never felt more relaxed.

We start talking, letting each other in like it's nothing—like we used to. I may be ashamed of the things I've done and of the things I let happen to me, but I know I can move past them. Being able to talk to my brother about it helps a lot, and I kick myself on the inside for not coming to him sooner.

I know things are still rough, and we've both got a long road ahead of us, but for just this moment, together there on the seawall, I know everything is going to be okay eventually. It's going to take time, patience, and a lot of healing, but it feels like we've finally started repairing the fractures that have slowly but surely been tearing us apart. And that's a feeling that's worth holding onto.

Thirty-Nine

Popsicles & Snowballs

Emerson

Basking in the warmth from the fire, I admire the night sky, adorned with twinkling stars as darkness falls around us, their light enchanting as we lose ourselves in their intricate patterns. Reclining on the soft sand, we gaze upwards, serenaded by gentle music blending with the soothing rhythm of the waves.

After talking to Eli about the last few weeks and what I've been going through, even what happened with Damon, a huge weight was lifted off my shoulders, finally allowing me to feel the peace I've been searching for. I thought he'd judge me, scold me, or even hate me, but that wasn't the case. He was supportive in every way I could've imagined, even told me that they had known all along what happened, but they were waiting on me to tell them.

I thought when my parents died that I was living in absolute darkness and misery. I thought it couldn't get any darker, but I was wrong. The darkest time of my life was being trapped with Damon those few days and then having to kill him in order to survive. But what made it even worse

was the fact that I felt like I couldn't go to my brother or the ones I trusted the most with my secrets. I felt hopeless and alone.

But all of that is behind me now. Talking to my brother helped more than I thought it would, and I'm so fucking glad I did it.

As the wind blows, I get a whiff of Seven, which is intoxicating and addicting, making my nose tingle. He reaches over and laces his fingers with mine, holding onto my hand tightly.

With Eli, Kane, and Stone working on transporting things from the beach house back to our places in the city, me, Ace, and Seven opted to stay behind and soak in as much of the beach life as possible before we head back home tomorrow.

Ace sits up, pulling a popsicle out of the cooler beside us, his dark eyes gleaming with mischief. Curiously, I watch him tear the wrapper with his teeth and slide it down, winking as he sucks the blue popsicle into his mouth. I'm not sure why, but I shiver, feeling heat engulf the sensitive spot between my thighs.

"Let me ask you something," Seven says, sitting up on the other side of me.

I sit up too, ripping my focus off of Ace and putting it on Seven, matching the sly smirk on his wet lips. "Shoot."

"What's going to happen tomorrow?" He tries to maintain his smile, but I can see how badly he wants to drop it.

The vulnerability oozing off of him tugs at my heartstrings, and his question ends up hitting me harder than I thought it would. Being here all summer, we've been in a little bubble, filled with nothing but freedom, sex, and the open road. We haven't had to deal with reality much, nor with the opinions of others outside of our little group. I haven't wanted to think about it, mainly because I was afraid of having to hear the one thing I didn't want to. I don't know if their feelings for me are real or just ones of lust and convenience, but the way I feel about each of them is very real, and I've been trying not to think about it too much.

What if they don't feel the same way?

"Princess, where did you go?" Seven's soft, deep voice sends a chill along the curve of my spine, making my toes tingle in anticipation.

He scoots closer until our legs are touching, and reaches up to gently cup my cheek in the palm of his large, tattooed hand. Once our eyes meet, it's fucking over, and I can feel the nerves begin to make me shake. There's something about the way that Seven looks at me that makes me want to drop to my fucking knees and do anything he fucking wants.

But I'm already sitting. So I try to keep my composure, not wanting him to see just how much he affects me.

"Answer me, Princess," he commands, flashing me a flirty look while pulling his lip between his teeth. "What's going to happen tomorrow when we get back to the city?"

"What do you mean?"

"You know what the fuck I mean. Was this all just summer fun for you, or do you really want to try and see where things could go with us?"

I could see that under his bold exterior, Seven was as vulnerable and doubtful as I was. For a minute there, I let myself get lost in his gaze before deciding it was time to face reality.

I could either keep playing this game and dodge his question or finally come clean about what I genuinely felt. We've had an incredible time together, but I knew that a decision needed to be made about where to go after the summer.

I take a deep breath and look Seven in the eye. "I don't want this to end," I admit, feeling the heat between my thighs spread to my cheeks, setting every inch of my trembling body on fire. "But..."

His face falls as he puts his finger to my lips to keep the words from spilling out. "No buts, Emerson... please."

Softly kissing his finger, I can see the fear in his eyes, clueless as to what I'm going to say. I feel Ace inch closer to the other side of me, placing his warm hand on the small of my back, jolting me alert.

"I was only going to say that I have feelings for all of you. Being so close to you this summer, it was hard not to catch feelings, so I can't pick just one." I feel relieved hearing myself admit it, but on the inside, I'm scared as fuck to hear the truth about how they feel.

Seven and Ace sit close on either side of me, their eyes filled with unspoken hope and apprehension.

I take a deep breath before continuing, "I want to see where things go, but I need to know if this is real for both of you, too." I look at Ace, gazing deeply into his dark eyes as he sucks and licks seductively on the popsicle, "I need to know we're more than just a summer fling."

Ace nods solemnly, his hand remaining on my back as he leans in closer. "I've got real feelings for you, Brat. I want to see where this goes too."

Turning to Seven, I search his intense eyes, silently begging for the reassurance I so desperately need. "What about you, Seven?" I hold my breath, waiting for his answer.

He lets out a long breath, as if releasing the tension he'd been holding in, then he meets my gaze with unwavering sincerity. "I fucking care about you, Emerson. More than I've fucking cared about anyone in a long time. I want this to be real, too." He smiles, easing the growing tension inside of me and giving my heart an excited flutter. "Besides, didn't I already tell your stubborn ass that you were fucking mine?" He smirks, and I instantly feel better.

Relief and joy surged through me. I lean in and kiss him softly, then turn to Ace and do the same. "I want this too," I whisper. "I want to see where this takes us, if we have a chance at being happy, even if our way is... unorthodox."

As the waves crash against the shore nearby, I feel a sense of calm and contentment within me. Tomorrow may bring challenges and uncertainty, but for now, I bask in the warmth of the moment, surrounded by two of the people I've come to care for deeply.

Seven captures my lips, kissing me fiercely with desperate lashes and flicks of his tongue. I feel Ace rubbing his hands up and down my arms, making sure I feel the love from both of them. I'm eased onto my back, my lips still locked onto Seven's, feeling my stomach and thighs tighten from the surge of pleasure flooding through my body. Slowly, my bathing suit is taken off and placed in a heap in the sand beside me, both men admiring my naked body, illuminated by the glow of the fire. I don't squirm from discomfort anymore. I relish their hungry eyes raking over every naked inch of my body, getting turned on from the aroused looks on their faces and the desire glimmering in their eyes—for me.

Seven drops his swim trunks and wraps his hand around his dick, gliding it up and down over his piercings, his eyes fixated on mine.

"Are you gonna open wide for me, Princess?" he grunts, squeezing the tip of his cock as he guides it to my mouth. "Are you gonna be my good little slut and swallow every drop of my cum that I paint your tight little throat with?"

I shiver from the utter filth of his words, undeniably turned on. Nodding, I whisper, "yes, baby. Fuck my mouth and give me a taste of you." I lick my lips as he rubs his cock head across them, urging me to open with a domineering look in his eyes that needs no other instruction.

As I open my mouth to suck him inside, Ace maneuvers between my legs, his fingers gliding up and down my pussy, swirling my wetness all over the place. Seven drives his dick into my mouth, thrusting until the pierced tip hits the back of my throat, making it constrict around him from an involuntary gag. My eyes roll back as I work my tongue around his shaft, feeling his cold piercings scrape against the inside of my cheeks.

Slurping on his popsicle while his fingers dip in and out of my entrance, Ace chuckles, letting a mouthful of ice-cold spit drop from his mouth onto my pussy, hitting my clit and making me shudder. "Be a good girl and spread your legs for me. I want to see how fast my popsicle melts in your pussy," he growls in a deep, seductive voice that makes my clit throb and my pussy drip even more.

I spread my legs on command, as wide as I can, trying to watch him and suck Seven's dick at the same time. His long hair falls in his face as he leans down, lowering his head, and pressing teasing kisses on my pussy with his cold lips. I watch nervously as he swirls his tongue around his popsicle one more time before he guides it to my pussy, sliding it into me with a smirk on his face that makes me fucking melt.

"Ah, shit," I gasp, letting Seven's dick fall from my mouth, feeling the cold object thrusting into my warm, wet pussy, something I never thought I'd experience.

"Cold?" Ace laughs, still pushing the popsicle inside me, his fingers dancing sensually across my lower belly.

"Fucking freezing," I answer with a laugh, propping myself up on my elbows to watch.

Seven watches too, stroking his cock at the sight of my pussy swallowing the popsicle. But he doesn't wait for it to be inside me all the way before shoving his thick, pierced dick back between my lips, fucking my mouth with dominant, desperate thrusts. I can feel the frozen ice melting as Ace starts thrusting in and out of me, the sticky liquid running quickly down my inner thighs. But fuck, it feels so good, intensifying every touch each of them gives me.

"You're fucking perfect, Brat," Ace growls, fascinated at how quickly the popsicle is melting inside me. "Your cunt is so fucking hot that this shit is about to melt already. I can't wait to suck it out of you and let you taste how sweet you are." He winks, fucking me faster with the melting popsicle.

My nerves are on fire. My body feels numb. My clit throbs. My nipples ache. I just want to come, but they're not making it easy. Every time I arch my back and try to buck my hips, Ace slows his thrusts. Seven keeps fucking my mouth, sliding as far down my throat as he can, grunting through thrusts as he gets close too.

I'm the center of their attention, and it feels exhilarating. I've never felt something so wild and intense before. As the warmth of the fire envelops us and the waves crash against the shore, I realize that there's nowhere else I'd rather be.

"Fuck, Princess," Seven grunts, and moments later I feel hot liquid gush into my mouth, but he pulls out before I can swallow all of it. Instead, he jerks off, his cum jetting in hot, thick spurts onto my neck and then down the front of my body, making a line from my collarbone to my pussy until he collapses in the sand beside me, panting.

I feel my pussy clamping around nothing, as the popsicle has melted now. Ace dips his tongue in and out of me, rubbing my clit fiercely with the pad of his thumb, knowing just what I need to send me over the edge. I raise my hips, bucking them against his mouth, while my hands grab and tangle in his hair. But before I can come, he pulls his mouth away, ripping a whimper from my throat.

"Wha..."

"Relax, Brat. I've got something planned." He winks, looking at Seven and then at me as he drags his tongue from my pussy to my neck, licking up the line of Seven's cum, his eyes piercing into mine.

Fuck, that's hot.

Pressing his lips to mine, Ace holds the cum in his mouth, teasing me. He then moves back down my body and rips my thighs open even more, spreading my pussy lips open with his fingers. Lowering his head, he presses his mouth against my entrance and spits Seven's cum inside me, flicking and thrusting his tongue against my tightening walls. Once Seven's hands wrap around my throat and his lips capture mine, I let go, feeling my climax rip through me without a single shred of mercy. I writhe in the sand, getting it in places I'll regret later, but I don't give a fuck right now. Ace fucks my pussy with his tongue, easing two fingers inside to add to the pleasure while slipping one into my ass. I come, and I come hard, grasping desperately at the sand as if it'll keep me grounded. But fuck, I feel like I'm falling. Seven chokes me as hard as he can—harder than ever—refusing to let go of my lips, his tongue exploring my mouth hungrily.

Ace sucks my cum and Seven's out of me, working his fingers like a fucking pro to bring me over the edge the rest of the way. Bucking my hips to chase the feeling, I scream out, hearing it echo in my ears as the final wave of intense pleasure rips through me, fully satisfying my every need. When my body goes limp, Ace comes up from between my legs and pushes Seven away, claiming my lips before I get a chance to catch my breath. Sure enough, he spits the cum mixture into my mouth, giving me a taste of the sweet and salty blue raspberry fluid, and I fucking love it.

Wiping the sweat from my brow, I lie back in a daze, my eyes closing as I listen to the sound of the waves and feel the warmth of the fire. Ace and Seven, still breathing heavily, collapse beside me, the three of us as close as can be.

"I can't believe you fucked me with a popsicle," I blurt out, laughing as I think back on the cold. sticky fun.

"You liked it."

"I did. I fucking did." I look at both of them, smiling, not wanting to leave this spot ever.

But reality sinks in and it hits me; we're fucking leaving tomorrow, and even though they assured me things wouldn't change, I can't help but feel that somehow they will.

FORTY

FIXED & FUCKED

Kane

As members walk into my office, they each drop their envelopes onto my desk and leave with nothing more than a nod. The music booms throughout the bar, while money piles up, but my mind is fixated on one thing, and it has been ever since we returned from the beach a week ago: Emerson.

Even though she eventually made amends with all of us, there's still a part of me that feels like we have unfinished business to handle. I haven't forgiven myself for breaking the necklace her old man gave her, even though she told me that she has. I fucking haven't.

Looking down, I watch the shiny pearls glide through my fingers, a smile creeping across my lips.

"What the fuck are you smiling at? Your cock?" Eli and Seven come into the office, drunk and smiling from ear to ear. Looking behind them, [illegible] and Stone follow, closing the door behind them.

"Nothing," I answer in a stern voice, discreetly slipping the necklace into my pants pocket.

The four of them look at me, waiting for me to instruct them on what to do next. It's like they're fucking lost, like this summer drained some of their brain cells and made them stupid motherfuckers.

"What do y'all fucking want?" I ask, lighting a smoke, blowing it directly into their faces.

"Everyone's back from their run, so what now?"

"Go the fuck home or go grab a damn drink. I don't give a fuck, Ace."

He laughs, heading for the door with my son on his ass like a fly on shit. "Fine, call if you need us."

"Just make sure you're here bright and early. We have our bike ride for the suicide awareness fundraiser."

They groan but nod, slipping out of my office without another word. Eli looks at me while Seven sits, obviously intent on staying behind.

"I'm going to head out with Nova, but if you need me, just holler," he says, tapping his pocket where his phone is.

"Will do. Hey, where is your sister?" I take another drag, feeling the mentholated smoke filter into my lungs, giving me a refreshing slap across the face.

"Last time I checked, she was out riding." He nods and walks out, leaving me and Seven alone, staring at each other as if we were in a fucking contest or something.

"What do you need?" I ask him, the pearls burning a hole in my pocket, just wanting to see the look on her face when I give them to her.

Seven looks at me with a smirk and says, "I think it's time you and Emerson settled things once and for all." Then he crosses his arms and leans back in his chair, waiting for my response.

I can feel my heart pounding in my chest as I look away, trying to ignore the weight of the necklace burning in my pocket. But I know he's right. It's time to make things right with Emerson. He only knows what's going on because he's the one who got the pearls for me. He was there for me to talk to, and I'm glad I did, but fuck, I don't need shit from him either.

"I know," I finally say, standing up and taking a deep breath. "I have some shit to finish up here, and then I'll take care of it."

"I'm supposed to meet her soon, so I'll let her know you're looking for her." He nods and walks out of my office, leaving me with a ton of shit to think about.

Grabbing a bottle of Jack, I sit back down and start drinking as I begin the count for tonight. All I can think about is Emerson, sweet little Emerson. And fuck, it's been that way ever since we left the beach house. I can't get her off of my mind, but I don't want to, nor do I have to.

I thought, much like everyone else, that once we left the beach, things would change between us, that they'd go back to how they were before, when all we did was fantasize about Emerson behind her back. But that wasn't the case. At least, it hasn't been so far. It's only been a week that we've been back in the city, but I've seen Emerson every fucking day.

When confronted about how we felt about her, she admitted that she wanted all four of us, but she didn't want a relationship. She loved each of us in her own way, and she hoped we could accept that. Of course, each one of us agreed and felt the same way, so really, it's like we never left the beach because things haven't stopped from how they were there.

We spend time with her together and we spend time with her apart, but the most important thing is that we all are there for her, not just as a lover, but as family, as it always has been.

Yes, there was some unfinished business between us, but I think it's time to put everything behind us and make things right.

Sometime after two am, I walk out of the back exit of the bar, the refreshing autumn wind smacking me across the face. I zip my leather jacket and shove my hands in my pockets, grasping the necklace as I walk down the dim alley to where we park our bikes. Leaves swirl off the ground and scatter throughout the night in the relentless wind, the temperature dropping by the minute.

Approaching the dimly lit parking lot, I hear Emerson's familiar laugh echo in the dead of night, and my cock gets hard instantly. As she comes into view, I see her and Seven sitting on his bike, facing each other, her hands held tightly in his. The way he makes her laugh makes my heart swell; it's obvious how much love they have for each other. He leans in and kisses her, ignoring her hair blowing in their faces in the wind.

Walking closer, I clear my throat, trying not to startle them, not wanting to get shot by accident. Emerson peels her lips off of Seven's and looks at me, her eyes gleaming under the flickering street light.

"Hey, Daddy," she says flirtatiously, winking as she hops off of Seven's bike and runs up to hug me, jumping right into my arms.

"You need to be fucking careful where you call me that, Little One," I warn, kissing her cold cheek.

"You good?" Seven asks, putting his helmet on.

"Yeah, thanks." I nod as he starts his bike, saluting us before he speeds away into the night, leaving us alone.

Emerson looks into my eyes, her legs locked around my waist, as I walk her to my bike, holding her tightly. I put her down on the seat and stand at the back of it, but she refuses to loosen her hold around my waist. So I kiss her, leaning her back so she's lying on my bike, hovering over her.

"I missed you," she mumbles against my mouth, reaching around so her hands are gripping my ass and pulling my pelvis against hers.

"I fucking missed you too, Little One. In fact," I say, reaching into my pocket to retrieve the necklace. "I have something for you."

She looks at me, her perfectly sculpted brows pinching in curiosity. She says nothing, but waits for me to finish, obviously nervous for what I might say. I raise my hand and dangle the pearls from my fingers, watching her eyes water and her jaw drop to the pavement.

"I had them fixed for you."

"You... you fixed my necklace? That's the one my father gave me." She almost chokes on her words, gazing longingly at the brand-new pearl necklace as if it were the most beautiful thing in the world.

"I did. I felt bad about breaking it. Every pearl is here too." I smile, unclasping it and hanging it around her delicate neck.

Her hands rise up and hold it immediately, and tears of joy fall down her cheeks, a smile curling on her plump, shiny lips. "Thank you, Kane. You have no idea how much this means to me," she whispers, trying to keep from crying.

I lean in and capture her lips, kissing her sensually as the night envelops us in its darkness. She kisses me back, rushing to undo my pants. She pulls my cock out and starts stroking, trying to pull me onto her even more.

"Fuck me, Daddy," she begs, her tone changing, almost desperate.

"Right here?" I work on lifting her skirt over her hips, pushing her soaked panties to the side, the cold air hitting her cunt, and making her gasp.

"Yes, right here. Fuck me just like this on your bike." She winks, putting her hands under her head while waiting for me to make the next move.

Looking around to make sure that we're alone, I grip my cock and push into her dripping cunt, pulling a seductive moan from her throat as I ease in slowly until I bottom out inside of her. Holding my handlebars for support, I begin thrusting my hips, fucking her with slow, long strokes, careful not to knock us or the bike over. She tugs her lip between her teeth and bites it, her eyes rolling back in her head.

I lean in, kissing her neck and tugging on her earlobe as she wraps her legs around my waist, increasing the sensation.

The cool night air dances around us, heightening the feeling of pure lust and desire. My veins pulse with electricity as she digs her nails into my back, begging for more as I pick up the pace, plunging in and out of her pussy with a fervor that matches the passion in her eyes.

Our breaths mingle in the cold, the sound of our moans and the squeak of the bike mingling with the distant sounds of the city at night. Emerson's back arches, her body trembling as she reaches the peak of her pleasure. I feel her walls clench around me and ride the wave of her orgasm, amplifying my own need for release. With a few more thrusts, I spill inside of her, kissing her deeply as we both come down from the high together.

After a moment of catching our breath, I help her straighten her clothes and smooth out her hair.

With a gentle smile, I whisper, "I'm planning on taking you somewhere special for breakfast tomorrow after the ride."

She grins, planting a sweet kiss on my lips and teasingly replying, "As long as it's with you, Daddy, I'll go fucking anywhere."

I help her onto the back of my bike, she wraps her arms around me, and we speed off into another night of the unknown, but as long as it's with Emerson, I couldn't give a fuck what lies ahead.

Epilogue

Emerson

Summer, A Year Later

The cold steel digs into my wrists, secured behind my back, each time Ace tugs on them, grunting in my ear. I squeeze my legs around Seven's body, using them to keep my momentum as I ride him, sliding up and down on his cock while Ace pounds into my ass, both men exploring my body with their hands and mouths.

The sun filters in through the closed blinds, casting a glow on the bed as we destroy it, our bodies moving in unison through every bounce and thrust delivered.

"Fuck, I love how wet this pretty cunt is in the morning," Seven groans, reaching between my legs to rub circles over my clit with his fingers. Cupping my breast in his other hand, he rolls my nipple between his fingers, not stopping until it's red and hard enough to cut through glass.

"Tell me again how much you love it," I beg, throwing my head back onto my shoulders, grinding against him, feeling my body tense as my climax rips through me.

"I fucking love how wet this pussy is, Princess." Holding my hips, he slams me down hard on his cock, knowing I'm about to come.

Ace reaches around the front of me and clasps his hand around my throat, still tugging on the handcuffs secured around my wrists as he plunges deep into my ass, filling it with warm ropes of his cum. Both men fuck me until they come, filling my holes with their seed to make sure I know who I belong to.

When they finally release me, I collapse onto the bed, spent and trembling. Seven and Ace exchange satisfied glances before they turn their attention to me, gently removing the restraints and cradling me in their arms. I can feel their warmth and affection enveloping me, a stark contrast to the earlier intensity. As I lay there, catching my breath and basking in their embrace, I catch a mischievous look on both of their faces and right away I begin to get nervous. I put my clothes on and sit, just as my bedroom door opens and Stone and his father walk in.

"What's all this?" I ask, looking around at the four of them, trying to find out what they're up to.

Pulling his sweats on, Seven tugs me onto his lap and curls his arms around my waist, flicking my earlobe with the tip of his tongue. "We have a surprise for you," he says, leaving it at that.

"What?"

"You'll see," Ace chuckles, tossing me my backpack. "Let's get going, though."

Nothing else is said as the five of us make our way downstairs, meeting Eli in the foyer, a grin on his face that has me even more confused. We walk outside, going right for our bikes, all parked along the curb, the hot summer sun shining down on us.

I don't ask any more questions. I just get on my bike, and we begin to ride, feeling the wind in my hair and the sun all over my skin, making me feel alive.

Over this past year, the five of us grew even closer, taking things further than any of us had ever imagined. Instead of living separately, we all live together in our own place in Boston, deciding to move in together just over six months ago.

I couldn't leave any of them, and, fuck, I tried to pick one. I debated for so long whether to stick with one or keep things how they were, and in the end, I couldn't give up any of them. Each one made me feel special in his own way. Each one brought out a different side of me that I fell in love with over time. Each one was good for me, and my selfish ass couldn't bear to part with them.

I CHOSE ALL FOUR OF THEM, AND THEY ALL CHOSE ME TOO.

The love I have for Seven, Kane, Ace, and Stone is unlike any other love I ever had for anyone, and I found myself wanting to see where life would take us.

They helped me through the darkest times in my life, and not once did they give up on me. Not once did they judge me.

And that meant more to me than anything they had ever given me.

They helped me with my trauma from losing my parents and the hell I went through with Damon, and I couldn't have asked for a better support system. They showed me how much they loved me daily, and they proved that they'd be by my side through anything—good and bad, happy and sad—they were always there for me, and I was always there for them.

I knew we would face challenges in the future, but we lived life one day at a time, embracing each other and all the things we had to offer. I knew that any problem that might arise, we would face it together, and that's exactly what we've done.

As the sun began to set over the horizon, the familiar street we rode along made a smile spread across my lips, and as I looked at the guys on their bikes beside me, I knew exactly where we were going: the beach.

The beach house was special to us in so many ways and held so many memories that shaped our lives in more ways than one.

Excitement coursed through me as I thought back on last year and all the fun we had. I knew that this summer would be even better because we had each other to spend it with. More memories would be made and our love would grow deeper; it was the best place in the entire world for us, and I was thrilled to see what this summer had in store.

We rode side by side, no need for words, as the wind carried our laughter and the sun warmed our hearts. Our home in Boston was waiting for us—a place where we could love and be loved, where each of us could feel special in our own way. I knew that whatever lay ahead, we'd face it together as a family.

As we approached the beach house, I felt a sense of peace and contentment settle over me. It felt good to be back in a place that held so many happy memories for us. Our home in Boston was special, but there was something about this beach house that made us feel free and unburdened.

And as I rode, my heart was full, knowing that I was exactly where I was meant to be and with who I was meant to be with.

THE END

KM ROGNESS

KM Rogness is an indie author who writes extremely dark, taboo, twisted, and over-the-top smutty Why Choose/RH romance novels. She's not afraid to shy away from real issues, and draws dark, raw, and gripping tales from personal experiences, putting a little bit of her own personal struggles and events in every book she writes. She pushes boundaries and tests limits, taking her ideas way out of the box.

Trying to bring awareness to topics usually not talked about, including mental health, abuse, assault, addiction, and the darkest, most disturbing topics, she captures her readers attention with only a few deep, captivating lines.

She loves how her readers can relate to the issues she writes about, and is appreciative of every single person who has reached out to her to share their story, often telling her how her books have helped them overcome certain elements and guided them through their darkest moments.

Currently residing in North Carolina with her husband, three sons, and a daughter on the way, she finds inspiration during rainy, stormy nights, and her own fucked up memories.

Her books feature intense themes and captivating possessive mmcs that will undoubtedly capture readers' hearts, after they've ripped them out and broken them into pieces.

She lives for the darkness, having absolutely no triggers, and you can always find a shopping list full of them at the beginning of every one of her books.

Her books are dark, dirty, and delicious, always promising an enthralling reading experience.

Other books by KM ROGNESS

Trick or Treat: A MMFMM Erotic Horror

Breaking Boston: A MFM Masked Stalker Dark Romance

Thank You, Fuckers.

I want to thank my very supportive and patient husband, Jon. Without you being 100% in my corner, I wouldn't have been able to follow my dream of becoming an author. Also, thank you for the years of experience that helped me create such a masterpiece. I owe it all to you. My boys, thank you for giving me the time I needed to write. I love you all so much. Thank you to my beta girls: Holly, Jasmine, and Chastity. You're not only amazing betas, but you're some of the best friends I've had the pleasure of meeting during my journey, and I love you fuckers so much. Thank you to my amazing street team and ARC team. Ya'll smutty fuckers have supported me so much, and I don't know where I would be today if it weren't for all of your help. Also, Molly, Ana, Lauren, Christine, Brit, CC, I love you ladies and want to thank you for being there for me since my Chapters days. You've been there through the ups and downs and had my back through everything. I love all of you ladies and I wanted to thank you from the bottom of my black heart. And of course, last but certainly not least, to all of my readers, followers, and friends, thank you for showing me and my books so much love. Y'all are truly fucking amazing.

K.M.
DROWNING
A WHY CHOOSE
FORBIDDEN DARK ROMANCE

Milton Keynes UK
Ingram Content Group UK Ltd.
UKHW031947281024
450365UK00008B/497

9 798227 429063